PARLEY

JAMIE McFARLANE

Cover Artwork: Sviatoslav Gerasymchuk

ISBN-13: 978-1500937614
ISBN-10: 1500937614

Don't miss the other exciting adventures in
Jamie McFarlane's
Privateer Tales

Rookie Privateer
Fool Me Once

CONTENTS

ACKNOWLEDGMENTS

Diane Greenwood Muir for excellence in editing and fine word-smithery. My wife, Janet, for carefully and kindly pointing out my poor grammatical habits.

My beta readers: Nancy Higgins Quist, Dave Muir, Jeff Rothermel, Carol Greenwood, and Robert Long.

Finally, Sviatoslav Gerasymchuk, an artist of exceptional skill.

MAYDAY

Red lights pulsed around the perimeter of the ceiling and a warning klaxon started whoop-whooping. I'd been staring aimlessly out into the star field in front of me, lightly dozing. That was certainly over now.

Report, I commanded my artificial intelligence (AI) and quickly scanned the vid screens in front of me. All critical systems were green.

Mayday distress signal received. Merchant ship under attack. Two hours to intercept. Combat data stream available. The ship's voice was that of a soft-spoken, middle-aged man. I'd experimented with different female voices, but found they caused my mind to wander at inopportune times.

Adjust course, wake the crew, render combat at engineering station, and turn off that damned siren.

We weren't necessarily going to get involved, but changing course now might save critical time. It was law that we respond to a mayday, but hostilities meant we could make a judgment call.

"Permission to enter the bridge," Marny Bertrand's alto voice requested from the door.

"Granted." When I looked over my shoulder, Nick's smaller form was right on Marny's heels. It made sense, as they had taken to bunking together in the original captain's quarters.

"What's all the fuss, Cap?" Marny asked. I was impressed with how put together she appeared. I knew for a fact she'd been sound asleep less than a minute ago. Nick, not-so-much. His straight black hair was slung unevenly to one side.

"Not sure, Marny."

I took a few steps back to the bridge's engineering station and they joined me in front of the holographic display. A ship,

3

obviously a freighter given its tug and barge design, floated just above the empty engineer's chair. Two thin attack craft were orbiting it, concentrating fire on the crucial ligaments between the tug and its three serially linked barges. A third ship, cutter-class, hung back several kilometers.

Identify ships, I instructed.

A translucent blue halo appeared around the freighter and the AI provided the details. *Freighter Baux-201, Mars Protectorate Registration, General Astral model A20-402.*

After pausing on the freighter, the blue halo jumped to illuminate the two circling attack craft. *Unregistered Fujitsu Darts, model FZ024.* The glow moved to the cutter. *Unregistered General Astral Cutter, CA-08.*

Are there any other ships within range that can provide assistance? I asked.

Mars Protectorate estimates ten hours for intercept.

There it was. *Sterra's Gift* was two hours away, which by itself was several lifetimes in space combat. Mars Protectorate Navy, at ten hours, wasn't even a consideration. If we balked at this, *Baux-201* was doomed. The freighter could hold off the darts for a while with their armor, but its fate was just a matter of time.

"Marny, how soon before those darts break through the linkage?"

Nick and Marny were studying the holographic display.

"Not really sure. I'm surprised the tug isn't firing back. Those tugs usually have at least a heavy blaster on 'em."

It was as if her words woke the captain of *Baux-201*. Two yellow charges erupted from a gun port on the back of the tug and streamed toward the darts. Each nimbly spun away, causing the charges to miss. The battle rendering lit up again as two more shots followed after the ships.

"Rotten luck," Marny said. "That'll never work. He'll never hit those darts with that heavy blaster. That's why the cutter is hanging back, it'd be a lot easier to hit."

"Will they stop the attack once they break the linkage?" I asked. I hoped Marny had practical experience with pirate behavior from her days as a gunnery officer in the Mars Protectorate Navy.

"Not likely. That cutter can't get any closer while the tug is still active. Are you thinking about getting into this? It will be over long before we get there," she said.

"Not if we do a flyby," I said. "They'd have no reason to keep attacking if we take out that cutter."

The AI had done a calculation based on us matching velocity with the attacking ships. That scenario, common in space travel, involved accelerating toward a destination, then flipping around at the halfway point and decelerating until you matched velocity and direction with your target. It was an efficient maneuver. If we could accelerate over the entire distance, however, we'd arrive significantly faster.

"Nick, can you get a calculation on that?"

"Yup," Nick said. He moved to sit at the station opposite engineering.

Hail Baux-201.

The forward vid projectors showed a dark-skinned, middle aged woman. Her black hair was neatly braided into narrow rows that closely followed her scalp and colorful beads hung from the ends. I knew from the moment I saw her kindly face that I wouldn't be able to abandon her.

"Captain Adela Chen," she introduced herself. "Are you able to render assistance?"

"Liam Hoffen. We're two hours out on standard approach. How long can you hold out?"

"Not that long, Captain. Maybe thirty minutes."

"We're considering a high speed flyby. Missiles are loaded and we could knock out the cutter. You'd be left with the darts."

"No good, Captain," she said. "Those darts would just eat me up after that."

"Understood. Call me Liam, Captain. We're going to emergency burn. Please keep the data-stream active. We'll get there as quickly as we can."

"Thank you, Liam. Godspeed." She cut the comm link.

"Nick, what's our minimum time?"

"Forty-eight minutes, give or take. We'll break the deceleration at five minutes out so we can upload *Baux-201's* data stream." It was faster than I had hoped for.

"Marny, you in? Could get dicey."

"You shouldn't have put her on the holo. Once they're real, there's no turning back. But yeah, I'm in. I'll warm up the turret."

"Nick, you in?"

"Yup."

"Execute your burn plan."

"Roger that."

On Nick's command, *Sterra's Gift* lurched forward. The inertial systems could normally absorb and redirect the effects of the engine's acceleration into simple downward force. Gravity would increase to 150% of Earth normal gravity, but a person standing in the ship wouldn't feel the forward acceleration. That was hard burn. In an emergency burn like we were now experiencing, the inertial system was unable to keep up with the demands.

I stumbled forward. My body felt like it weighed a couple of hundred kilos. When my hands found the back of the port side pilot's chair, I pulled myself into it, drawing the combat straps over my shoulders and snapping them into place. We still had plenty of time before arrival, but I wanted to be ready.

Project combat on forward holo.

The always listening AI moved the unfolding combat scene from the engineering station to just in front of the twin pilot chairs and beneath the armored glass that swept up from the nose of the ship to the back of the bridge.

For the next twenty-four minutes a constant data stream would show the battle as it took place. At mid-point, *Sterra's Gift* would flip over and start decelerating and we'd lose the stream due to engine interference.

"Marny, once the linkage is broken, what then? That cutter can't haul those barges, can it?"

"No. It's about half our size. Even if we had a decent way to hook up, we'd have quite a bit of trouble with those barges."

"Yeah, that's what I thought. Won't they ruin the linkage?"

Nick chimed in. "Those barges can be linked on both ends. That's how they decelerate. The tug lets go and reattaches to the other side. In a pinch, they rotate the entire line of barges, but it's a lot easier to detach and reattach. They probably have a tug off somewhere waiting for combat to be over."

"She doesn't stand a chance, why hasn't she just ejected?"

Marny responded, "She's buying time by creating a standoff with the cutter. It can't approach while she's manning her blasters. She's also slowing down the darts."

A possible explanation hit me. "How much crew on a tug?"

Nick answered. "Minimum two, four if you squeeze."

"Any lifepods?"

"Just one. Checking to see if it's been deployed ..." Nick paused. "It's gone, Liam."

"She's protecting her crew," I said. My stomach tightened at the realization.

Hail Captain Chen.

"Tell me you found a way to get here faster, Captain Hoffen." Adela's face was tight but she managed a small smile. We were closing in on the halfway point and it wasn't looking good for her. It didn't escape me that we would miss this fight by less than twenty minutes. It was a lifetime.

"Send me the trajectory of the lifepod. I promise you we'll do everything we can to protect it."

Her holographic image held my eyes for what seemed like minutes. "That's my daughter on there. She means everything."

"On my honor, Captain," I replied.

Rotation in thirty seconds, the AI reminded me.

"Trajectory transmitted. Stay safe, Captain. Chen out." She cut communications.

Sterra's Gift's engines slowed and the constant, nearly crushing acceleration diminished and finally stopped. A slow rotation, end over end, and the engines spooled up again. The crushing force of acceleration returned. We now had to sail blindly toward the combat zone.

"We got the lifepod," Nick said.

"Good. When we drop out of burn, I want to unload two missiles on the cutter. Can you make that work, Nick?"

"Yup."

"Marny, how's that turret looking?"

"Ready to rock! Give me something to shoot."

We sailed in silence for the first twenty minutes of deceleration. *Sterra's Gift* dropped out of burn just long enough for us to get an updated data stream.

Show current status.

Status not available, the AI replied.

Show stream at ten times speed.

The holographic rendering of the attack started right where we'd left off. After forty seconds, the darts finally finished their job, severing the linkage between the tug and the chain of barges. I watched with resignation as the darts turned their attention to Chen's tug. I slowed the recording to watch in real time. I felt I owed that to her. We'd been less than ten minutes too late.

It was more than I could take. "Why wouldn't they simply blow the tug before separation?"

"They couldn't risk the explosion." Marny replied. I hadn't realized I'd asked the question out loud.

It took the darts less than a minute to tear the tug to shreds as it drifted away from the string of barges. It was horrific to think of Adela Chen, still on that ship, being murdered.

"Turn it off, Cap." Marny's voice sounded distant.

"I can't."

"You have to. Get your ass in the moment, Cap. This ship won't fly itself."

She was right, I was wallowing. I turned off the recording. "Roger that. Thanks, Marny."

"Dropping out of burn in thirty seconds," Nick warned. It was unnecessary, since I could see the countdown on my vid-screen.

I pulled the flight stick back from its cradle and rested my left hand on the throttle control.

"I'm bringing us in hot, Nick. We'll concentrate on the cutter first. The darts can't get home without it."

I aborted the deceleration a few seconds earlier than planned. This would cause us to do a very high speed flyby of the cutter as well as make it harder for the ship to take evasive maneuvers.

Too late, the smaller cutter became aware of our approach. They'd fired up their engines and were burning hard on an escape vector perpendicular to our path. I arced toward their escape route. The darts, in turn, adjusted to chase us.

"Missiles away," Nick said.

Track missiles on holo projector.

Both missiles had to make minor adjustments in their less-than-two-second flight, but that was expected. The cutter had detected the launch and attempted to dodge.

Only one missile hit, but that was sufficient. Kinetic damage is king in space combat. The energy is amplified geometrically by speed. By not fully decelerating when we fired, the missiles hit the cutter with much greater velocity than if we'd simply been chasing the cutter in matched combat. Missiles have explosive charges, but if we'd hit the cutter with a missile-sized rock, it would have done just about the same amount of damage.

A quick survey showed the top third of the now slowly tumbling cutter had been vaporized. The contents of the ship were exposed to vacuum and the shock of impact would surely have killed everyone on board.

Center Sterra's Gift on display. I'd lost visual contact with the darts, but knew they were out there. The AI identified their holographic images trailing us, not far back. The ships were accelerating hard and would overtake us in less than a minute unless I fired the engines back up. Thing was, we weren't some little tug. We were an armored ship with a full load of ammo for our turret. They could outrun us, but our gun range was just as good as theirs. Bring it on!

I flipped *Sterra's Gift* around. With the cutter out of the mix, our odds were pretty good. I accelerated hard in their direction. It struck me that this particular maneuver had been executed by warriors throughout the ages. We thought ourselves so advanced, but when it came down to it, we were just knights tilting down the line with a lance tucked under our arm.

Hail those darts. I couldn't figure out how the AI always knew what I meant, but it never failed.

"You want to surrender?" The voice was haughty.

"Stand down. We'll take you into custody. At least you'll live," I said.

He cut off communications.

Send message to darts. "If you don't fire on us, I won't fire my missiles. You light us up, we'll come at you with everything we have."

We continued to accelerate toward each other.

"Marny, if you can hold it a little, wait until we are fired on."

"Aye, aye, Cap."

"Nick, get a plan for our last missile for both of those darts. Fire it at the first one that shoots. Make it your best shot, it's all we'll get."

"Roger that."

Just as we got into turret range, one of the darts veered off. It was a confusing move. The dart had limited range, so it couldn't expect to get somewhere safe. The ship had been piggybacking on the now-destroyed cutter and really had nowhere to go.

The other dart started firing at us. Although still at long range, we were both moving fast enough that I wasn't thrilled about taking shots head-on. Armor was heaviest on our belly, so I rotated up slightly to take the hits.

"Hey! No fair." Marny protested the move, since she no longer had the ability to shoot.

"I'll nose over thirty-five degrees in five … four … three … "
Just as I executed the maneuver, Nick fired our one remaining missile and tracers stitched a path through space from Marny's turret. The dart dove out of the way, but I followed its descent. Marny anticipated my move and her fire lanced through the small ship, taking out its engine. Nick's missile was slower to respond to the dart's path, but with the craft's engines now inoperable, it caught up quickly. The explosion was brilliant.

RESCUE

The remaining dart accelerated hard at an oblique angle, not wanting to meet the same fate as its partner.

"Where can it go?" I asked no one in particular.

Nick was first to answer. "There has to be another ship. They blew up the tug, and that small cutter we hit first certainly wasn't going to move those barges very far."

"Nick, would you send our combat stream to Mars Protectorate? They'll want to log that debris." One thing all sailors wanted to keep up to date was the massive database of debris vectors in the system. Military ordinance disintegrated after a few days in vacuum. Wrecked ships were another thing entirely.

"Yup. The cutter is on a good line for a close pass with Mars in a few months. Some salvage company will be happy to see that coming."

"Let's see if we can find where that dart ran off to," I said.

We still had a lock on the dart, although it was zipping away at a high rate of speed. I pushed the t-handled throttle forward, stopping short of the emergency burn rate. The cost of fixing the engines after using emergency burn was still etched in my mind from our last adventure, where we'd been running for our lives, and I'd already done enough damage getting here.

"Nick, can you get a scan on where that dart is headed? See if there's a ship out there."

"Working on it."

The dart must have picked up on our pursuit as it suddenly veered off course. I had to make a decision: follow the dart or follow its original path.

"Nick, project the dart's original vector. I want to see what's out there."

"Okay. I've got nothing yet."

"Understood. Let's give it a few minutes. He hadn't started decelerating yet so it must be further out." My reasoning was that the dart would attempt to meet up with a fourth ship. Spacers generally flew directly at their intended destinations. Given the speeds and distances involved, even small adjustments in angles became significant over relatively modest periods of time.

"Got 'em!" Nick said. "Sending to forward projector."

Sure enough, a tug appearing on the vid was accelerating hard away from us. Our superior speed and maneuverability made its action a futile gesture.

"Dart's coming up on our flank," Nick said.

Send message to dart. "Same deal pal, we won't fire at you if you keep things calm."

We didn't get any response from the dart, but the tug spun on its horizontal axis and loosed a volley of bright yellow blaster fire at us. I'd been expecting it and dodged the fire easily.

Hail hostile ships. "We have missiles locked on. You won't get a second warning. Stand down your weapons and heave-to." It was a bluff, but I didn't believe they had the ability to scan us sufficiently to tell. However, I was more than prepared to pound both ships into dust at this point.

For a couple of minutes all three of us sailed along together with no one taking any action. I suspected the dart and tug captains were in deep discussion.

"Let us take the dart and I'll surrender the tug." It was the captain of the tug who'd finally answered.

I didn't hesitate. Combat was far from a sure thing. "Deal. Send command codes for the tug immediately or we'll settle this the way I'd originally planned."

Fujitsu Freighter Model FF718 command codes received.

Lockdown all ship access. Stream all available interior video. Lock all interior doors.

"We had a deal, Captain. What are you doing?"

"Sit tight. If everything checks out, you'll be on your way soon enough."

Keep comm open, but mute outgoing audio.

"Marny, what should our protocol be here?" Marny was a decorated, retired Marine. Of the three of us, she would know how best to handle the situation.

"First," she said. "Run the video log back ten minutes. Make sure he didn't do anything funky."

"On it," Nick said.

"Once that's clear, let him take a walk over to the other ship. They might make a final run at us once he's loaded, so we stay alert until they take off."

We all watched the video at 5x speed. The tug's interior was tiny in comparison to *Sterra's Gift*. Down below, there was only a bunk room that slept two and a small alcove with stand-up galley and a head. The cockpit was on a second level with not much more than two reclined chairs.

We watched as the captain stuffed a couple of packages into the engine compartment and one beneath the pilot's chair.

"Probably scuttling charges." Marny said.

Restore audio transmission.

"You have one chance to fix what you did. Play dumb and I'll leave you locked in there for the Navy."

We watched the live vid feed as the captain removed each of the three packages. He held them up, each in turn, as he disabled the charges.

"All systems are reporting satisfactory," Nick said.

"Move to the airlock. Leave the charges on the floor. You are not allowed to take anything with you," I instructed.

That earned me a scornful glare, but he complied. I instructed the ship to cycle the lock and the captain stepped inside. Once he was free of the ship, the dart swooped in close. Its canopy lifted with a puff of atmosphere and the captain climbed in.

Terminate communications.

"Why'd you let 'em go?" Marny asked. She sounded annoyed.

"Maybe I'm naïve, but I just don't want their blood on my hands. It's one thing when we're under attack, but he was willing to stand down. We could have demanded to take them all into custody, but then it would have meant a fight."

"A fight we'd have won."

"I think you're right, Marny, but I'm not out here to win. I'm out here to live. The odds of survival for all of us went way up when we put the guns down. I'll take that every time. Thanks for not challenging me in the middle of a fight."

"I might not agree with what you did there, Cap, but it's your call. I just want to know where we stand."

"You okay with it?"

"Can't say I'm not pissed. Those boys deserve what they had coming."

"Couldn't agree more, Marny. I got to be honest with you, though, I hope none of us get what we've got coming."

That broke the tension as I heard her guffaw. "Okay. You got me there, Cap."

"Nick, can you slave the tug to us? I'd like to get back and search for that lifepod."

"Already done. You'll have to take it slow, it doesn't have a lot of acceleration."

I set a course to intercept the lifepod that was ejected from *Baux-201*. I wasn't looking forward to the coming conversation with its sole occupant. Ten minutes later, we pulled up alongside the pod. It was tumbling end over end and the person inside had been ignoring all of our attempts at communication. I was worried about the pod's integrity and the wellbeing of Captain Chen's daughter.

"Nick, is the pod still sealed?"

"Yup. It reads green."

"Shouldn't it have some way to lose the spin?"

"You'd think. Maybe it's busted."

"Okay, I've got this," I said.

I nudged *Sterra's Gift* ahead of the tumbling cube. If I wasn't careful, I could seriously injure the inhabitant. I flipped us end over end so that we were gliding backwards at the same speed as the cube, but now pointed directly at it.

"What are you doing?" Nick asked.

"Hang on. I've done crazier things."

I ever so carefully popped the navigation arc-jets of my ship. The main engines weren't anywhere near subtle enough for what I wanted to accomplish and I watched our relative speed on the vid screen. The cube was now approaching us at half a meter per second, which is a quarter of the speed a person walks.

The cube tumbled into the ship, making contact. As it did, I nudged the arc-jets so the ship rotated up slightly into the spin of the cube. The cube's flat surface provided it with nowhere to go and the slight difference in our relative speeds didn't provide enough momentum to cause the cube to bounce away.

"That's pretty neat," Nick said.

"Thanks, bud."

"Marny, would you meet me in the port cargo hold? Nick, you have the helm."

"Roger that," he said.

"Aye, aye."

The port cargo hold was amidships, nestled just in front of the three large engines. It was one of two formal cargo spaces on *Sterra's Gift* and was empty since we hadn't had a chance to contract a full load before leaving Baru Manush.

I met Marny in the hallway in front of the door leading to the hold. I looked at her face to see if she was holding a grudge. She was all business, but I didn't see anything out of the ordinary.

"What's the drill, Cap?" Marny was my height but had at least twenty-five kilos on me, not a gram of which could be attributed to unnecessary fat.

"We'll go outside and push the lifepod into the cargo hold. I don't know what we're getting into. Should be Captain Chen's daughter. Not sure why we can't get her on comm."

"Okay, give me a minute." Marny disappeared into the armory and reappeared in a fully armored vac-suit with a blaster rifle slung over her shoulder and a pistol strapped to her thigh. She was intimidating as hell in armor. Her normally muscular shape took on frightening proportions with the armor hugging and accentuating her every curve.

"Think we'll need all that?" I asked.

"I'll get you trained yet, Cap. You're thinking backwards. What's the worst thing that could pop out of a pod?"

"Ah, I get your point. Here's the plan …"

We entered the cargo hold together and waited for the atmo to be cycled out.

"Nick, we're opening the port cargo hold door. Are we still good?"

"Roger that. The lifepod is floating off the port side about ten meters, you can't miss it. Still not able to raise it on comm."

Open port cargo hold exterior door. Reduce gravity to oh-point-two in cargo hold.

I always appreciated an unobstructed view of space and this time was no different. I felt free having nothing between my vac-suit and the expanse of space. I made the tiny gestures that communicated flying instructions to my AI. Blue cones appeared on the bottoms of my boots and on the palms of my hands. I leaned over and jetted out of the hold.

I didn't immediately see the lifepod, but a subtle blinking amber light in my peripheral vision indicated its direction. I turned my head until the light centered in my vision. My AI projected an outline around the lifepod, but I would have found it, regardless. The flashing blue lights along each side made it hard to miss.

It was a simple matter to push the pod back to the cargo hold. As an asteroid miner, I had a lot of experience moving much larger machines around. The lifepod was a tight fit, but we managed to maneuver it through the doors.

Close door and re-pressurize.

"Let's hope I didn't leave the door on the bottom," I said.

"You didn't check?" Marny asked.

I chuckled to myself. "Over on this side." I was standing in front of the door. I hoped that the .2 gravity had allowed the inhabitant to settle slowly to what was now the floor. Marny joined me. The pressure was almost restored in the hold.

"How do you want to do this?" I asked.

"Knock a couple of times, then open it. I'll cover you. With all that tumbling, I suspect they're unconscious." I did as she suggested and the door opened easily. Most lifepods didn't have a locking mechanism other than to hold a seal against vacuum. With atmosphere on both sides, the lock released. Marny held the blaster rifle loosely, but she could raise it instantly if the situation required it.

I poked my head into the lifepod and quickly scanned. Everything was in order except that I'd put the pod into the hold upside down. The sole occupant was strapped into a chair attached to the ceiling, her arms and legs hanging down. I stepped in. "Frak. Marny, I need your help."

She joined me in the pod and looked up at the dangling form.

"Nice. I've seen worse. If you jet up and release the harness, I'll catch her."

In .2 gravity, the girl would float down at roughly the speed of a piece of paper in normal gravity. I did as Marny recommended and she easily caught the limp body.

"Let's get her onto the couch in your quarters," I led the way out of the pod and opened the cargo hold door into the main hallway. Marny followed me back to her quarters and gently set the girl's body down on the couch.

Medical emergency override, release the helmet of the unconscious passenger. Normally it wouldn't be possible to open someone's face shield on a vac-suit, but AIs could negotiate in the circumstances of a medical emergency.

The mirrored face shield withdrew into the suit and the hood relaxed, electrical stimulation no longer keeping it rigid. I knelt next to the couch, desperately hoping she was alive.

The first thing that struck me was just how bad an idea it had been to lean in so close. A wave of putrid air hit me hard and I gagged. It had been a long time since I'd barfed in my suit, but believe me, memories of that experience never leave you.

I saw with relief that she was breathing.

"Nick, can you take us back to the *Baux-201* site and start looking for Captain Chen?" It would be a terrible blow to her daughter, but leaving the woman to float in space like so much trash would be even worse.

"Roger that, how many were in the lifepod?"

"One girl, about our age. She's breathing." I looked down at the girl. She looked a lot like her mother, same beautiful face, warm brown skin, and hair that was woven into tight rows of beaded braids. Her hair was much longer than her mom's and had bad things in it at the moment, no doubt a result of her violent spinning episode.

Marny had left and returned with our med-kit. She placed a diagnostic device on the girl's forehead and another on her chest. They both showed green.

"She's got a suit-liner on. Let's at least get her out of the suit and clean it. It would be awful to wake up to this smell," Marny said.

"How about you start on that and I'll find something to help get her cleaned up."

"Chicken."

"True enough."

I rounded up an extra pillow and a couple of clean blankets as well as a bucket of warm soapy water and a pile of cleaning towels. This girl would have enough to worry about when she awoke without also having to deal with the embarrassment and mess of having violently thrown up.

I was grateful that by the time I got back, Marny had successfully removed the vac-suit. It lay in a pile on the ground. Together we worked to clean up the girl's face and hair. It didn't take too long and by the end I thought the smell had been mostly mitigated. We covered her with blankets.

"I'll run her suit through the cleaner and then sit with her," Marny offered.

"Thanks, Marny, but I'd like to be here when she wakes up."

"Understood. You did a good thing, Liam. I know I gave you a hard time, but she wouldn't be alive if we hadn't come."

"I'm not sure she'll see it that way."

"That's not why we do it," Marny said.

TOUGH DECISIONS

We found Adela Chen's body in the wreckage of her tug, still strapped into the pilot's chair. She had been shot up pretty badly. It was so senseless and caused me to question my decision to not drag those frakking pirates to justice.

Nick sent the combat data streams to the approaching Mars Protectorate frigate. They were still several hours out and requested that we remain in the vicinity.

"Cap, she's comin' around. You might want to get in here." Marny had stayed with the girl while Nick and I looked for her mother.

By the time I arrived, Captain Chen's daughter had pushed herself up to a seated position. Her wide-eyed stare locked on me as I entered the room. Marny, obviously uncomfortable with the situation, stood by the door. Unfortunately, Marny was still in her armored vac-suit.

"Thanks, Marny. Would you mind giving me a few minutes with Miss Chen?"

"Aye, aye, Cap." Marny looked relieved and quickly exited the room.

"Miss Chen, I'm Captain Liam Hoffen. You're on *Sterra's Gift* and you're safe."

Seating options were pretty limited. She was on the couch. I wasn't about to sit next to her, given her current state of confusion, but I also knew that standing was the wrong answer. I opted to kneel down and sit back on my heels.

"My mom?" She looked at me with tears already forming. The memory of Adela's body inside her ship was still fresh in my mind. This girl looked so much like her. I felt a tear slide down my cheek.

"She didn't make it." I was completely unprepared for this kind of conversation.

Adela's daughter took a shuddering breath, held her face in her hands and sobbed. It was more than I could bear to watch, so I got up, sat next to her and pulled her in gently for a hug. I was prepared for resistance, but she melted into me. We sat like this for several minutes while she wept.

Finally, she pulled away to sit up and I slid back just slightly to give her some room. Marny, who had changed back into her normal vac-suit, re-entered the room and pressed a handful of tissues into my hand. I passed them to the distraught girl.

"Thank you, Marny," I said.

The girl finally spoke, "Ada." I wasn't sure if she was telling me her mother's name or introducing herself. So I looked at her, hoping she would continue.

"I'm Ada Chen. Can I see Mom?"

"Yes. Of course. We're at your disposal. We're currently holding position off the ship's wreckage at two hundred meters. Mars Protectorate is five hours out."

"I need to see her."

"Do you want to EVA?" I asked. EVA was spacer shorthand for Extra Vehicular Activity.

"Yes."

"Would you allow me to accompany you?"

"Yes."

"Would you like to clean up first?"

"No. I need to do this."

"Okay. Your vac-suit is on the table. I'll meet you in the hallway when you're ready."

A few minutes later we were jetting through space toward the wreckage of *Baux-201*. The string of barges had separated from the wreck and was hovering about a kilometer away. Ada was quiet. I hesitated when we got within ten meters.

"I'll give you your privacy," I said.

"Thank you."

I waited, floating in space and surveying the scene. What a

waste. I hated pirates. Their greed and disregard for life was horrible. For a load of whatever was on the barges, they were willing to destroy two lives. All for a small cut of ill-gotten gains. I understood more clearly why Marny had been pissed at me for not firing on the remaining two pirates and allowing them to escape. Rationally, I still thought it was the best approach, but emotionally it was clearly not what I wanted.

"I'm coming out." Ada's voice cut through my internal conversation.

"Is there anything you want to bring back with you? I can help." I said.

"I've got it." Ada jetted toward me, pushing a loosely bundled set of cases.

Once we were back on the ship, I showed her to Bunk Room #2 (BR-2). Marny and Nick must have been working while we were out, as all of the cargo we'd stored there had been moved. The bed had fresh linens on it and a towel was folded neatly in the center of the lower bunk. It was a thoughtful gesture.

"I'll be on the bridge. You're welcome to join us there if you want. It looks like Marny or Nick already has you set up here."

"Thank you." Ada wasn't processing very well yet. It was understandable. I left her alone and joined my friends on the bridge.

"Nice job with the bunk room guys. Thanks." I didn't know which of them had been responsible, but I was grateful. It didn't take much to empathize with Ada. She was my age and the recent attack on my home mining colony made it easy to imagine the loss of one of my parents.

"It sucks," Marny said.

"Agreed. Nick, did you send a message to Belcose?"

"Not yet."

"I'll do it." I left the bridge and entered Nick and Marny's room - originally the captain's quarters. Nick and I were co-owners of the business and while I had been designated captain, it made more sense that Nick and Marny take the larger room. The issue was, when we'd received our Letter of Marque from Mars

Protectorate Navy, they'd installed specialized communication equipment in the captain's quarters. Bottom line was ... every time I needed to make a private call, I had to take over Nick's room.

I shut the door behind me to spare Ada from the details of what I would share with Lieutenant Gregor Belcose, my contact with Mars Protectorate Navy.

Attach all recent combat data streams to the following message.

Greetings Lieutenant Belcose – Sterra's Gift has rendered aid to the merchant ship, Baux-201, which was eventually destroyed. Captain Adela Chen was killed by the action of a well-organized pirate team. We arrived too late to help Captain Chen, but were able to rescue her daughter, Ada Chen, and in the process destroyed two pirate ships and captured a third. I believe we will end up requesting a prize claim for this captured ship and will take this up with the captain who takes control of the now secured combat area. We intend to continue to render assistance to Ada Chen until the Mars Protectorate Navy instructs us otherwise. I have attached combat data streams for all of these actions.

I'm concerned about discovering pirate activity this close to Mars since we are less than a week out. On a personal level, I hope you and Captain Sterra are doing well.

Hoffen Out.

I heard Ada in the adjacent shower room. It was a good sign that she was taking care of herself. I rejoined Marny and Nick on the bridge.

"I know the timing is bad, but we should probably talk to her about the cargo. The way we treat this could have a big impact on her," Nick said.

"I'm not following ..."

"It depends who owns *Baux-201*. Tugs are pretty commonly owner-operated. If that's the case and the cargo is lost, then they'll forfeit their bond. If they don't own the ship then it's probably not as big of a deal. Either way, we should help her figure that out before the Navy shows up. We could rightfully salvage the load and demand its value, as well as the value of the actual barges from whoever owns it. We'd have to get a lawyer again," Nick never ceased to amaze me with his understanding of these types of details. I wondered if he ever slept.

"That sounds pretty mercenary," I said.

"Right, but if we leave it here, what's going to happen to it? Probably get picked up by pirates. Point is, you're not going to feel good about it unless she's part of the conversation. It really depends if her mom owned the ship and held the bond."

"Ugh, got it. Not sure she's ready for this."

Nick had forwarded me some of the easier to understand legalese related to salvage rights. The laws were essentially the same as they had been since the Roman Empire. As salvager we could ask for repayment equal to the value of the load, including the barges. If we went that path and the Chen family had a bond, they would not only lose their tug but also their bond. Most small trading families couldn't take that type of loss and survive.

I waited for a few minutes after Ada got out of the shower and then knocked on her bunk room door.

"Come in." Her voice sounded small behind the door. I pushed it open. Ada sat on the edge of the bed and was drying her hair with the towel.

"I'm really sorry, you've been through a lot, but we should probably talk about some things before the Navy gets here. We have some decisions to make that could affect you."

She looked up at me with distrust in her eyes. I didn't blame her, it was way too much to take in.

I continued. "At least let me tell you how we read it."

She nodded and I leaned against the door frame. "A lot of this hinges on whether you and your mom owned the tug and if you hold the bond on the load." Her answer showed in her face before she had a chance to say anything. She probably wasn't much of a poker player.

"Okay …" she said, trying not to give anything away.

"Let's just say that's the case."

"It is," she interrupted.

"Well, that's mostly bad. As it stands, the company you contracted to will collect the bond since you have no way to complete the delivery."

"What about the other tug? Is it yours?" Ada asked.

"No. It belonged to the pirates. We have captured it, however, and will make a claim on it."

"Is that it? Are you trying to take our load?"

"It's okay to be mad, Ada, but you need to know we're not the bad guys. We responded to your mayday. We're merchants, just like you."

She looked chagrined. "I'm sorry. It's just, well, I've never had to deal with this before. Mom always handled this stuff."

"Is your dad still around?"

"He and Mom started the business together, but they split up a few years ago. He still owns half. All our money is wrapped up in the tug and those bonds. We're wiped out without it."

"We'll get you hooked up with our comm gear so you can talk to your dad. Before that, let me tell you what I'm thinking. You're probably required to report this to whomever you contracted with, so you should do that first. My guess is they'll tell you they're taking your bond. Tell them you might be able to sub-contract out the delivery and find out if they'll still honor your agreement. Your dad might pass that by a lawyer if it gets dicey. The problem is, we need to resolved this before the Navy gets here."

"You keep saying that. Why?"

"I don't want to make a claim of salvage on the barges and your load if we can simply help you get them delivered. A decision needs to be made while the Navy is on-site. Mars Protectorate Judiciary will settle everything while they're here and they don't go for long, drawn-out processes. If you want us to sub-contract delivery for you, I need to know so I avoid filing the salvage claim."

"Wouldn't you make more money if you salvaged them?"

"Yes."

"Why would you do this for us?"

"It's the right thing to do."

"Shouldn't you make something? It doesn't seem fair to you."

"Okay, what was your net on this run going to be?"

"Forty thousand."

"If we deliver on time, then you pay us twenty. Talk it over with your dad and let me know. We'll give your AI full access to the comm system and I'll leave you to it. Come find me when you know something."

HARD BALL

"Hey, Liam. Can we talk?" Ada's voice came from the doorway of the bridge.

"Sure, come in, we're all friends here. You've already met Marny, and this is my partner, Nick."

Nick stood and shook her hand. It was less awkward than I might have expected.

Ada took a breath and said, "We've got a problem. I talked to my dad and then to a lawyer. The contract was oddly written and it doesn't allow us to sub out its fulfillment."

"Did you contact the company?" I asked.

"Precast Products. Yeah, our lawyer contacted theirs and they aren't budging. We stand to lose three hundred fifty thousand in bonds not to mention the loss of *Baux*." The stress in her face was clear.

"That sucks." I said.

"We've got an incoming hail from the frigate *Banny Hill*," Nick said.

"On forward holo."

An older naval officer appeared, centered and forward of the two pilot's chairs. His features were strongly oriental. He had short black hair that was graying at the temples and the fit build I had come to expect from naval personnel.

"Greetings, Captain," I said.

"Greetings. Lieutenant Commander Pablo Veras. With whom do I have the pleasure of addressing?"

"Thank you, Lieutenant Commander. Captain Liam Hoffen. You are being broadcast on my bridge in front of my crew and a survivor of the attack."

"Appreciate the heads up, Captain Hoffen. We're currently a

thousand kilometers from your location, would you submit to a turret lockdown?"

Accept turret lockdown from frigate Banny Hill. "There you go, Lieutenant Commander."

"Thanks, Captain. We're only a few minutes out and aren't tracking any hostiles in the area. Do you concur?"

"Roger that. All's quiet."

"We'll get right down to business once we arrive, if you don't mind. Thanks to your combat data streams we will process the scene quickly and let you get on about your business. We'd like to dock up with you and provide a temporary catwalk between ships. Is this something you would be amenable to doing?"

"Certainly. Have your engineer work directly with my partner, Nick James."

We tracked the frigate as it arrived. It didn't immediately stop next to us, but slowly sailed a long arc around the combat area. At forty-five meters, the *Banny Hill* wasn't a lot longer than *Sterra's Gift*, but it was three times as thick and shaped more like a triangle, with several decks above and below the centerline. The amount of firepower on display on the flat side of the triangle was outrageous - turrets and missile tubes fairly littered the side that faced us. I imagined the other side was similarly outfitted. I would hate to run into the *Banny Hill* under the wrong circumstances.

The Navy pulled alongside *Sterra's Gift* and extended the pressurized catwalk. It didn't take long for two figures to cross over and press the 'hail' button on the exterior side of our airlock.

A stout Marine in full armor stood in front of Veras as I cycled the locks. With the pressurized catwalk, we didn't have to worry about de-pressurizing and re-pressurizing, but safety dictated that at least one door be sealed just in case either ship were to move suddenly and disconnect the catwalk.

"Permission to come aboard?" Veras requested from behind the armored Marine.

"Permission granted. If you'd join us on the bridge, we can make introductions there."

"Lead on."

When we arrived on the bridge, Marny snapped to attention and announced, "Captain on the bridge." Once the Marine had surveyed the bridge and apparently decided we were of a limited threat he moved to the side and stood rigidly. We all shook hands and made introductions.

"If you are amenable, Captain, I would like to interview Ms. Chen first. We can either do that back on the *Banny Hill* or, if you have a private space, we could do it there."

I offered him the use of the captain's quarters. Ada looked at me with concern.

"Ada, I believe Lieutenant Commander Veras would like to meet with you privately to make sure that you aren't being coerced or held against your will. I suspect he will also want to take a statement from you on the events that occurred here today. I know it's a lot to take in, but he is honor bound to make sure you are safe, first and foremost."

I caught Veras's eye and he nodded affirmatively. Ada, mollified, walked off the bridge with Veras and his Marine guard in tow. I was pleased to see that the door remained open. The Marine took up a position where he had a clear view of Veras and Ada, while blocking our exit from the bridge.

"Nick, any comm?"

"Not a thing. Are you going to claim salvage?"

"Not sure what other option we'll have. I'm guessing it'll tie things up for a few months, greedy bastards."

"Are you serious about heading back to Colony 40?" Marny asked.

"We can talk it over, but it would give us the greatest leverage. I bet Precast Products wants to call my bluff and see if we'll actually file the salvage claim."

"Why wouldn't we?" Nick asked.

"I've got an idea that might keep Ada and her dad from taking too much of a financial hit."

We waited for Veras and Ada to finish. I was itching to get moving again. All of this sitting around was driving me nuts. Finally, Ada returned to the bridge.

"How'd it go?" Her eyes were red and her cheeks puffy. "No fun, eh?"

"He'd like to talk to you now."

Veras stood when I entered the room and we shook hands again. "I had a nice conversation with Commander Sterra on the *Kuznetsov*. She speaks very highly of you."

I wasn't sure how to respond. "Thank you."

"My staff reviewed the combat data streams and provided we don't find anything to the contrary with the physical inspection that is currently taking place, Mars Protectorate will find the crew of *Sterra's Gift* acted within the law. Further, you and your crew will be commended publicly for quick and decisive action which resulted in the preservation of the life of one Ada Chen."

"I sense a 'but' in this conversation," I said.

"Not really. I just don't understand why you let those pirates go. They fired on your ship and you were well within your rights to take action. To some, it will look like you wanted that tug and didn't care if a couple of pirates got away."

"It seemed like the right idea at the time. I'm not sure I would do the same thing again."

"Are you going to request the tug as a privateer prize? I couldn't help but notice its proximity."

"Yes."

"Surely you see how that looks," he said.

"Let me put my cards on the table. I'm not concerned with how other people view this, but I am concerned with how you see it."

"Oh? By all means, put your cards on the table, then."

"Did I consider the tug when making the deal with the pirates? Yes. Was I worried about exchanging fire with two ships? Yes. I was out of missiles and we were outnumbered. Did I think we could win? Absolutely. Did I think we might take casualties? Absolutely. The people on this ship are my family and if I can keep someone from shooting at us, I'll do it every time. Am I a merchant? Yes. I'm looking out for me and mine."

"Some might say you had less than honorable intentions."

"They'd best not say that to my face. The reason we responded to the mayday was simple. Adela Chen was being attacked and about to lose everything, including her life. Do the math. I launched three hundred thousand m-creds worth of missiles before I even knew there was a tug. Smart money said - fly on by."

"Alright, no need to get hot." He gave me a slight grin. "I have to ask the questions and get them recorded. For the record, I think you should have blown them to bits, but I don't have mouths to feed. As for the matter of the tug, it is not registered which, as you most likely know, means it was probably being used in criminal enterprise. I am awarding Loose Nuts Corporation the Fujitsu Freighter – Model FF718 as a prize under the Mars Privateer Act."

Off the record. Veras stopped the recording.

"Between you and me. I get that you had a hard decision to make. What I want you to think about is what those two pirates are going to do now. Do you think they'll turn away from their illicit activities? How many others will die at their hands? You can comfort yourself all you want that you didn't put your crew in danger. I think that's crap."

Veras's words hit me like a ton of bricks. My face flushed, was I just greedy? I started to talk but he cut me off.

"Look, you're young and just getting started. I saw you in action back on Colony 40 and read about your attack on the pirate base near Baru Manush. I believe you came here to help Captain Chen. You are an honorable man. The thing I've got stuck in my craw is that, dammit, you let me down. Like it or not, you've got a lot of people watching you and we need heroes, Captain Hoffen, not mercenaries. Straighten up."

Veras pulled his jacket straight. *Back on the record.*

I was too stunned to respond. He couldn't have shut me up better if he had whacked me in the forehead with a two kilo spanner.

"As to the matter of the string of barges, would you like to file a claim of salvage?"

My mind whirled with emotion. How could he switch gears so quickly?

"Yes."

"Very well."

"No, wait."

"Pardon?"

"Could I have a minute with Ada Chen?"

"It's a little out of the ordinary, but I don't see a problem, I would like your conversation to be on the record, however."

"Okay."

"Sergeant, would you request Ms. Chen's presence?"

Ada entered the room and looked uncomfortably between us.

I started, "Ada, Loose Nuts Corporation has recently come into possession of a Fujitsu Freighter Tug. It so happens that we don't have any pilots available currently to fly this tug for us. Would you be willing to contract with us to pilot it back?"

"Uh, couldn't you or Nick sail it?"

"No, we have our duties aboard *Sterra's Gift*." I winked at her, hoping she'd clue in. She looked at me with some confusion.

"Well, okay, yes."

"We can discuss a price later," I said. She just looked at me. I glanced at Lieutenant Commander Veras conspiratorially.

"The Loose Nuts Corporation declines to file a claim of salvage on the string of barges. It is well beyond our capability to maneuver."

Veras's face broke into a wide, knowing smile. "I see, Captain." He turned to Ada. "Ms. Chen, since you are the only other captain in the area capable of filing for a claim of salvage, would you like to do so?"

Ada caught it. "I would."

"So granted. And Captain Hoffen, for the record, that was a very honorable thing to do."

Veras stood and I stood with him. "With that, our inquiry is complete. We have a second piece of business to discuss."

"Oh?"

"Yes, but we need to have the conversation on *Banny Hill*. Security issues, I'm sure you understand. Would you join us at 1900?"

"Certainly. Uh, there's also a small matter I was hoping to get your help with."

"How's that?"

"The pirates left three unarmed scuttling devices on the Fujitsu tug. We don't really know what to do with them."

"Now that's something we can take care of. Sergeant Hawthorne, please coordinate a disposal team and while you're at it, make sure there aren't any additional surprises."

"Aye, aye, sir."

After escorting Veras and Hawthorne back through the airlock, I rejoined the crew on the bridge.

"Captain on the bridge," Marny said. I couldn't help but notice it wasn't with quite the verve it had been when Veras and Hawthorne were on board.

"Is that strictly necessary?" I asked.

"No, but I like it," she said.

"How'd it go?" Nick asked.

"You probably should have been in there with me."

"Yeah, probably. Felt like you had it though."

"Okay. They did award us the tug. Ada has salvage since we are contracting her to fly the tug back for us." I looked to Ada who nodded her agreement.

"Veras wants a meet on the *Banny Hill* at 1900."

"What's that all about?" Marny asked.

"He wouldn't say - something about security. I'd like you both there."

"Anything else?" Nick asked.

"Navy agreed to remove the scuttling charges from the tug. They'll probably need to coordinate with someone."

"I'll take that," Marny offered.

"One more thing. We need to come up with a name for the tug. Any suggestions?"

I was surprised when Marny spoke up first. "In the Navy there is a long history of naming smaller ships after heroes. Ada, I know it's probably too soon, but what would you think if we called her the *Adela Chen*?"

"Yes, I'd like that."

TWO POINT FIVE KILO TONNES

The corvette *Kuznetsov* was the only other naval ship I'd been on and it seemed very similar to the *Banny Hill* from the inside. On the outside, they couldn't be more different. Where the *Banny Hill* was shaped like an overstuffed angle fish (according to Marny) the *Kuznetsov* was shaped much more like an arrow. On the inside there were immaculately maintained hallways with sharply dressed, hustling sailors.

Sergeant Hawthorne met us at the airlock and led us to a meeting room. Once in the room, I recognized the setup from a previous meeting with military personnel. We'd arrived a few minutes early and were the first in the room. Hawthorne posted himself at the door and took the position I associated with Marines; feet spread to shoulder width apart, hands clasped behind the back and a mile long stare, straight forward.

Marny had excused herself from the meeting, insisting someone stay aboard and look after things. We probably would have been okay, given our present company, but she felt strongly and I didn't see any need to push it. Nick and I knew better than to sit down right away. Some senior ranking officer would undoubtedly come in and then everyone would stand up. I knew from past experience this would be a perfect opportunity for Nick and me to find a new way to embarrass ourselves.

Right at 1900, Lieutenant Commander Veras entered the room, followed by a woman we hadn't yet met. Hawthorne snapped to attention at their entry. Nick and I had done enough research to discover that no expectations were placed on civilians under these circumstances, but I still felt weird about it.

"Dismissed, Sergeant," Veras said.

"Captain Liam Hoffen, Nickolas James. May I introduce you to my first officer, Lieutenant Qiu Loo." Her first name sounded like 'Tso.' We took turns shaking her hand. She had a thin, spacer build with strong Oriental features.

"Pleased to meet you." She had a clear voice and a firm grip.

"We aren't much for decorum here, grab whatever seat you like. Qiu, would you fire up the holo-comm?" Veras asked.

"Yes, sir." she said.

I wasn't particularly surprised when Lieutenant Gregor Belcose's muscular shape appeared from the waist up on the holo projector. He was our primary contact with Mars Protectorate Navy since we'd been issued our Letter of Marque, giving us privateer status.

"Greetings, Lieutenant Belcose," Veras said.

"Thank you, sir. Greetings to you, as well." Belcose was sitting rigidly, somehow able to communicate a sense of almost being at attention.

"At ease, Lieutenant. Let's keep this informal."

"Thank you, sir." Belcose shifted slightly but he seemed anything but informal.

"We're all here. Let's get on with it."

"Yes, sir. Mr. Hoffen and Mr. James, our intelligence division has requested that we find suitable clandestine transportation with possible light fire support for an upcoming mission. Commander Sterra, upon hearing of your prize claim of the Freighter *Adela Chen*, suggested your team would provide the perfect cover."

"That was fast, we just named her an hour ago." I tossed this out, hoping to give Nick a moment to process.

"I have to be honest, I just saw the name pop up, I doubt Commander Sterra is aware of it yet."

"What does this have to do with the *Banny Hill*?" Veras sounded impatient.

"Nothing more than we discussed, sir." Belcose had not let down his guard much.

"Lieutenant Loo, I'm not needed here." Veras stood, and she rose with him. Nick and I pushed up from the table.

"Gentlemen, good luck to you." He held out his hand. Nick and I shook it in turn and he exited the room.

I wasn't sure what to make of all that, so I turned back to Belcose's image. "What does light fire support mean?"

"If our intelligence asset is compromised, you might have to get creative in getting her out of there."

"At the risk of being annoying, what's this got to do with Nick and me?"

"We think a mining colony's been taken over by Red Houzi. We've lost several assets to so-called accidents. Somehow they always figure out who we are. With your new freighter, no one would think it odd that you show up. It's a great cover for our operative."

Nick stepped in. "Aren't all the colonies tied up with M-Corp contracts? What's a tug going to do for us?"

"Jeratorn's not," I answered.

"Jeratorn is barely under Mars Protectorate from what I hear," Nick said. "I've heard it's anarchy. Are you nuts?"

"It's not that bad," Belcose said. It was telling that he didn't completely deny that Jeratorn was out of control.

"I still don't get why you're thinking about us," I said.

"Harry Flark," Belcose answered.

That got my attention. Harry Flark had been the administrator of Colony 40, our home, when it was attacked by pirates. It was never proven that he had anything to do with the attacks but I, for one, was certain of it.

"What about Harry Flark?"

"He's the new station administrator on Jeratorn."

"What happened to the old one?" I couldn't help but ask.

"We're not sure."

"How many people are you looking to transport over there? And how long would we need to stay on Jeratorn?" Nick asked.

"One person, ten days on the outside."

"You cover fuel, and we'll need repairs, missile replacements and a short term, high value bond, preferably not issued by Mars Protectorate, I'll send a list," Nick said.

"Just like that?" I asked and looked at Nick.

"No chance you'll turn down a shot at Flark. If we don't have to pay for fuel, I don't see how we could ignore this."

"That's almost in PDC space." It was no secret that the People's Democracy of China and Mars Protectorate were uneasy neighbors.

"We might need a couple of temporary crew," Nick said. I felt like I wasn't completely in the room.

"We'll cover it," Belcose answered.

"So we'll pick someone up on Mars?" I asked. Nick gave me his, 'prepare to feel stupid' look, which confused me all the more.

"That'd be me." Qiu Loo said. "And Belcose, I'd like to be clear with you that I'm not on board with this civilian crew. I've lost too many colleagues and we don't know where the leak is."

"Oh …" I wasn't sure how to respond to that. She clearly didn't trust us, but it was a sure bet we weren't her leak.

"The decision's been made, Lieutenant. This is a first rate crew and they're good in a pinch. More importantly, they've got a vested interest in seeing this through," Belcose responded.

"I understand and I get it. I just want everyone to be on the same page. This isn't how we should be doing it. Don't forget, it's my ass on the line."

"Do you want to pull the plug?" Belcose asked.

She paused for a full minute before responding. "No. There's too much at stake. You better be right about these guys."

"I am," he said and turned to Nick and me. "What do you think?"

"She's right. We're not even close to being Navy," Nick said. "But if Flark was responsible for the attack on Colony 40, I'd like to be part of taking him down."

"So you'll take the job?" Belcose asked, looking at me.

Nick didn't often drive a conversation, much less a deal. If he wanted this mission, then I would back him. I nodded slightly.

"We're in," Nick answered.

"You mean after we discuss it with the crew, right?" I said with a slight grin.

"Frak, right! After we discuss it with the crew."

"I'll have Sergeant Hawthorne escort you back to your ship and I'll be along in twenty minutes." Loo said.

Back on the bridge of *Sterra's Gift*, we found Marny alone.

"I think Ada's down for the count," she said.

"Thanks for staying with her," I replied. "Any word on the tug?"

"They've got a team aboard right now. Team leader said they'd be done within the hour."

"Nick, you have any idea how to link up a tug with those barges?"

"Same idea as the ore tenders at the refinery. You get close and the tug takes care of the rest."

"I don't want to wake Ada and I want to get out of here as soon as Qiu gets on board."

"Qiu?" Marny asked.

"We've got a job offer," Nick quickly interjected.

"Saddle up!" Marny replied.

"It might be kind of crazy," I said.

"Oh, do tell ..."

"Well, truthfully there aren't a lot of details. We're dropping a passenger off on the colony of Jeratorn, using the tug as cover."

"I can help." We all turned to see Ada standing in the bridge's doorway.

"Come on in. Only Nick and Marny ask for permission." I enjoyed the uncomfortable look on Marny's face. She wanted to correct me, but I suspected Ada's recent hardships kept her quiet.

"I thought you turned in," Marny said.

"Can't sleep." Ada sank down into one of the chairs.

"We've arranged to bring your mom home with us," Nick said.

"Where is she?"

"She's in the cargo hold next to the lifepod. Do you want to see her?" Nick asked.

"No. Not like that."

"We'll be getting underway in the next hour or so," I said.

"Let me help," she said again.

"Ada, I don't think …"

"What do you know about sailing a tug?"

"We'll get along."

"I'm sure you think that. You might even be right, but each of those barges are two-point-five-kilo tonnes. The tug merely makes suggestions - you can't make quick adjustments. You won't be allowed to dock anywhere on Mars and you'll have to hire an operator once you're within a thousand kilometers of any port unless you have your Class-A license."

"Ada, it's just so soon."

"Mom wouldn't have gone with that. Besides, what difference does it make which ship I'm on?"

"Any word from the Navy on the tug?" I asked.

"They're clearing out now," Nick said.

"I'd like to get rolling with the tug, you come along with *Sterra's Gift* once Qiu shows up?"

"Yup. Take some bars with you. Who knows what kind of food they've stocked."

"Ada, if you're riding with me, grab your gear and meet me in the airlock in five."

Coming from *Sterra's Gift*, the *Adela Chen* was like stepping into a closet. Surprisingly, the ship was in immaculate condition. It was obviously a new ship and every surface was spotless, not the smallest bit of grime or trash to be found.

The layout of the ship was straightforward. The airlock was at the back of the living space and right next to the galley. The galley was a meter and a half wide by three meters long. Built into the long wall of the galley was a suit freshener, large refrigeration unit, meal preparer (called a galley-pro), coffee machine and water supply. There was a half meter wide countertop that folded down at a standing height as there was no room for chairs. It was extraordinarily efficient, if not particularly comfortable.

The bunk room had a wide two-person mattress on one side, with a fold-down single mattress above that was currently in the up position. A small nook held a permanently attached overstuffed chair. Opposite the beds was a bank of built-in drawers and shelves hidden behind latched doors. The large bed was neatly made and a couple suit-liners were folded on the shelves.

A narrow ladder connected the living space to the cockpit. The cockpit was nothing more than two well-padded chairs with a small console between them and a bank of vid screens in front.

"Where's the flight stick?" I couldn't imagine a ship without some sort of flight yoke.

"What would you use that for?" Ada asked. The smile on her face made me almost forget how horrible her day had been.

"How do you steer?"

"I'm just messin' with you. We had a stick, but you really don't use 'em that often. These babies are a one-trick pony. They push. Sometimes we push a little more on top, on bottom or one side or the other, but mostly we just push."

"How do you fly around?"

"Yah, you're not really getting the concept."

"Right, we just push."

"Now you're getting it."

"Teach me?"

"Told you, you'd need me."

"Which side you want?"

"Always sat on the starboard. Mom liked to sit on the port side."

I watched as Ada grabbed a bar above the starboard side chair and nimbly swung her body over the back and settled in. I imagined that she had executed this maneuver a million times. At .6 gravity I was in my element and mirrored her move. I wasn't as graceful, but made it into the seat just fine. Surprisingly, it was considerably more comfortable than my chair on *Sterra's Gift*.

Hail *Sterra's Gift*.

"Heya Liam, you all loaded up?"

"Roger that. We're going to get underway shortly."

"Sounds good. We still haven't heard from Qiu. I wonder if she ran into problems with Veras. He didn't sound too happy with the arrangement."

"Yeah, you get a contract from Belcose?"

"Sure did. Covers fuel to/from Jeratorn, full missile load, repairs and a million cred bond for six months."

"Man, you're hardcore."

"Wish I could take credit. He rolled over too easily. It feels like we're walking into something bad. Might want to step away from all this. We can reject the contract, it's not too late."

"Not with Flark in the mix. Belcose knew he was involved in the attack on Colony 40, but held that little piece until now. Pisses me off, but it worked. I want that piece of crap. You want out?"

"Nope."

"Okay, come find us. We're gonna get under sail."

"Roger that. *Sterra's Gift* out."

"You care if I put some music on?"

"Sure, what do you have in mind?" Ada asked.

"Trust me, you'll like it."

Play Dave Dudley Six Days on the Road.

The twangy sound of cowboy Dave Dudley filled the cockpit.

Well, I pulled out of Pittsburg, Rollin' down the Eastern Seaboard.

Six days on the road and I'm a gonna make it home tonight.

ONCE A ROOKIE ...

"The first thing you need to understand is that you're not in charge," Ada said.

"I don't even know how to respond to that." I grinned at my double entendre.

Ada ignored me and pushed forward. "Second thing is the tug merely makes suggestions. Once you get those girls moving, it's real hard to stop or change their direction."

"Okay, how do we get over to the barges?"

"All the controls are built into your chair. This ship is configured with twin sticks. You pop the sticks up out of the chair's arms. We didn't have them on *Baux* but there're people who swear by 'em. Mom used to get into arguments with other pilots all the time. I think they just wanted something to talk about."

Ada noticed I was unsuccessfully looking for the sticks in the arms of my chair. "Just push on the panels there on the end of the arm rest," she added.

That did it for me. A joystick swiveled out from under the arm as soon as I depressed the small panel.

"So not a coffee holder?"

"Probably not. Now, pull both joysticks back so your arms are bent and your elbows can rest on the chair again. Make sure you're comfortable. The AI will register this as your home position."

I pulled the sticks back so my arms were slightly bent. "Good enough?" I asked.

"No worries, you can re-register the sticks if you don't like where you have 'em."

"You gonna let me sail her?"

"Only way you're going to learn. I've already registered my Master's license with the ship so I can override you if things get out of control," Ada said.

"It'll override my status as owner?"

"You're such a control freak."

"Okay, I had that coming. You've a Master's license?"

"Override only works if we have a string hooked up. Been sailing since I was ten, homeschooled in space."

"Sounds lonely."

"Not at all. We weren't always sailing 'cause Mom and Dad took turns. I was home at least half the time."

"Where's home?"

"We have an apartment in Puskar Stellar."

"Is that where Precast Products is located?"

"Sort of. Precast has offices in several major cities on Mars. This string's headed for their orbital refinery over Puskar Stellar. They make parts for the big shipyards."

"You land the tug on Puskar?"

"Nope. You can, but they're not very good at atmospheric entry, even on Mars. We have a private slip that's not too far away from one of the Space Elevators. Saves a bunch of fuel by not burning in and out."

"Hadn't thought about all that."

"You would, once you paid for the fuel to lift that tug off the planet."

"Any harm with me flying this around a little?"

"Inertial systems?"

"Check."

"Gravity systems?

"Check."

Ada had a list a kilometer long but I appreciated that she had it committed to memory. She definitely had some items that Nick and I should add to *Sterra's Gift*'s checklist. She finally ended with, "Coffee brewing?"

"Negative."

"We'll have to fix that, but I can overlook it for now. Take it slow, it's going to feel slippery compared to what you're used to. These engines are waaay overpowered for flying around without a load."

"Alright Captain Chen, hang onto your seat." At some point while we were going through Ada's checklist, she'd managed to get her own joysticks deployed.

"Slow on the helm, Mr. Hoffen."

The *Adela Chen* was pointed directly at *Sterra's Gift* and we were only back half a kilometer. The *Banny Hill* was on *Sterra's Gift's* port side. I had no idea what I was dealing with, so I pushed both sticks forward slowly with no tilt in any direction. As I suspected, the ship started moving forward. Much to my surprise, however, we accelerated very slowly. I pushed the sticks even further forward and we did accelerate faster, but still nothing like I was used to.

"Good," Ada said. "Now give us a little declination and head under those ships."

I complied and tipped the sticks forward in unison. The ship nosed over very quickly and before I knew what was happening, we had rotated nearly one-hundred forty degrees, or so much that we were almost pointing backwards.

To Ada's credit, she didn't say a word. I figured I was mostly there already, so I slowly pulled the sticks back until we had rotated all the way around and were now pointed down at about ten degrees.

"Incoming hail from Sterra's Gift."

On comm.

"That what you had in mind, Liam?" Nick's voice was half amused, half concerned.

"Only the last ten degrees."

"Roger that. Anything we can help with?"

"Negative. Captain Chen is giving me some free rein."

"Roger that. Let me know if you need us to move."

Terminate comm. I wasn't going to dignify that with a response. We passed beneath the two ships with a considerable safety margin.

"So remember, I said slippery. Try some rotation, but take it real slow," she said.

I nodded and tipped both sticks over slightly to the port. The ship gently rotated to the port but stayed on the same line.

"Good. Straighten it out."

I pulled it back and flew straight. I had some experience with a twin joystick system, just not something with this kind of power.

"Oh, good, you've got it," Ada said, with surprise.

"I just wasn't expecting that much power."

"Everything changes when you hook up to a string of barges. Just run her around to about a hundred meters behind the string."

I did a decent job of sailing up behind the set of three barges, but found I was low by twenty meters. I tipped the ship back ninety degrees and nudged it upward, but twenty meters was too fine of an adjustment for the large engines. I spun back down and tried again. I ended up thirty meters below - things weren't getting better.

"You're missing something." Ada had been quiet, letting me work through things.

"Oh, thank Jupiter. What am I missing?"

"What do you suppose would happen if you'd rotated port with your starboard stick and starboard with your port stick?"

I felt like the rookie I was. "Ahh, crap, of course." I gently tipped the sticks away from each other. The ship lifted slowly into position.

"Nice touch." Ada said.

"How do we link up?"

"Slide us in so we're just twenty meters off."

I complied. It was coming easier to me.

"Okay, we're almost done. Stow the dead-heads. The ship will hook up the glad-hands and the tongue."

"Glad-hands and tongue? Sounds like a bad dance."

"Very funny, there should be a push button or rocker switch on the console between us for the dead-heads."

Sure enough there was. In this day and age of virtual everything, there was a frakking rocker switch right there on the console. I'd probably seen ten of them in my life on very old equipment.

"What? We don't trust the AI to handle the dead-heads?"

"Provides a good visual reminder when you're not loaded."

"Because the AI does such a bad job of managing this stuff?"

"Just do it," Ada said.

I flipped the switch. It had a satisfyingly hefty feel to it and clunked audibly when I pushed it over. Three tongues extended from the end of the barge. Each tongue was three meters wide and a meter tall. They extended from the barge and toward our ship and fell well below my sightline. Ada flipped on a vid screen that showed the tongues sliding into receptacles in the ship. Three bright green lights glowed on the forward bulkhead. A few seconds later yellow bars flashed below each of those green lights.

"That a problem?" I asked.

"No, the top lights are showing the coupling status. The bottom ones are the glad-hand connections. They haven't connected yet. You can't fly with tongues connected if you don't have the glad-hands hooked up.

"What's a glad-hand?"

"Communication, power and hydraulic couplings."

"Why not say that?"

"You sail a ship for a living and you want to know why things are named funny? When's the last time you actually filled your sails with wind?"

"What? Oh … Very funny."

The vid screens showed thick cables being stretched between the ship and the barge. Once they were connected, all light patches showed green.

"And, we're ready to sail. Too bad the first mate hasn't laid in a route for us."

"How hard do you burn?"

"With this heavy of a load, let the AI make a recommendation. It'll make a big difference."

Calculate navigation plan to Precast Products. Leave 15% reserve fuel.

The AI showed a plan on the centered vid-screen.

Ada didn't like it. "Six days. Dang. Most of the time we use a Rate 4 consumption calculation. It's what gets figured into most of our contracts. You just dropped a burn rate that's well into the Rate 1 category. You could save a bunch if you backed off a bit."

"But this trip we're going to get you home fast." I was surprised that Ada hadn't overheard the conversation about the Navy paying for fuel. I didn't think I needed to point it out again.

Engage navigation plan.

The ship's massive engines spooled up. It was a much different feeling from the one we got on *Sterra's Gift*. I would have expected us to lurch forward, given the sound of it all. However, it didn't seem like the ship was doing much of anything.

"Well. Let's get that coffee rolling. We should set a watch schedule and I'll take first," Ada said.

"Sorry, I'm not going anywhere for a while. How about you try to get some rest?"

"I'll start coffee, but I'm going to run the sheets through the freshener first. You should start working on your tug certifications. You will get some good hours on this trip."

"How many hours do I need for a Master's license?"

"You don't want to know. Six thousand in the seat."

"Ugh."

"Two tests and five hundred hours gets you an Operator's license. Most of the outlying colonies are fine with that."

"Oh, that's not too bad."

"Nope. AI records your hours. Believe it or not, you don't have to be awake for half of 'em."

"That's stupid."

"Wait 'til you start taking the tests."

"I'll help with the coffee."

We pulled out of the seats. It felt weird to leave the ship to accelerate on its own, but there was virtually nothing we could do to help it along. With the heavy load in front of us, changes in direction would happen slowly. If we needed to dodge something quickly, we'd be out of luck.

I helped Ada pull the sheets off the bed. It was immaculately made with corners crisply tucked in. I folded the top bunk down and pulled its sheets off before running them all through the suit freshener, while Ada loaded up the coffee maker.

"You take the bottom bunk," I said. "I'm a pretty light sleeper and will probably spend most of the time in the cockpit."

"Sounds good. I guess I am pretty tired," she admitted.

"Sleep as long as you need. I'll be topside." By the time we had the sheets cleaned and back on, the coffee was ready, for which I was grateful. I grabbed a cup of joe and a couple of meal bars and headed back up to the cockpit. It felt good to be underway again, if not a little strange. The heavy thrum of much larger engines would take some getting used to.

THE TROUBLE WITH WOMEN

Our navigation plan showed that we would accelerate for two days and then decelerate for four. I was more than happy to use the Navy's fuel to cut our trip time down.

Tabby, my sort of girlfriend, had been at the Mars Naval Academy for less than three weeks and I was hoping to see her when we arrived. She hadn't communicated much since we parted ways back on Colony 40, but the contact we'd had was more than enough to let me know she wasn't trying to dump me.

Tabby, Nick, and I had known each other for virtually our entire lives. We'd grown up going to school together, played on the same pod-ball team, and palled around for the last seventeen years. It wasn't until Tabby was about to ship off to the Naval Academy that she'd finally let me know I'd been an idiot to not have pursued a relationship with her more seriously.

Compose video to Tabby, center on my face.

"I hope your start at the academy has been okay. You'll never believe it but Nick has fallen hard for that new crewmate, Marny. But, that's not really the big news. We ran into another problem. It seems like trouble finds us. Anyway, it's really a bad deal; a pilot and her daughter got attacked by pirates, even though they weren't very far out from Mars. The daughter, Ada, made it okay but the pilot, her mom, ended up dying. It was terrible. We did, however, make a prize claim on the freighter we captured. Anyway, we are expecting to be on Mars in six days. If you can break free from school for a day or two, I'd love to see you. We'll do something awesome. I'd really like you to meet Marny. Oh, you'll notice I'm flying in a different ship. This is the tug we captured. Ada's been teaching me how to fly it, and I'm going to work on my license. Anyway, let me know about getting together. I really miss you, Tabby."

I felt like an idiot. My thoughts, when talking to Tabby, were jumbled and I seemed to just ramble. I hoped she'd be able to make something out of what I said.

Incoming hail from Sterra's Gift.

"Liam here," Ada wasn't in the cockpit with me so I played the audio over the speakers.

"Qiu's on board and squared away. She wants to know when we'll leave Mars for Jeratorn." Nick said. He struggled to pronounce her first name.

"Think T.S.O. - nothing like it's spelled. The time frame will depend on when repairs are complete, but I'll get to work on lining up a load. We've been hitting it pretty hard lately and I'm going to try to meet up with Tabby."

"Cool, I'd like to see her too if that works out," Nick said.

"I left her a message, we'll see what she comes back with. We should plan to pull some pay out for both of us so we can live it up. You set the amount. We also need to square with Marny."

"Yup. Already on it. Marny's been paid out and I dropped five thousand creds in our personal accounts. Marny said she was going to introduce me to hot springs. I can't wait."

"I'm not sure I want to hear this. By the way, have you looked into the TradeNet subscription?"

"Yup, done. So after everything, we're running at ninety thousand m-creds without being paid for the load of pirate loot."

"I was thinking, wasn't there some artwork in those crates we liberated from the pirates on Baru Manush? Isn't it likely stolen?" I asked.

"Yup. We'll have to find a dealer who can do a provenance search. It'd probably be easier to find an auctioneer who deals in this stuff. The navy will validate our video evidence of how we procured the art, although some of it might get tied up. All in, just be better to let the pros deal with it."

"How much will they take off the top?" I asked.

"I'm showing the big boys take fifteen to twenty percent."

"Sounds like it'd be worth it."

"I'll set it up," he said.

"I was wondering, have you gotten any security updates from

the pirate base?" We'd captured a Red Houzi base about a month ago and we hadn't come up with a plan to do anything with it. There was at least ten times as much loot left at the base as we'd been able to take with us.

"It's all quiet. Not even a flyby as far as I can tell. We've got to get back there," Nick said.

"Any thoughts on how we should go about that?"

"We have a tug now, we should just rent a barge and get Jack to help. Do you think your dad would be willing?"

"Why not? We could cut 'em both in on the haul." I hadn't said anything to Nick yet, but I wanted to set up our own base somewhere using buildings and guns we scavenged from the Red Houzi base.

"I'm in. How is Ada doing? She had a pretty rough day," Nick said.

"Hanging in there. She's sacked out right now. Can you find us? I sent you our navigation plan."

"Check your sensors. We're right on top of you."

The displays weren't set up like I was used to, something I would soon resolve. Sure enough, *Sterra's Gift* was fifteen kilometers above us.

"Would have bit me ..." I muttered.

"Hey Liam, you did the right thing back there. Ada'd be dead if you'd turned away. I don't give a crap what Veras and Marny said about the other thing."

"Thanks bud, it means a lot coming from you. But, don't let Marny hear you say it, I think she can take you."

"Nah, she knows. I get where she's coming from. When she was in the Navy, she had to clean up a lot of messes those pirates made. It was hard for her not to take 'em out when she had the chance."

"I've got a bad feeling about this. I'm not sure we're dealing with the same class of pirates."

"What do you mean?"

"This ship is immaculate - like Navy immaculate. There isn't a single thing out of place."

"What are you thinking?"

"Not sure. I guess it's just different. Also, we're six days from Mars. That's striking pretty close to home."

"Yeah, I suppose, but it was just dumb luck that we were close by."

"No. I know. I'm not sure what I'm saying. We're missing something. Anyway, I have a class to start working on."

"A what?"

"Oh, Ada's got me all fired up to get my Operator's license. I need two tests and five hundred hours on the tug."

"You have the hours."

"What do you mean?"

"You need five hundred hours sailing under load. What do you think you've been doing with all that ore from your claim to the refinery?"

"You think that counts?"

"I know it does."

"That's pretty cool." I couldn't believe that all of those years working Dad's claim was going to pay off for something like this. "I'm going to sign up for the coursework and see what kind of loads are available between Jeratorn and Mars. Ask Qiu if she can help us with scheduling at the dry dock."

"Good point. I'll ask her. I'm out."

"Roger that. Over and out."

I was shooting for an Operator's license in the greater-than-a-hundred tonnes class. With license in hand, AI oversight was all the Mars Port Authority would require when entering their controlled space. Docking fees would be higher too, but I didn't have the time to finish my Master's license. Fortunately, with Ada along, it wouldn't matter on this trip.

The first course was estimated to take forty hours of classroom work and was followed by a test. At least I would have something to keep me busy and if I got after it, I might be able to complete it before we got to Puskar Stellar. The course was already available on the freighter's systems. All I had to do was transfer five hundred credits to M-Corp.

I fired the course up on the main vid screen. The first order of business was to take a placement test. The AI would adjust to my current understanding and drill me on the information I was weak on. I scored horribly and got a forty five percent.

To me, the questions were over the top. I didn't see what difference it made if I understood the buoy systems, since I would have an AI plotting my route or what difference it made if I could recognize the light patterns of the different types of ships. Even so, I thought I knew most of it. My score certainly didn't reflect my confidence. I decided to spend two hours working through the material before I switched gears to other tasks. Ugh, I thought I was done with school, it sure was going to be a long six days to Mars. I'd rather have toilet fixing duty.

Two hours later, I was grateful to be able to close the course. I needed more coffee and could use a quick trip to the head. When I passed by the bunk room, I heard the soft sound of sobbing behind the door. A lump formed in my throat. Ada had seemed so brave through it all, I'd momentarily forgotten her loss. I considered knocking, but decided to give her some space for now.

Several hours later I woke up in the pilot's chair. I had hit the studying again but must have dozed off. Sleeping at the helm was just part of the job for an independent freighter captain. You had to be a light sleeper just in case something came up. At the speeds we sailed, the AI's default actions would almost always be the preferred responses, and they would come in milliseconds. It was especially true with this amount of mass. There was no dodging with three, two-point-five-kilo tonne barges in front of us, and Jupiter help the dumb-ass who got in our way.

I slid down the metal ladder. If you did it just right, you could place your feet on the outsides of the bars and slide. It was a harder maneuver for me since my left foot had been lost back on Colony 40. The military grade prosthetic did a lot of things well, but providing feedback about pressure on my ankle wasn't one of them. I landed a little harder than I intended but it was okay.

"Want some breakfast?" Ada was up and working in the small galley.

"You find the meal bars?" I asked.

"No, there's quality food here. Biscuits and gravy, bacon and eggs, and pancakes and that's just the breakfast stuff."

I was hungry and pancakes sounded really good. "Why not? Throw me in some pancakes."

"Orange Juice?" she asked.

"Seriously?"

"Sure enough."

"Absolutely." Marny was going to be jealous. I would be sending her a picture.

"Anything crazy going on up there?" Ada asked.

"We're six hours from deceleration. How hard is it to flip this bad boy over?"

"I'd better be there, but you've got good hands. You could probably do it."

"Before I got on this tub I might have agreed with you, but I've got to admit, I'm a little intimidated."

Ada smiled. It wasn't flashy, just a friendly, connected smile. Man, could she light up a room. "That's a good attitude to have on a tug." I couldn't help myself, I felt a little proud of myself for saying something smart. I hoped I didn't have a dopey look on my face. Her slightly raised eyebrows indicated the opposite.

"How about you get some shut-eye. I'll wake you up before we circumvolve."

"We what?"

"Flip over."

"That wasn't so hard to say, was it?"

"No, but flip over isn't on your test."

"Oh, it's gonna be like that, is it?"

"We'll see." She smiled again. I didn't know what was worse, the thought that she was going to be testing me the entire trip, or that every time she smiled, my brain tried to shut down.

As comfortable as the pilot's chair was, the upper bunk was even more so. I set my alarm for five hours so I could shower before circumvolving. I slept like a rock and probably woke in the same position I'd gone to sleep in. I really had no idea.

I pulled off my vac-suit and removed my prosthetic foot. I hadn't even thought about it in the last couple of weeks. It was amazing how well the technology worked. I checked the stump under the medical cap. It was clean and looked like my leg had just grown without a foot. A little freaky, but I was starting to get used to it.

In .6 gravity I found it easy to hop over to the shower. Before getting in, I put my suit in the suit-freshener and laid out a clean suit-liner. The hot water was wonderful. I was still taken aback by how spotless the entire ship was. Even the shower had absolutely no grime or soap buildup. Maybe the ship had a cleaning bot. It wouldn't explain everything, but it would explain the shower.

I pulled on a fresh suit-liner and hopped back to the bunk room. I was wiping down my prosthetic when Ada knocked and pushed the door open.

"Oh …" Her hand flew up to her mouth like she had caught me doing something awkward. She spun out of the room and pulled the door closed.

I mentally kicked myself for not remembering to warn her. Most people were okay with my missing foot, but it took them off guard when they saw me holding the prosthetic. I hopped up and pulled the door open.

She was standing there, right outside the door, staring at me, her mouth agape. I could tell she wasn't quite sure what to say.

"It's a prosthetic. Pirates blew off my real one back home. Don't feel bad, takes most people a bit to adjust. I should have warned you. Believe it or not, you feel so much like all the rest of my friends, I kinda forgot you didn't know."

"Oh..." Her eyes glistened like she was ready to cry. "That's about the nicest thing anyone's said to me in a long time." She pulled me in for a hug. Unfortunately, I wasn't particularly well balanced when she did. She wasn't expecting to carry my weight and as a result, we both fell over.

"Oh frak," she said and her hand flew up to her mouth again. "Sorry."

I looked up at her. I'd had the good sense to twist us around so neither of us hit anything hard. I was real glad no one else was there to see it, however. It was the very definition of a compromising situation. We both started laughing.

"I'm so sorry. I didn't think about that."

"Payback's a bitch," I said.

She slugged me in the arm. "No cussing."

"Okay, okay. How about I get dressed and I'll see you topside in a couple."

"I just wanted coffee." She was still a little embarrassed.

I reattached my prosthetic and pulled on my vac-suit. She sure smelled good. Frak, I really needed to get those thoughts out of my head.

I met her in the cockpit. Whatever embarrassment she had felt was gone by the time I got up there.

"The AI could do this for you, but you might as well get the experience. It's generally considered best practice to stop the burn, detach, fly to the other end, reattach and then start the deceleration. It introduces fewer non-linear stresses on the string. That said, we don't have that option since the pirates destroyed the coupling on the other barge. Any idea how you might accomplish circumvolving?"

"Seems like the most obvious way would be to use the joysticks in a way which would cause us to lift."

"You're a quick one. That's it, exactly. The AI will warn you if you start to twist, but generally if you're close, it will just make up the difference."

"Ready?" We had already dropped out of the burn and the AI was waiting for us to flip over one hundred eighty degrees to start our deceleration.

"Make it so."

I shook my head and tipped the joysticks in. We slowly flipped over. Fortunately, the vid screen showed me the horizontal line I was aiming for and I slid down into position. At this point anyone who had grown up on a planet would be in real trouble because we were now technically pointed downward. But as spacers this wasn't much of a problem for us.

"Good job," Ada said.

"Thanks. So how do you guys set up your trade routes? TradeNet?"

"If we can't line up something better, we use TradeNet. Recently, we'd been hauling for Precast. It was good money. They supplied the string and we ran out to the small mom-and-pop claims and hauled ore for 'em."

"I'm trying to figure out if I should use TradeNet as my primary or as a backup."

"Out of the box, you'll need to use them," she said. "You won't be able to make the contacts otherwise."

"Perfect, thanks."

I started punching in details about the trip we wanted to take and spent the next two hours setting up a few different scenarios. Most of the work I had to do was just inserting our two ships into the TradeNet system. I set an alert on cargo headed to Jeratorn as well as an alert for barge strings coming from there.

Ada seemed to enjoy helping me with the Operator's license studying. She knew most of it, but there were a few things she'd forgotten. It wasn't really a terrible way to pass the time.

With only two days left to Mars, I received a communication from Tabby.

"Heya, Liam, that's so exciting that you're coming here. We get Saturday afternoon and Sunday off. I just have to be back before 2200 on Sunday. Is Nick coming? I'm super busy, but I'll make sure I have my weekend clear. I gotta run to class. See ya this weekend."

I breathed a deep sigh of happy relief. I wasn't sure I'd survive if I didn't get a chance to see her. I knew in my heart she was the one for me, but I'll be darned if gorgeous women weren't always showing up in my life and causing unwanted distractions.

By the time we were a day out, I'd studied about as much as I was going to. I was scoring in the high nineties on the practice tests, but Ada informed me that the actual test was harder. I only needed a seventy percent to pass and even then the score wasn't recorded, only the pass or fail.

"If you blow this you can't take it again for forty-five days and it's another two hundred fifty m-creds." Ada said. I could hear my mom's school teacher voice sometimes when she spoke.

"Yup. I'm doing it." An hour and a half later I finished the test and passed. They didn't tell me how I scored but I didn't really care.

"Now you just need to finish your hours," she said.

"Let's see how many I have." I punched it up so it would display on the screen.

"What? That doesn't look right." Ada looked at me curiously.

The display read thirty-five hundred, twenty-four hours.

"You've got a year and a half in the chair already?"

"Ore haulers. Life of an asteroid miner."

"That's fantastic. Pay for your license then."

I did as she suggested. It was rather anti-climactic.

"You're licensed to bring us in to dock now. With me on board, you won't even have to get AI oversight."

"You think that's a good idea?" I asked.

"Why not. I've done it hundreds of times. You have to learn sometime. Anyway, Precast's dock isn't near anyone really. It'll be easy."

"Are you dropping off the barges with Precast? I thought you'd filed a claim of salvage," I said.

"Oh, I forgot to tell you. Because of your deal, they waived the penalty on our original contract."

"Nice. So what'll you do after all this?" I asked.

"Know anyone looking for a freighter captain?"

"What about you and your dad's business?"

"He's done. He wants to retire. He's giving me part of the insurance payout from the loss of *Baux*, but I'm out of a job."

"I don't think you want to get involved in our next gig. We're headed into pirate territory."

"So, what? You don't want me along?" Man, she could go from happy to grumpy in a hurry.

"No, I'm not saying that. It's going to be really dangerous."

"And I can't handle it?"

"No, you're plenty tough. It's not that."

"Then what?"

"I like you Ada. I don't want to see you get hurt." It didn't come out the way I wanted it to.

"Liam, I understand the risk, but I want to do something that matters. And I don't think about you that way."

Oh crap, I'd really messed this up. "No, I didn't mean that."

"What, so you don't like me?"

"No. I mean yes. But not that way."

"So do you or don't you?"

"What? Like you?" I felt like a fighter who'd taken one too many punches in a fight.

"No, need a captain for the freighter?"

"Yes, of course we do."

"Good then, it's settled. Wake me up when we're a thousand kilos from the dock." She pulled herself out of the chair and slid down the ladder.

TIME TO GET BUSY

"Look Captain, we need to get this resolved. I feel like you're stonewalling me," Qiu Loo said.

"Have you spent much time on a mining colony? If we show up there with a half loaded ship and no contract to haul ore, we're going to draw a lot of unwanted attention. I'll get a load put together, but it takes work."

"I still don't feel you're prioritizing this mission, Captain."

"Let's be clear, Lieutenant. I don't know what this mission is, other than dropping you off."

"Is that why you're dragging your heels? You're miffed about not being read in?"

"Not fair, Qiu. I'm not dragging my heels. You're definitely holding back on us though. If all you want is a taxi, then there are a hundred cheaper ways to get that done. You asked us, remember?"

"This discussion isn't productive."

"Agreed. We'll have the *Adela Chen* docked by 1500 and then Nick and I have some things to get through. How about you and I sit down with Nick after that and we can talk about schedule and expectations?"

"I'd like that," she said.

"Hoffen out." I terminated the comm. Damn, but she was exhausting.

We were about twenty thousand kilometers from Mars. One of the great features of the Fujitsu tug we were flying was the ability to change the orientation of the cockpit by rotating around the ladder opening. For the final two hundred thousand kilometers I'd swiveled around so I could catch the first view of Mars. The glow from around the engines was so bright that it wasn't until we were within fifty thousand kilometers that I was finally able to make it out.

The scale of a planet is hard to understand if you're from one of the colonies. As we approached Mars, it just kept growing. Precast Products' refining platform orbited Mars at eight hundred kilometers. At that distance, the planet would likely fill my entire view from the cockpit.

I slid down the ladder and knocked on the bunk room door. "Ada, we're getting pretty close, you want to come up?"

She opened the door. "I'll be right there. I was thinking, once we unload the string, you could use our slip on Puskar Stellar's orbital station. It's not big enough for both ships but you could leave the freighter there until we take off again."

"Are you sure you still want to come?"

"Yes. Are you sure you want to have this conversation?"

I knew when to let it go. "Nope. See you topside."

After a few minutes, Ada slipped into the other pilot's chair.

"Oh, good, you rotated the cockpit. We'll slide in like this at Precast," she said.

"I'm going to tell Nick to meet us at your dock at Puskar. Do they have any public slips?"

"Yes, loads of them. I'll send him the info." Ada shot a message over to him from her reading pad. Less than twenty seconds later she announced, "That was fast, he already responded and said they'd meet us there."

"That's Nick all right."

We both watched as *Sterra's Gift* cut across our field of vision, accelerating toward their destination.

"Time to get busy," Ada said.

"Pardon?" I had a dumb smirk on my face.

"Oh … Oh you're terrible." Her medium brown skin gained a slight shade of crimson. "Not what I meant. Initiate contact with Precast and they'll give us the exact spot to drop the string."

Establish contact with Precast Products, request docking instructions, I said to the AI.

"Good, that'll do it. Our job from this point out is pretty

straightforward. They'll give us a zone to drop it in, we just need to make sure the load has a zero delta with the refinery."

"We just leave it?"

"Yes. They have their own tug system that takes the material to the refinery."

"How do the barges get back to the colonies?"

"Precast will contract them."

"You have a contact at Precast I could talk to?"

"You really want to talk to them? They're jerks."

"Your lawyer was the idiot. That was a heck of a clause to mess up."

"I suppose ... I have a contact." She swiped at her reading pad. "There you go."

I sent them a message with instructions about our intended destination and timing, as well as proof of our bond.

As with most complex things on a spaceship, the AI did the vast majority of the work. It was our job to make sure we had instructed the AI correctly. The *Adela Chen* and its string of barges slid neatly into the pre-arranged location and the engines spun down. I instructed the AI to disconnect us and returned the cockpit to its normal forward orientation.

"Well executed, Mr. Hoffen, and congratulations on your first official heavy freight load."

"Congratulations to you as well, Ms. Chen. I hope everything works out with Precast."

"Out of my hands now," she said.

Set course for Chen Family slip at Puskar Stellar orbital docking station.

"You'll want to let the AI take it in from here," she said.

"Why's that?"

"You'll see."

Engage autopilot.

The freighter pulled back gently, turned a graceful arc, and sailed toward the planet. Ada took joy in pointing out many of the different landmarks of Mars, both natural and manmade. The closer we got, however, the more traffic increased. It finally became almost unbearable. If I'd been flying manually I'd have been terrified. As it was, I felt a cold sweat break out on my back. I'd never been so grateful to stop sailing as I was once we finally docked. It would have been one thing with *Sterra's Gift* but the controls of *Adela Chen* were still too unfamiliar to me.

"You get used to it, but I didn't think a rock jockey like yourself would be expecting the traffic."

I punched her arm gently. "Careful who you're calling rock jockey."

The spaceport above Puskar Stellar was gigantic - I estimated four kilometers long and a kilometer wide. At the center of the station, a tethered space elevator extended downward to the city of Puskar Stellar. I hoped we'd get a chance to visit. I'd never been in a city that was home to millions of people.

"Cheap seats out here. We have a time-share arrangement. It takes longer to get over to the elevator but the price is right," Ada said.

"We've got to be a couple of kilometers out."

"Two point four kilometers to be exact. Don't sweat it, there's a tram we can catch."

"I've got work to do on *Sterra's Gift*. We're planning to sail in ten days. That work for you?"

"Yes. I'll be ready. Let me know if anything changes."

"Roger that."

I helped Ada carry her bags off the ship to a tram platform.

"Thanks Liam ... for everything." She gave me a quick hug and stepped onto the tram.

It was 1630. Frak. My meeting with Qiu was in less than thirty minutes.

Give me a route to Sterra's Gift.

My AI projected a route, overlaying my vision. It was subtle, but it appeared there was a line of green vapor leading from my current position to where I needed to go. It was the sort of thing that could be configured according to a person's needs. Some people preferred to have it show up on the ground or as a blinking orb in the distance. The variety was endless. A small contrail of vapor was my current thing.

I jogged through the concourse. It wasn't that far and I traveled light – just my blaster pistol in a holster strapped to my waist. I placed my hand on a panel next to an airlock. The gangplank between the slip and the ship's airlock was pressurized, so all I needed to do was unlock and push my way in.

Marny saw me in the hallway and gave a conspiratorial grin. "Heya, Cap. Welcome aboard. Oh, and you're late."

I rolled my eyes at her but quickened my pace all the same.

"Captain on the bridge," Nick said when I entered.

"Heya, buddy." It had only been six days but I'd missed him.

Qiu Loo was seated at the engineering station. I nodded to her. "Lieutenant Loo."

"Captain." I tried to read her expression but got nothing.

"Would you give us a few minutes, Lieutenant?"

She didn't respond other than to stalk off the bridge. I closed the door behind her.

"Any advice on that?" I looked toward the door.

"Nope."

"Okay. Let me deal with it. Any luck on finding an auctioneer for our load?"

"Yup. Stevedores will be here in an hour."

"Any problems on the legal end?" We'd liberated the cases from a pirate base. I had no illusions that they were anything but stolen goods.

"Ordena's on it, he's working with the auctioneers."

"What's that going to cost?" We'd first met Jeremy Ordena on Colony 40. He was a sloppy looking, easy to underestimate, slightly greasy lawyer. I had mixed feelings about working with him, but no doubt he would get the job done.

"Five percent."

I sighed but didn't argue.

"How about repairs and munitions load-out?"

"We're scheduled for 1000 tomorrow at the Coolidge Yard. Navy's giving us a good deal on armor. We'll have to pay cost on the supplies."

"How much?"

"Fifty thousand."

I whistled.

"New stuff according to Belcose. Very hard for smaller slug throwers to penetrate. Also, we'll super harden the captain's quarters and the non-glass portion of the bridge."

"How long will they have the ship?" I asked.

"Eight days and that's only because Loo put 'em in a headlock. They're going to run triple shifts on it."

"That's progress. How about you get us a nice place to stay? Tabby's staying with us Saturday night."

"Which Saturday? Tomorrow?"

"Tomorrow for sure, I didn't ask about next week."

"That works out well, the shipyard orbits over the town of Coolidge, which is near the Naval Academy. I'll stick to that area and find us accommodations."

"Perfect. Let me grab Loo." I found Qiu and Marny chatting in the galley and asked them both to join us on the bridge.

"Lieutenant, it looks like you were successful in getting us an expedited repair schedule. According to Nick, that puts us at eight days. I need to know when you will fill us in on the details of this mission."

"We've been over this. The mission is too sensitive to read you in."

"No, I get it. Fact is we have no interest in the mission per se, but we need to understand what 'light fire support' means. You can't possibly expect us not to prepare for that."

"Fair enough. If I'm successful, that won't come into play."

"And if you're not?"

"The most likely case is I simply get dispatched."

"As in ..."

"Killed. Yes."

"How many hostiles are you estimating?" Marny asked.

"Could be as many as fifty."

Marny whistled. "That's a frak-tonne of baddies. Are you extracting some sort of payload?"

"Personnel extraction," Loo answered.

"Do we have any budget for crew?" Marny looked to Nick.

"Budget should handle up to two additional," Nick replied.

"Lieutenant, can you hook us up with some gear? Mostly standard tac stuff. I can work with your quartermaster once we have crew set," Marny said.

"We'll need it back," Qiu Loo said.

Marny winked at Loo. "That's the spirit." Qiu wasn't completely sure what to make of her comment.

"We'll be ready to go in ten days unless there are delays on the repair." I said.

"What if you still can't find a load?" Qiu asked.

"I'll make it work. Worst case is we leave the tug behind."

"Seems like that'd be a good idea in either case," she said.

"Not your call, Lieutenant. I'll stay out of your business if you stay out of mine."

"Understood. Anything else?" she asked.

We all stood with her and I extended my hand as a friendly gesture. She was hesitant but accepted it. "See you in ten days," I said.

We all watched her exit the bridge and I gave a sigh, then said. "Let me spend some time working on loads, then I'll come find you guys."

I still couldn't see any perfect matches for our load configuration. If I was willing to deadhead the tug to Delta there was a two-barge string that needed to come back. Delta was a lot closer to Jeratorn than Mars, but it was a weak proposition.

Filling *Sterra's Gift* was going to be ridiculously easy. There was enough material headed to Jeratorn to fill our cargo hold at least twice and we'd make decent money on each trip. I suspected the *recent pirate activity on the station* description in TradeNet was causing most captains to avoid it. I'd keep looking during the next ten days to see if I could get the tug a load.

I walked back to Nick and Marny's quarters. Nick looked up from a reading pad he had sitting on the small table. I sat on the comfortable L shaped couch that partially surrounded it.

"What else do we need to accomplish?" he asked.

"This'd be the perfect time to work on our team skills. Also, you boys are a little soft. We need to get you into an exercise regimen," Marny said, completely serious.

Nick and I looked at each other and started laughing.

"So, let me get this straight. When Nick says shore leave, your immediate thought is to get us into better shape? Are you sure you've been on leave before?" It felt good to laugh.

Marny looked at us skeptically. "We can still enjoy ourselves, I just want a small budget, and four hours a day."

"Four hours?" I was flabbergasted.

"How much budget?" Nick sat up straighter.

"I could get by with three hours and squeeze it all in for thirty-five hundred."

"You're serious?" I asked.

"Oh, come on, Cap. Tell me you wouldn't like to be on the giving side once in a fight instead of on the receiving side."

"Okay," Nick agreed.

Damn his infatuated little ass. "Start Monday?" I could at least negotiate.

"Sunday. I promise if Tabby is who you've described, she won't want to miss day one."

I groaned. "What time on Sunday?"

SHORE LEAVE

Planet-side, in the town of Coolidge, it was 2200 local time on Friday night. Marny explained that the locals used the position of the Sun to adjust their clocks so midday was always 1200 and midnight was 2400. Moreover, they used a twelve hour clock that reset at those two points. I couldn't have come up with a more ridiculous idea if I'd tried, but Marny insisted that's how it worked.

The naval shipyard was connected to Coolidge by the same type of elevator / tether that most modern space ports deployed. While *Sterra's Gift* was capable of landing on Mars, we left her at the shipyard for repairs and upgrades.

The physics of a space elevator is terrifying. Each pod is a relatively small, four meter round, three meter tall capsule. Once loaded, it simply drops, in vacuum, accelerated by magnetic fields. A local gravity generator keeps the inhabitants stuck to the floor and magnetic forces keep the pod from touching the sides of the elevator.

The Coolidge Naval Yard was in orbit at five hundred twenty kilometers. From that elevation, it was a ten minute ride to the planet's surface. With *Sterra's Gift* in the shipyard, the elevator was an inexpensive way to get down to Coolidge, not to mention both Nick and I desperately wanted to ride on one.

The three of us stepped off the elevator platform, found a restroom and immediately changed into our civvies. Nick sported black jeans, a black collared shirt and a light brown blazer. I wore a black coat, white shirt and blue jeans. We had both opted to wear shoulder holsters with flechette pistols. Marny warned us that Coolidge, as a military town, was likely to enforce the 'no laser blaster law' most towns had. Marny wore tight fitting blue jeans and a colorful tunic with a Mao styled collar. She didn't wear an obvious weapon, but I'd be willing to bet she had easy access to something.

"Boys, dinner's on me tonight," Marny said. We were standing in a large open area in the most spacious building I'd ever been in. The ceiling had to be at least twenty meters above our heads. Intellectually, I knew atmosphere wrapped around the entire planet but my spacer sensibilities were overwhelmed by the wanton waste of space. The atmosphere to fill this room alone …

"Cap … you with us?" Marny asked. I was lost looking around the room.

"Uh, sounds good. You know some place? I thought you were North American Navy." I said.

"Sure enough, but I've been here plenty. We're allies, you know." She winked at me.

The elevator terminal wasn't overly busy. In the ten minutes we'd been here, perhaps twenty pods had arrived. The area was nowhere near the capacity it was made for, even if you just considered the floor and not all the openness. I wondered if it was built this way just to mess with spacers like myself. If that was the goal, they'd certainly succeeded.

"Cap. This way, big fella." Marny had a grin on her face and Nick stood next to her with his arm wrapped around her waist. They didn't show much affection on the ship, but apparently on leave, all bets were off.

As we neared the exit doors, we could see through the glass that it was very dark outside. I heard a loud rhythmic noise, as if the glass was being pelted by thousands of pieces of debris.

"Looks like we're gonna get wet," Marny said.

Nick and I looked at each other and simultaneously yelled, "Rain!" We bolted for the door, pushed our way through and ran out into the street. There was water all over everything and it was coming down heavy enough that it was hard to see much farther than ten or fifteen meters.

Marny watched with a bemused expression from under the terminal's awning. She had hold of our bags, since we had impulsively dropped them. "Let me know when you've had enough." She had to shout over the sound of the rain.

It grew old after a few minutes and we rejoined her. I was appreciative of our clothing's ability to resist absorbing water. My hair was wet and I had water running down inside of my shirt and undies, but that would dry soon enough and it was worth it.

"I'll call a cab." Marny still talked louder than normal due to the rain.

A silver vehicle pulled up next to the awning and a door opened. We all piled in and Nick and Marny got into some sort of wrestling match. Their playful happiness was infectious and I couldn't help but sit back and enjoy just being in the moment.

"We have a place to stay tonight?" I asked.

"Yup," Nick answered. *Take us to the Concord.*

"You're really going to love this place, I've never stayed, but I've been in it a couple of times," Marny said.

"Will it be raining there too?" Nick asked.

"Yes my gorgeous little man, it'll be raining there too." Marny apparently couldn't resist getting back to wrestling with Nick.

I couldn't have been happier to have the cab start descending. The building we approached was a minimum of forty stories tall and made entirely of reflective glass. It was dark outside and giant flood lights attempted to light up the building's exterior. The rain, however, was heavy enough that the lights had a difficult time illuminating the large building.

The cab gracefully pulled to a stop beneath a wide canopy and its doors opened. It was 2200 local - which Marny insisted on calling ten o'clock - and the luxurious lobby of the Concord Resort was still very active. The people in the lobby appeared to be of two camps; either they were dressed for a fancy evening in suits and gowns, or they were dressed for play in shorts and t-shirts. I couldn't see a single person in a vac-suit, which struck me as unusual.

We must have looked like we were lost since a man dressed in a uniform approached us and offered assistance. "Are you checking in?"

"Yup," Nick said.

"Nigela would be happy to help you with that at the registration desk." He gestured toward a long series of tall counters atop ornate wooden cabinets. A woman stood behind one of the counters and looked up at us expectantly.

"Thank you," I said and we traipsed over to the desk. Checking in was painless and we found the glassed-in elevator that whisked us up to the thirty-second floor.

The suite Nick booked for us was, by spacer standards, extremely spacious. There were three large bedrooms, each with a bigger bed than I'd ever slept in. A living room joined all of the bedrooms together and a bar/kitchenette took up a portion of one wall. One entire side of the suite was glass from floor to ceiling. The only thing that broke up the glass was a door.

For me, the first order of business was to see what was on the other side of that door. I discovered, to my amusement, that it led to a balcony. The heavy rain initially made me wonder if the balcony had any sort of barrier to keep people from simply falling off the edge. As it turned out there was a perimeter wall, it was just made of some nearly transparent material. I wasn't interested in getting closer to the edge or getting soaked again, so I soon came back inside.

"Were you able to see anything?" Nick asked.

"Not at all," I said. "The rain is coming down so hard I can barely make out anything beyond the exterior wall. You guys getting hungry?"

"Marny's already on it. She's gonna order food, then take a shower."

"Which room's mine?"

"Two rooms left, grab one." Nick said.

It was an easy choice. One room was near the door we entered and the other had an entire wall of glass with rain pelting off of it. I might not sleep well, but I sure would enjoy experiencing weather. I wondered if it might actually snow. It wasn't out of the range of possibility at ten degrees.

I must have fallen asleep because the next thing I knew Nick was waking me up.

"Keep sleeping or eat?" he asked. I hadn't eaten for at least ten hours so there was no decision to make.

"Eat," I mumbled and groggily got up. It took a couple of minutes to recover from my short nap. Once I caught a whiff of the food, I woke up very quickly. In the living room there was a large pizza that had to be at least five centimeters tall with a crust that towered to seven or eight centimeters in places.

"You boys are in for the treat of your lives. This is made by real Italians." Marny pronounced the last 'eye-tal-yuns.' "And for drinks, we have what's been the best beer for more centuries than the North American Alliance has existed."

I hadn't noticed the three frosted glasses sitting next to the pizza. Next to those glasses were eight tall sealed black bottles. Marny caught my eye, opened one of the bottles and poured out the dark umber-colored liquid into a glass and a two centimeter creamy foam formed on top. I accepted it, took a seat on one of the couches and started to drink.

"Hold on there, Cap. Let's make a toast," Marny said.

I waited for her to finish pouring their drinks.

"To Adela Chen," she toasted. We clinked glasses.

I took a long drink of the beer. It tasted like nothing we'd had in previous ports or back on Colony 40. Its smooth, buttery taste made it the finest drink I'd ever experienced. I looked to Nick. He didn't seem to be enjoying his.

"What is this magic elixir? Nick, you don't like it?" I asked.

"It's not bad." Nick put his glass back down on the table and snaked a piece of pizza.

"Guinness, and you'll learn to love it, Nicholas," Marny said. He just looked sideways at her.

The pizza was equally awesome but after a third beer, the day started to catch up to me.

"Guys, I'm gonna turn in," I couldn't help yawning.

"You sure, Cap? Nick and I are gonna go swimming."

"Swimming, really?" I asked.

"Yup," Nick had a huge grin on his face.

"That's almost tempting, but I'll wait for Tabby."

"Suit yourself. Did you set your alarm?" he asked.

I hadn't, so I did. I lay down in the bed and understood why I'd fallen asleep so quickly before. It was luxurious. I'd never slept in a bed this comfortable, with blankets and pillows so soft. I fell asleep immediately.

The next thing I knew, the alarm on my reading pad was going off. I'd given myself an hour to shower, dress and get over to the Naval Academy. It took a moment in the shower to realize I was standing next to the glass exterior of the building. My first concern was that I was naked. Fortunately, there were little glowing letters at eye level that read 'window is opaque.' I finally realized that opaque meant 'unable to be seen through'.

The rain from last night had stopped and I could see that the hotel was on the edge lake so large I was unable to see a shore on the opposite side. Closer to the hotel were a multitude of sailboats with colorful sails deployed. Further out were larger ships going about their business. I had to tear myself away from staring out over the water. I wanted to be on time to pick up Tabby.

Neither Nick nor Marny were in the living room and I suspected they had been up fairly late last night. The pizza was still on the table, so I grabbed a cold piece and headed out. The elevator had the same external lake view as my shower and I gawked the entire way down.

I carried a reading pad since I had no other way to communicate with the AI while dressed in my jeans and dress shirt.

Hail a cab, I said. Exiting the hotel through the large sliding doors, I was surprised to see flowering plants growing in abundance in large pots. For the most part, flowers weren't overly common on a space station. I'd seen them before but generally in small groups. It was one of a hundred new experiences I'd had since arriving on Mars. A taxi-cab was waiting for me under the large awning. When I approached, the small silver vehicle opened its door.

Mars Naval Academy, negotiate with Tabby Masters for pickup. By letting my AI know where I was going and who I was picking up, it would be able to get specific directions. The AI wouldn't actually need to talk to Tabby, but simply communicate with her AI. The cab gently lifted from the surface and joined the traffic. I estimated we were flying at an altitude of six hundred meters. It provided a great view of the planet beneath me.

This part of Mars was covered by forest that had been seeded many centuries ago when Mars was terraformed. The abundance of plant life was surprising to me in that I knew Mars hadn't originally had any indigenous plants. Everything I saw below had been seeded from either Earth or one of the four 'new' planets. According to what I'd read, however, the plants and trees adapted to the Martian environment and had become unique to Mars, only faintly resembling their ancestors on Earth. I supposed that was true of people also. Nick and I were a lot like Marny but our small spacer builds were significantly different from her heavily muscled frame.

The Naval Academy was thirty minutes away from the Concord Resort. For the last twenty minutes the air traffic had thinned out and there were fewer and fewer structures below. I'd been flying over land for the entire trip, but the low white buildings of the academy were all lined up in neat rows along the shore of what I assumed was the same lake as the resort.

The cab set down next to a building on the outside of a ten meter tall fence. Cabs probably weren't allowed to fly over the grounds of the academy. It would cost me additional to have the cab wait, but we were far enough from town that I didn't want to be stranded out here. The academy was in a remote area and we certainly wouldn't be able to walk back.

A wide rock path led to the doors of the visitor's center and before I'd made it to within twenty meters, Tabby burst through the door and ran toward me. She was wearing a beige uniform and still sported the buzz cut she'd left Colony 40 with. We hugged fiercely and I lifted her as we spun around.

She whispered in my ear, "No kissing in public while in uniform."

"Do you have a bag?" I asked.

"Let me grab it."

I took her hand and let her lead me back to the visitor's center. She'd left a small bag by the front door. I carried it for her and we jogged back to the waiting cab.

Privacy mode. I instructed the cab.

"Do you even notice it?" she asked.

I looked her up and down trying to find some detail I'd missed. Her skin was tanned and her face had a harder look than I remembered but mostly she was covered by her uniform. She picked up on my confusion.

"No, you dork. Your foot. I can't tell you're wearing a prosthetic at all. Do you notice that you're wearing it?"

"Oh," I said, relieved. "Almost never. It's funny, I was sitting on the bed putting my clothes back on when Ada saw me cleaning it and I ... "

Tabby interrupted me by slugging me hard in the arm.

"What was that for?" The punch actually hurt. Then I thought about what I'd said. "No ... it's not like that."

"Then how is it? Is she cute?" Tabby looked at me sternly.

"Oh, yeah ..." I caught it before the punch landed and was able to deflect most of it. "Seriously, it's not like that. Ada just lost her mom to pirates. I'm telling you that was the last thing on her mind." I dodged a strike. "What ..."

"What about *your* mind?" Tabby said. She was actually starting to get pissed. I was in trouble.

"Nothing like that. Ada's a nice girl ..." Tabby started to agitate, "No, listen, I worry about the same thing with you. All these good looking Navy guys you hang around. But really Tabby, all I think about when I'm near a beautiful woman is you."

Tabby looked somewhat mollified. "So you're saying ..."

The canopy darkened and I knew no one would be able to look in at us. I pulled Tabby in close and kissed her. Initially, she was a little hesitant but I wasn't letting go. Finally, she melted into me. I was more than a little disappointed when the cab started its descent on approach to the hotel.

"This looks nice," Tabby said.

"The rooms are crazy, Nick set it all up. Let's go up and see if he and Marny are awake."

"Are they a thing?" Tabby asked.

"That'd be an understatement."

"I thought she was an Earther, how's that work?"

"Just does, I guess. She's probably half again his mass though. Calls him 'her little man.'" I led Tabby onto the elevator.

"That'd be funny. Nice view here."

I palmed my way into the suite.

"Tabby!" Nick ran over and hugged her.

"Morning, Marny." I didn't want her to feel left out.

"Morning, Cap."

Nick released Tabby and drug her by the hand over to meet Marny.

"Tabby, this is Marny, the one I've been sending you comms about."

Marny held her hand out to shake Tabby's but Tabby was having none of that and gave Marny a big hug. I was surprised, since generally Tabby didn't take right to people.

"I'm so glad to finally meet the woman who has been keeping my guys safe. Thank you, and I'm honored to meet you." For Tabby, this was gushing.

Marny smiled, which is what I'd have expected either way, not too much rattled her. "Glad to be part of the team."

"What have you guys planned for the day?" I asked.

"Too many things, so little time. We were thinking about heading over to Puskar Stellar and checking out the Open Air District," Nick said.

"How far away is that?" I asked.

"'Bout an hour, they have a super-fast magnetic levitation train. It's in the same terminal as the space elevator from dry dock," he said.

I looked at Tabby and she responded, "Works for me, I just need to get changed."

I didn't care what we did as long as she was part of it. Two hours later we exited one of the numerous stops the train made in the city. It was mid-afternoon and the sun was shining, the weather was holding at fifteen degrees. I'd brought my coat along and Tabby had switched to a pair of very tight jeans and a loose sweater.

"Meet for dinner at 2000 local?" Nick asked.

"Sounds good." I looked to Tabby for confirmation. She nodded.

"Try to stay out of trouble, Cap," Marny said with a grin.

Puskar Stellar's Open Air District is the perfect place to walk around when you have time to kill. Interesting old buildings lined the brick streets, and vendor booths covered by colorful umbrellas and tents were set up in front. It all made for an inviting environment and reminded me of when family trading ships would visit Colony 40 - only about a thousand times bigger.

"We should get swimming suits for tonight," I said.

"I was thinking about getting an earwig communicator," she replied.

"What's that?"

"Just about everyone has one - look around. See the little piece of jewelry on that woman's cheek leading back to her ear?" Tabby nodded in the direction of a woman seated at a small table, chatting blithely to no one in particular.

"Oh, like a vac-suit HUD."

"Right. We can't wear them while doing physical training or even in some classes, but other than that they're acceptable. Most people have one since nobody wears a vac-suit down here."

I pulled out my reading pad. *Find vendors who sell personal communication equipment.* The pad displayed several nearby shops. We read a few reviews and decided to take a longer walk to get to Ballance Electronics, as they had the top reputation in the area.

A woman, several years older than the two of us, watched as we browsed, then headed our way. We'd found a cabinet loaded with several dozen different models of the earwig. Most of them were very thin, but apart from that there was quite a bit of variation.

"Would you like to try one?" she asked.

"Why so many different models?"

"Three things: style, projection quality, and adaptive holding," she said.

"What's adaptive holding?"

"It's only available on the newer models and it's a nano-adaptive surface that latches onto your skin and molds itself to your contours even as you talk. They are almost impossible to knock off, partly because the edge bevels out with the adaptive surface. " She took a breath. "Sorry, that's probably more than you wanted to know. It's easier to just try it on." Her face was a little flush.

"Sounds like you really know your stuff," I said.

"They're just really cool," she replied.

"How much are we talking?" Tabby asked.

"Eight hundred is top of the line, unless you get jewel inlay, which we don't do."

Tabby whistled. "That's a lot. What do you have in the three or four hundred range?"

"Lots of good ones. The only real difference is the adaptive feature."

"Could I try the blue one?" Tabby pointed to one that was the same deep blue color that was part of the Mars Protectorate Navy uniform.

"What year are you?" The girl asked while she stepped behind the counter and pulled out two sleeves with blue earwigs.

"First year."

"Not from Mars?"

"Perth Mining Colony."

"Glad you came in. You'll appreciate not having to rely on reading pads." She held an earwig next to Tabby's ear and then put it back in its sleeve. She held another one up and appeared satisfied. "That should do it. Just hold it up next to your ear and then push it in gently. This one has an early generation of the adaptive technology and makes a perfect fit every time."

Tabby pushed it in and adjusted the earwig so that the fine

blue wire led from her ear, along her cheekbone to just in front of her eye.

"It tickles," she said, with a slight smile.

"You get used to it. That's because it is held in place entirely by the connection in your ear."

"You should at least try on the adaptive one," I said. The woman looked to Tabby, who nodded affirmatively.

They both looked the same when sitting on the counter, but when Tabby pushed the new device in, the difference was immediately evident. It was as if the earwig melted into her ear and onto her skin. Where the previous earwig had filled her ear, this one simply lined it. Additionally, it melded into her skin along her cheekbone and looked more like a tattoo than a piece of equipment.

"That's too cool," I said.

"I wanna see," Tabby said.

The woman who was helping us pinched at something in her vision and mimed tossing it at Tabby. It was a familiar gesture that established a video link between them.

Tabby ran her fingers over her cheekbone while staring off into space. I could tell she was watching the HUD. "That's incredible. Any trouble with water?"

"Not at all. Most people never take them off."

Tabby pulled it out of her ear reluctantly. "A little more than I can afford, student and all."

"With a boyfriend who never gets to see you," I said. "We'll take two."

"Liam, you can't. They're expensive."

"Think of it as an investment in me being able to talk to you more. Let me do this. Please?"

After a few minutes and a private conference, Tabby finally relented.

"So … since you saved all that money on an earwig, maybe you could get a swimsuit?"

"If I didn't know better, I'd say you have an ulterior motive. Oh wait … I do know you better. I'll get one if you do." She poked me in the chest with her finger and looked up at me with a smile. It was a moment I wanted to last forever.

We wandered through the streets holding hands and chatting about whatever came to our minds. We ended up finding a push cart filled with swimwear attended by an older woman. Tabby finally found a two piece she felt she could live with. To my disappointment, she wasn't at all impressed with the bikinis and their lack of coverage. In the end, it didn't matter too much to me.

WORK HARD, PLAY HARDER

Dinner with Marny and Nick was a blast. But I wanted to spend as much time alone with Tabby as possible. Marny warned us that the plans she had for us started at 0800, so Tabby finally convinced me at 0300 that we should get some sleep. She agreed we could sleep in the same bed, but insisted that was all we would be doing. I'd like to say I didn't try to convince her otherwise, because I did, but I also respected her desire to 'save it for marriage.'

A loud rap on the door caused both Tabby and me to jump out of bed. "Frakking Jupiter, are you nuts?" I yelled at the door.

"0800 Cap, time to lose some of that baby fat." Marny's voice filtered through the door.

"What are we doing, anyway?" Tabby was standing in front of me in a white lacy camisole top and matching panties. I had a very difficult time focusing on what either her or Marny were saying.

"Hoffen ... you're staring and you're not answering."

I looked up guiltily. "Uh ... Cripes, I have no idea. And if you're gonna wear that, I'm gonna stare."

"Complaining?"

"Not even close."

"And ..."

"Oh, right ..."

Marny rapped on the door again.

"Ten minutes, Cap. We've got an appointment."

"I really don't know. All she said was that you wouldn't want to miss it."

I opened the door. "What should we wear?" Marny was sitting on a tall stool in the kitchenette drinking a glass of orange juice.

"Doesn't matter."

Fifteen minutes later we were all headed down the elevator. Tabby and I had to settle for a meal bar for breakfast, but that didn't bother me too much. I was used to them.

Once we were in the cab I couldn't take it anymore. "Alright Marny, it's time to spill. What's the big secret?"

"I already told you, we gotta all get in better shape, learn to work like a team."

"What's that got to do with Tabby?"

"What? I can't be part of the team?" Tabby slugged me. I kind of wished she'd find a new way of expressing herself.

"Nothing at all, other than I get an extra day of training this way and I guarantee you'll love it." Marny smiled sagely at Tabby. Smart women made my life … interesting.

"Nick? You know anything about this?"

"Nope. Where'd you get those comm units?"

"Found 'em last night. The HUD projection is super clear."

"Better than your suit?" he asked.

"A lot. I'll take you over there if Marny ever gives us a break."

"Really? We haven't even started and you're already whining?" Marny shook her head and laughed at us.

It wasn't long before the cab slowed over the top of an area filled with large nondescript buildings. We dropped down between two of them and landed next to a gray steel door.

"Anyone carrying any weapons?" Marny asked.

Oddly I wasn't. I hadn't even remembered to wear my flechette when we'd gone to Puskar Stellar. We all shook our heads in the negative.

"Good. Follow me." Marny climbed out of the cab and walked up to the door labeled TAC-10A. We followed her into a room with a rack of blaster rifles and a shelf with wrap-around goggles.

"Here's the mission. Everybody grab a rifle and a pair of goggles. There are twelve bogies spread throughout the building. There are also friendlies. We get scored on kills and time - negative scores for friendlies and getting hit by a baddie. The good news is if you get hit, your weapon just stops working for thirty seconds. The bad news is you can get hit again during that period of time. Cap, first run through is yours. Each of you will get a shot at this so let the leader set the strategy. Okay?"

"Are there real people in there?" Nick asked.

"Nope. All holographic. Believe me though, you'll think they're real, but I don't think we'll get to the point where we want real."

"Why's that?" Tabby asked. I was glad that she was engaged.

"It's a testosterone factory. You have to get one of the other teams to play the baddies and most of the teams here are either private security companies or S.W.A.T. teams. They like to play hard. Anything else?"

"Why aren't you leading?"

"I need to see what you do under pressure so we can fix what's broken and enhance what you naturally do well."

"Last question. What's a good score?" I asked.

"Try to keep everyone up. That's what we'll focus on. Ready?"

We all nodded.

"Team is yours, Cap. From this point forward we'll follow your lead."

"Roger that, Marny. Since we don't have a map of the area we'll have to build it on the way. I want Tabby in the lead, Nick on her left shoulder, Marny you have the rear, facing backward as much as possible. This will be our base formation. I'll change that depending on what we run into." I sounded a whole lot more confident than I felt. I also knew, from playing sports, that your team picked up on a lack of confidence and it affected their play.

Create channel one: Tabby, Nick, Marny and me. Build a tactical map as we discover terrain. Highlight positions of team members using blue dots, red dots for baddies and green dots for those I identify as friendly non-combatants.

"Tabby, when we approach a blind corner I want you to take a knee and do a quick peek before we go around. If you start fatiguing let me know, so I can switch Nick in."

"Check," Tabby said.

"We have no idea what's on the other side of this door. Tabby, take a knee and keep your body behind the door frame. Nick, cover left through the door and stay real close to Tabby. I've got right and I'll slide around to the right, looking left. Marny, if it's open straight ahead I need you to cover that. Say 'hold' if you don't know what to do, otherwise, Tabby, open the door."

I pulled the blaster rifle tightly in to my shoulder and snugged up to Nick. Tabby swung the door open to expose a narrow hallway leading to the left.

"Nick, we're going to look down this together. You're going to slide out until you can see the middle of the hallway as far as it goes. You get everything to the right. If you see something, say 'contact.' I'll stay on your right and focus on the hallway to the left. GO."

Nick slid around Tabby and the doorframe and I moved with him. The tactical map on my HUD started to fill in as I gained more visibility on the twenty meter hallway.

"Contact left," I said. My peripheral vision caught a figure disappearing through a door about five meters down on the left side. It was the only door in the hallway which ended in an L-shaped turn going to the right.

"Tabby, go ahead on point, I saw someone enter the door on the left. Marny, follow on my six." My heart was hammering in my chest enough that I could hear it in my voice.

"Tabby, when you get to the doorway I want you to kneel and cover right through the doorway without entering it. Nick, stay right of Tabby. Once she gets to the doorway, swivel past with your gun pointed in. You'll use the opposite side as cover. I'm going to cover down the hallway. GO."

We followed Tabby down the left side. It was hard not to try to get a view through the opening and keep my eyes down the hall. She stopped at the doorframe. Nick peeked and then attempted to cross to the other side.

"Contact!" he said. His gun flashed as he fired into the room. My tactical display filled in with the rectangular layout of the room, including two red dots, both on the right. Nick slid to the other side of the door. I could see his blue dot on the tactical display, he hadn't been hit.

"Tabby, they're in front of you. Engage." Tabby poked her gun in and must have gained visual as she started firing. One red dot blinked out and the second moved quickly to the left, running across Nick's field of view. He fired and the other dot blinked out.

"Marny, cover forward down the hallway." I slid up on Tabby's right shoulder, looking into the room, sweeping from right to left. There was a small amount of furniture in the room and I didn't initially see anyone.

"Nick, I'm going in. Cross behind me once I do. Tabby, follow on my right shoulder. Marny, use the door frame as cover for down the hallway." I was exhausted just spitting out all the instructions - there had to be a better way. It occurred to me that combat on the ship was easier, mostly because we all knew our roles.

We worked our way into the room. I wanted to make sure we didn't have any hidden baddies. We moved around the desks, taking time to look beneath them when …

"Cap. Contact in the hallway." Marny said. I looked to my tactical display in the HUD. A gray dot appeared at the end and disappeared. Crap, it wasn't clear if that was a baddie or friendly.

"Clear," Tabby said.

"Clear," Nick agreed.

"Marny, stay on the doorframe and cover down the hallway. Tabby, take a knee next to Marny and aim down. I'm on point. Nick, on my six, next to the right wall. GO."

We fast-walked down the hallway. Seeing Nick's rifle between me and the wall didn't seem right but I knew that stopping wasn't a good idea. I hoped he wouldn't have to fire it. My face was awfully close to the end of the barrel and he had no freedom of movement. That said, he was protected by my body. Ugh, not ideal.

When we reached the corner, I knelt down and crept up. I peeked around quickly and came face to face with a person. "Contact." I had no idea if it was a baddie or friendly and I popped back. "Might be a friendly." I spun my rifle around, peeked again and jammed the stock of the rifle into the person's stomach, grabbing at their shirt to pull them around. My hands passed through their clothing and they disappeared.

The advantage of my two peeks around the corner was that I now had a tactical perspective of where the hallway led. I wasn't sure if it was a good thing to have slugged the person who disappeared, but I put it out of my mind as something we'd cover later. There were two doors, five meters down, one on each side. So much for being able to deal with them one at a time. Ten meters beyond that the hallway ended in a 'T' with a railing that obviously overlooked a lower level.

"Marny, Tabby, advance to our position. There are doors on both sides across from each other. We're going to clear these rooms simultaneously. I want Marny and Tabby on the right side. Nick and me on the left. If the doors are open, we will aim across the hallway into the opposite doorway until we control the room. If we contact before getting to the door frames, front people will take a knee and concentrate fire on the contact. Back people will cover and help if possible, but we are in the open. Take your room as quickly as possible. First person in, sweeps the room from opposite side to close, second person crosses behind to the opposite side of room. Questions?"

It seemed a lot to communicate and I was proud that no one had any questions and moved out like I'd directed. I was in front of Nick so I slid over to the left side of the hallway, I could see his rifle pointed down the hallway. Nick and I would be able to see the doorway on the opposite side of the hallway before we got to the one on our side. The door was open so I aimed into the room. I saw the end of a blaster sticking out.

"Contact, right side." As soon as I could see further into the room, a second figure appeared. "Second contact, right side." I took a knee and fired off three rounds. I missed but the figure didn't move quickly enough and I finished him off. Tabby was in front on the right side and took a knee, Marny looked over her shoulder down the hallway.

"There's one more on the right side hiding behind the doorframe. Let's move forward. Nick, you cover right when I reach our doorway. I'll have to clear our side. Tabby, Marny move forward with us, your baddie isn't moving yet." The blaster rifle still hadn't moved. Before I made it to the doorway, a third contact appeared on the right, inside the room.

"Contact." I fired at the figure and it blipped out. Four down, eight to go. I was sweating profusely.

"Contact," Tabby said. She fired across my line of sight.

"Tabby, you clear?" My tactical display showed that she had dropped the baddie.

"Roger."

"Let me clear my opening. You have a baddie right behind your doorframe."

I moved up to my doorframe and peeked around. There wasn't anyone directly across. I swept from right to left, stepping into the doorway. There was another baddie, but I brought him down, barely feeling the small lance of fire in my back. I spotted a third baddie in my room and tried to fire. My gun did nothing.

"Frak!" I jumped at the baddie, I would tackle her. She fired at me again, clearly hitting me. My arms passed right through her and I fell to the ground sort of at her feet, sort of behind her.

Nick entered the room and brought her down. I picked myself up and scanned the room. There wasn't enough furniture in here to hide anyone. "Clear," I said.

"We're clear," Tabby replied. I looked at the count. We had cleared a total of seven. There should be five remaining. I was dead, although I would be active again in twenty seconds.

"Nick, Tabby, position on the doors, aim diagonally to the end of the hallway. I have fifteen seconds to reset."

"Contact left," Tabby said. "Friendly."

"Let him go." I marked the target as friendly on the tactical display. "Marny, you and I are going to stick to the walls on opposite sides and go down the hallway. If we have contact we both drop prone. Roger?"

"Aye, aye."

"GO." My timer was complete and my gun was active again. We didn't make it five meters before three figures popped around the corner at the end of the hallway.

"Contact!" Three red dots appeared in my tactical display. I tossed myself forward onto the ground. It was impossible to fire, but at least I didn't get hit by the initial salvo. Tabby and Nick returned fire and Marny dialed in a target on the way to her stomach. All three figures dropped.

"Marny, we'll crawl to the end of the hallway," I said.

"Aye, aye Cap."

We made it to the end of the hallway without incident. My tactical display agreed with my assessment that the T was a balcony.

"Nick, Tabby, advance on our position. Stay clear of the balcony railing, might be baddies below."

"Roger."

"Check."

I peeked around the corner to the left. I was able to see all but the far right corner of the balcony from my position. I was still on the ground, not wanting to give my position away to anyone below. The balcony ended in an open stairwell. I thought I could stay hidden if I crawled over there, but if I did that I wouldn't be able to deal with the stairwell. We had three baddies left.

I pushed myself backward - back the way we'd come. I didn't have to tell Marny to do the same, she followed suit and we stood up.

"Two left. I believe this level is clear. There's a stairwell on the left. I'll take point with Tabby on my right shoulder and Marny stacked up behind her until we get to the stairwell. We need to stay away from the balcony. Nick, you stack up on Marny. I'll hug right as much as possible in the stairwell to give everyone a clear firing lane. GO."

We moved to the stairwell without being detected. I wasn't sure if that was good or bad. We started down the stairs and a figure appeared. I fired and Nick fired. The figure disappeared but I had a sinking sense it might have been a friendly. Whatever it was, two more peeked in and popped back.

"Fire short bursts at the stairwell door and follow me. GO."

We started firing and didn't see any more baddies. We had to get through this bottom door. "Tabby and I are left, Marny and Nick right. They know we're here, so short bursts to keep 'em suppressed. GO."

We moved through the doorway and caught one of the baddies in the open. Tabby and I moved around left and I was sure Marny and Nick had moved to the right. The tactical display showed two more baddies pop up on the right and they dropped just as quickly.

"That's twelve. Clear the room," I said.

Tabby and I moved around the room and met up with Marny and Nick on the other side. There was a door at the end with a sign that read 'End.'

I pushed the door open and walked through. I was exhausted. It had taken us a total of …

Two men spun around from behind a wall and opened fire on us.

"Contact!" I said. My gun wasn't operational. Tabby's obviously wasn't either, as she'd followed directly behind me. Marny and Nick returned fire and tagged the two remaining baddies.

"What the frak?"

"Clear," Marny announced.

SO WHEN DOES VACATION START?

"That's fourteen by my count," I looked at Marny suspiciously.

"Oh, did I say twelve?" She tossed an innocent look back at me.

"What about that sign? It said 'End,'" Tabby declared. "Let me guess, that was an object lesson."

"Guilty," Marny said sheepishly.

I was annoyed at the result, but the message was well-delivered.

"Okay. Nick, you're next," Marny announced.

"Can we have a couple of minutes?" I asked.

"Paying by the hour, Cap."

I sighed. We exited the room and saw the sign, TAC-10B on an adjacent door. The second run went much the same as the first, except we didn't get surprised at the end. It was quite a bit easier for me since I wasn't the one having to think my way through the entire exercise. Finally, it was Tabby's turn. I'd like to say she did a lot better, that her weeks at the academy had instilled in her some inherent squad leadership capabilities neither Nick nor I had. However, in the end, we didn't do so well. It wasn't her fault. The fact was, we were tired and just started getting sloppy.

The trip back to the hotel was quiet. Nick, Tabby and I were frazzled. Marny, as expected, looked as fresh as she had first thing in the morning. Thankfully, she wasn't gloating.

"How'd we do?" I didn't hold out much hope for a glowing report.

"Perfect. It's not the sort of thing you can be good at right out of the box. Overall, I'd say you did better than most on their first time out. Mostly I wanted to introduce you to the struggles of running a squad, especially if that squad hasn't trained together. The three of you work well together. I can tell you did team sports. Wish you were part of the crew, Tabby."

"Wish I wasn't missing the part where you teach us how to do it right," Tabby shot back.

"You'll be running your own squad soon enough."

Tabby nodded, lost in thought.

"Anyone else up for hot springs?" I asked. The night before, Tabby and I had discovered the resort's giant hot springs.

"Oh heck, yah!" Tabby said.

The afternoon passed quickly and before I was ready, it was time to take Tabby back to the Academy. The two of us sat in the cab, just outside the visitor center.

"I didn't know if we'd ever see each other again after the attack on Colony 40," Tabby was looking at me intently. I felt like she had something she needed to say.

"I'm glad you could break free for the weekend."

"So, are you okay with this?" Tabby asked.

"This? As in us?" I asked, gesturing between us with my hand.

"Yeah. Not knowing when we'll see each other again?"

"Are you? It seems kind of unfair to you," I hated saying it, but I had to give her a way out if she wanted it.

"Is that how you feel?"

"You know better than that."

"Do I?" she asked.

"Tabby, I've always believed you're too good for me, that I've no right to expect you'd want to be with me. I felt lucky just being your friend. I guess I still kind of feel that way."

She just looked at me for a couple of moments. "So what? You just want to be friends? Frak, Hoffen. Sack up and just come out with it."

I didn't know how she always got me so twisted up and how we could go from awesome to completely off the rails. Worse, I never seemed to say what I intended and now we were headed down the worst possible path.

"That's not what I meant at all," I finally said.

"So what did you mean?"

"I meant ..." I put my hands on the sides of her head and

pulled her toward me. She resisted, but I didn't relent and met her half way. I kissed her the way I'd been wanting to since I'd picked her up the day before.

Tabby finally relented, wrapping her arms around my back and pulling me on top of her. After a few moments we came up for air.

"*That's* what I meant," I said. "And for the record, Tabby, I hate this. I want you with me every day. But if the options are what we have now and nothing at all, I'll take this. I chased you to Mars, I'll follow you wherever you go until you tell me to go away."

"Only one way I'll do this," she said. "Completely honest and monogamous."

"Hah. I can't have a girl in every port?" Which was not the right thing to say.

Tabby drew back and slugged me hard. That one was gonna bruise. "Not even one, Hoffen. I'll know and I'll hunt you down and end you. Then we'll be done."

"Won't I be gone, since you ended me?" Again with the wrong thing. It earned me another slug, but that was fine by me.

"I have five minutes. Don't break my heart, Liam." Tabby opened the door and started to climb out. I leaned into her and stole a final kiss. She ran toward the gate and looked back over her shoulder before she passed through and gave me a sweet smile. It was a memory I would treasure.

The ride back to the resort seemed to take forever. I knew I would see her the next weekend, but I couldn't escape feeling melancholy.

Marny was stretched out on one of the couches with her head resting in Nick's lap when I walked back into the living room at the Concord.

"Guinness in the fridge, Cap."

I grabbed a bottle and flopped into the couch across from them. "What's on deck for tomorrow?"

"Tomorrow we deconstruct what we did today. You guys did better than I'd expected. It wasn't hard to tell you'd worked together before. I wish we could keep Tabby." Marny stopped and looked at me guiltily, "Frak. Sorry, Cap."

"Nah, I get it. We're better with her," I said.

"Not necessarily better, just she fits the team. It's hard to find that kind of synergy. So tomorrow we're going to work on theory. It'll work fine with three. We'll also work on common four-man formations."

"Just for the record, I don't want to be doing much of this," I said.

"Practice?" Marny asked.

"No, practice is fine. Chasing people who have guns, I'd like to avoid."

"We practice so we're not making it up as we go."

"I'm in... I'm also exhausted. See you guys in the morning."

"Yeah, we're headed to bed shortly," Nick said, not even smirking at me.

I checked my queued comms. There was a never ending stream of small details that Nick and I dealt with as budding entrepreneurs. I felt fortunate that Nick handled most of them. The one item that was solely in my wheelhouse was to line up loads and destinations.

Loading *Sterra's Gift* was going to be easy, but the *Adela Chen* was still proving to be problematic. I'd made initial contact with several corporations hauling in and out of Jeratorn. However, the responses so far had only been of a generic 'thanks for your inquiry' type.

Of primary interest, however, was a comm from Ada.

Liam, I know this is short notice and I completely understand if you can't make it, but we are having a memorial service for Mom on Monday afternoon. It will be informal, but Dad would love to meet you guys and ... well ... no pressure. Talk Later – Ada

It struck me again just how stoic Ada had been this past week. I still felt awful that we hadn't been able to save her mom. The only comfort I could take from the whole mess was that Ada was now safely home with her family. I appreciated that she'd attached the address of the memorial to her vid-comm message so we could be there.

The next comm was from Qiu Loo. I was a little surprised, since I wasn't expecting to hear much from her. The note was flagged as urgent.

Captain Hoffen, we may need to cut leave short. There are things I can't discuss on comm that could change our priority. I have contacted the shipyard to see about further expediting the repairs and modifications. Please tentatively plan to leave next Sunday, 1400.

I tried to tamp down my annoyance. She was busting to get going, but I didn't think she was the type to pull a stunt. Qiu Loo was much more of an in-your-face, don't-care-what-you-think type of person. I walked back out into the living room. Nick and Marny were still on the couch.

"Did you get the messages from Ada or Qiu?" I asked.

"Haven't checked since we got back to the suite. What's up?"

I explained the messages.

"What do you think Qiu's on about?" Nick asked.

"Any ideas, Marny?"

"I agree with you, Cap. Qiu's not yanking our chain. A lieutenant isn't going to get the shipyard to do bupkis without having some real juice. The fact she's been at them twice means somebody high up is pushing."

"That's my read too. You guys going to Adela's memorial?" I asked.

"Wouldn't miss it," Marny said. Nick nodded agreement. "Doesn't get you out of practice though, so set your alarm for 0700. We don't want to be late to the memorial."

I sighed and turned back into my room.

At 0600 the next morning I jumped right out of bed without an alarm. I thought I'd be sore from all the bending, crouching and crawling from the day before, but I felt pretty good after a long hot shower. I decided it was time to stop feeling sorry for myself about the situation with Tabby. I had the love of the woman I most cared about in the universe and we'd make everything else work out.

"Cap. Bacon and eggs? I make a mean omelet." Marny greeted me cheerfully.

"You cook?"

"Nope. Room service." She lifted the silver lid off a plate containing a large breakfast. I was starving. I wondered if the smell was why I'd woken up so easily.

I sat down, plate in hand. "How're we going to do training today?"

"Two parts. First, we'll walk through each of the scenarios. The studios are set up to replay the encounters. I'll point out what we could have done differently as we walk through. After that, I'll reprogram the scenarios to run, using the changes we talk about and you can see how things would go differently."

"What, with holographics and stuff?" I asked.

"Yup, the studio is all holographic with programmable physical props like walls, trees, ponds, you name it."

"That's pretty intense."

"Tuesday – another indoor. Wednesday – low gravity station. Thursday – outdoor. And Friday, we'll volunteer to be baddies."

"Why would we do that?"

"What? Be baddies? It'll give us a chance to see pros in action."

"We get to be the bad guys?" Nick asked as he joined us. "Frakking about time!"

Working through the scenarios was humbling. Watching from behind our holographic figures, it became imminently clear how messed up our formations and approaches were.

"Listen to your instructions here, Cap. See how much information you're having to communicate? That's because we don't have a common frame of reference, like we do on the ship. You can't make any assumptions, so you have to think about every bit of minutiae. You're overloading on details and that means you can't think clearly. You recovered, but try to remember how you felt right then. That's why we're doing this, so we can create a common set of phrases and hand signals to describe complex actions. It allows you to focus on things that are different, not on everything all at once. Let's move to the next room."

Marny was complimentary at our approach to the first room. "You hit that pretty much textbook. If I didn't know better, I'd have thought you trained on that approach. Nice job, Cap. Let's move down the hallway."

Our holographic images moved out of the first room and we watched Nick walking on my right side with his gun against the wall. If something bad happened he wouldn't be able to move his gun anywhere and it would be going off right next to my ear.

"As uncomfortable as it sounds, you'll have to switch shoulders in that situation. We'll work on it so you are comfortable. You had the correct side but once you got to the corner, if something happened, Nick would have had no way to support you," Marny said patiently.

"Since you were already out of position when you reached the corner, you couldn't possibly execute a correctly pie'd corner." Marny grabbed my holographic figure and slid it around and directed the AI to make my blaster rifle point down the hallway.

"If you ran into problems, Nick couldn't have done anything to help you without stepping into your line of fire. It worked out in this case, but we need to fix it."

She walked us through all three scenarios like this, patiently explaining where we had messed up and where we had done a good job of improvising. We were such rookies, I was surprised she was even trying to train us.

At the end, Marny made all of the adjustments she wanted and then re-ran the encounters. We flowed smoothly through the building and easily cleared the rooms. The concepts ranged from complex to fairly obvious. When standing next to a life-size version of yourself during the explanation, the concepts became clear very quickly.

"Why do I feel like we're just scratching the surface?" I asked while flying back to the resort. We all wanted to take a shower before the memorial.

"That's right," Marny said. "But it's like everything else, there are big ideas you can learn right away. Then, there are nuances that take forever. We're going to focus on those big strokes. I appreciate you both being willing to do this, I think it's important."

"You're an important part of the team," Nick said.

I agreed with him, but it was still a little bit much for me to take in. "I just hope we don't have to use our new skills."

"You already have Cap, unless you've forgotten about our incursion onto that pirate base."

"I know and that was terrifying."

"Tell me you weren't just a little bit excited."

"Yeah, it was crazy, but you're right. I can't say I wasn't loving parts of it."

LIMIT YOUR DOWNSIDE

Only a few people showed up to *Adela Chen*'s memorial service. It was a little sad. I was used to large services on Colony 40. On a mining colony, everyone knows everyone else and when someone dies, it's the right thing to show up and pay your respects.

Mr. Shan (Sam) Chen, who we met upon entering the chapel, started the service by talking about how he and Adela had met. The story was pretty common. They'd met through the introduction of a couple of friends and one thing led to another. Adela worked for her family's shipping business. It wasn't too long after that they'd gotten married, scrimped and saved and finally put a down payment on their own freighter. He went on to describe their life, struggling to make it, the joy they experienced with having Ada and even the stress of being married.

The story in and of itself was very ordinary, but there wasn't a dry eye to be found in the small crowd. Through his story, Sam was able to communicate great love for his wife and a profound sense of loss at her passing. They had been good friends, even after their separation. It made me wonder about my life with Tabby and if we would be able to find time to develop that same closeness. I suddenly missed my mom and dad.

It was equally hard to listen to Ada talk about losing her mother. She was gracious and acknowledged us in coming to their aid, but it was hard to feel good about anything, considering how much she had lost. I was never a big fan of these services because of the way they made me think about things I'd rather keep at arm's length.

We'd been invited to dinner with Ada and her dad. The restaurant was nicer than any I'd ever been in. Mr. Chen, who I couldn't bring myself to refer to as Sam, told us it was the same restaurant where he'd proposed to Adela.

"I can't possibly express how grateful I am that you brought my daughter back," Sam said for the umpteenth time. He'd been reminiscing about his first solo trips with Ada. Apparently, she had been quite a little terror on the ship, all full of energy and nowhere to run around.

I'd run out of ways to verbally acknowledge his gratitude and apparently so had Nick and Marny.

"So what's next for you youngsters?" We'd been at the restaurant for the better part of two hours.

"We're trying to line up a couple of loads to Jeratorn for early next week," I said.

"That sounds risky. Lots of rumors of pirate activity in and out of there."

"Plan is to convoy out with our cutter. Loads are selling at nearly double the normal trip rate." I didn't like that this painted us as opportunistic, but we were under a confidentiality agreement with the Navy.

"You said trying. If loads are selling so well, what's the problem?" he asked.

"TradeNet has nothing for the tug," I said.

He nodded, knowingly. "The vendors pulled all of their deliveries from TradeNet coming from Jeratorn."

"Why'd they do that?" I asked.

"Too many bond payouts, most likely. They'll open it back up once things settle down."

"Any ideas how we can line up a load?"

"I don't think you should be going out there. Especially not with my Ada."

"Dad," Ada interrupted. "That's not your call."

"Seriously? After all this? We talked about this."

"Ada, he's right. I shouldn't have brought it up. I'm so sorry." I silently berated myself for not considering the circumstances.

"What will you do if you can't find a load for the tug?" she asked. I knew my answer was going to annoy her, but I didn't see a way around it.

"We have a contracted load for *Sterra's Gift* already, so we'll be taking the cutter either way."

"Dad. I know how you feel about this but I'm getting a gig no matter what."

"But Jeratorn?"

"With an armed escort. Would you rather I crew for Belstak? I doubt their heavy blasters even work. Liam's tug is a brand new Fujitsu-FF718, top of the line. It doesn't get better than that."

Talk about an awkward moment. Somehow at a memorial, I'd caused Ada and her father to argue. I looked to Nick uncomfortably, unfortunately he was staring at his plate. I needed to say something.

"This won't be our only load. We'll be back in less than a month," I said.

Ada and Mr. Chen both looked at me. Ada was first to respond.

"What, so we're supposed to pass all routes through my Dad?" So much for getting out of this cleanly.

"I can't lose you too, Ada." Shan Chen's eyes glistened.

"I'm a sailor, Dad, it's who I am, not what I do." She laid her hand on his arm. "Don't hold me so tightly."

"I don't like it, Ada."

"I know, but you need to do this for me."

"You could do a spec run," he offered.

"What's that?" I asked.

"Rent a three-string and work directly with the mining co-op. You find a buyer once you're en route to Mars."

"We don't have that kind of money. A three-string has to be half a million in ore alone."

"More like three quarters of a million. You don't need to have it all. For that matter you don't need to have any of it as long as you have enough bond. You just need investors."

"That's a lot of money to come up with in a short period. What kind of terms do you normally get?" Nick asked.

"Do you have three-quarters of a million bond?" He asked.

"Yup." Nick answered.

"That makes it easy. How much do you want to put in?"

"We've got nothing," Nick said.

"That's not a problem, it just affects your profitability. The way I'd structure it is for expenses to come off the top. Investors get half of the remaining and you split the rest with your crew."

"Give me a minute," Nick started punching on his tablet. "If we do standard crew and ship shares we'd stand to clear about eighty. That's assuming we get a second crew for the tug."

"That might be a little high," Sam said. "Mind if I see?" He motioned to Nick's reading pad.

"Ah, right, the public bid-ask is wrong on ore. You won't get that, but it's close. Discount that ten percent and you should be pretty accurate. I'd be interested in investing a quarter of a million as long as it's backed up by a bond."

"How do we sell it once we get back?" I asked.

"Your man, Nick, already has it," Sam said. "There's a public commodity market. Once you have the load and are headed back, you start watching the market. You lock the price based on a window of time. So look here," He slid the tablet over so I could see it. "This is the forty-eight hour price and these are the tonnages at that price. Say, today you had seventy point five kilo tons of iron, that's what they'll pay for it, minus that ten percent I was telling you about."

"How do we set a price with the co-op?"

"Good question. That's all about timing too, based on when you pick it up."

"So what if the market goes down between when we buy and sell?"

"Then it's a bad time to be in a commodities market. It'd have to sink a lot though. Undelivered ore is discounted almost fifty percent. We can also put in a zero loss clause. Basically, if it all goes to crap, the investors have to pay for expenses. Ship comes out at zero."

"I can see why people like TradeNet," I remarked.

"You'd think, but TradeNet is expensive, so it's almost always the least profitable. Don't be so quick to dismiss the gamble. It's more work, but you almost always come out ahead. The trick is to figure out how to limit your downside. Since I'm investing, let me help you when it comes time to lock in prices."

"Thank you. I think we just got a free lesson in trading." I grinned across the table at him, hoping to put him a little at ease with what we were doing.

"I couldn't be more invested in your venture, between Ada and most of my capital. I'll get you a contact for the co-op. They know me so that should help."

"Would you mind forwarding me a boilerplate contract?" Nick asked.

Mr. Chen pinched the air in front of him and tossed it at Nick's tablet.

"I'll get our lawyer to look at this and then send it back to you," Nick continued.

"That'll work. How about you let me negotiate with the co-op? Like I said, since I'm an investor, our objectives line up together."

"That makes sense to me," Nick said.

Walking out of the restaurant, I had a good feeling. I couldn't think of a better way to honor Adela Chen than to talk about sailing. Nick and Marny went to the electronics shop for earwigs and by the time we got back to the resort it was late again. We took a dip in the hot springs but found ourselves back in bed before midnight.

The rest of the week turned into an easy rhythm; up at 0800, light breakfast, training with Marny in squad tactics in the morning and different outings in the afternoon. I loved hanging out with the two of them. Our group felt oddly like it had once been with Nick, Tabby and myself, with the obvious addition of having to avert my eyes occasionally.

Friday morning I had that sense I get when things are about to change. And boy, I couldn't have been more right.

"Morning, Cap," Marny said in her usual cheery tone. "Breakfast is on the counter and then I need you to put on an armor suit."

Marny was already decked out in her black combat armor. I

marveled, once again, at her transformation from normal person to warrior. The combat armor's tight fitting, but slight additional bulk, accentuated her extraordinarily muscular build. I'd seen her in action before and knew this wasn't simply for show.

"Why do we need armor? I thought we got to be the bad guys today," I asked.

"Most of the time it's just for safety. Today, however, we are up against a martial only team."

"What's martial only?" Nick asked from the couch.

"No ranged weapons unless they are thrown."

"Ugh, not sure I want to get a knife in the throat," Nick's face went a little pale.

"We'll have helmets on and they'll have safety weapons. Nothing to sweat about."

We looked pretty awesome walking through the lobby of the resort and drew more than our share of attention. It was a short cab ride to our destination, but we unloaded at a new location. The last four days in a row we'd gone to the same building that kept reconfiguring itself to Marny's designs. I'd been the most impressed with the forest encounter, enough so that I'd made Marny and Nick go on a hike in the forested hills near the resort Thursday afternoon. But this morning we didn't know what we were going to be in for.

"The way this works is we're extras in their encounter. The players won't know if we're real or holo. The holo actors will respond to our actions so be careful about giving away your position. When you've taken incapacitating damage, your helmet will light up bright blue. Do not try to re-engage the players once you are blue. Also, once you're down, the AI will show you an exit after the players have passed. Follow the path the AI gives you, you might be able to re-enter the encounter."

Marny had bright red patches on her shoulders and Nick and I didn't.

"What's with the patches on your shoulders?"

"I'm announcing that I'm open to martial combat. If one of the players wants a tussle, I'm willing to cooperate."

"Are you nuts?" I asked, even though I was a little impressed.

"Aye Cap. That I am. Only way to stay sharp is to know the next one's gonna hurt."

We pulled on the helmets that were sitting on a shelf in the first room we entered. I grabbed a flechette pistol. I figured if I brought a blaster rifle I'd never get a chance to use it. These guys would want to fight close up and were probably good enough to make sure that happened. I needed a gun I could quickly maneuver.

My AI interfaced with the scenario and a map popped up. It was different than what we'd run, but I suspected there were millions of variations. I loved the way this one was organized. Instead of a hallway with adjoining rooms this was some sort of large mechanical room. There were giant pipes, small alcoves, stairwells and catwalks. From my perspective, I'd prefer to drop a bomb, because you'd never successfully clear it. There were too many hiding places.

My thought was, whoever we were up against was going to be really good. Obvious hiding places wouldn't fool them for a moment. I checked to see where the holo actors were located. There were some out in the open but a number of them were tucked away in shallow alcoves.

I picked my first spot - wedged behind a large pipe and had a good view of two of the holos hidden in alcoves. I couldn't see how anyone would be able to take out those two without me getting a decent shot on them. All of the holo actors were wearing the same helmets we had. A couple of them even had red patches on their shoulders. I was sure this was to keep the playing field as level as possible.

Players have entered the scenario. Prepare for contact. The AI's warning was ominous and caused my blood pressure to rise. It felt more like the start of a pod-ball game than the incursion Marny and I executed back near Baru Manush. Marny was right, since they couldn't really hurt me, it made a difference.

I kept the pistol up near my chest. I wanted to give myself the best chance I could at actually getting a shot off. My confidence with the fletchette had grown significantly in the last several weeks. Marny worked with me on the ship and I was able to get at least thirty minutes of practice in every day, even while we were on shore leave. The nice thing about the flechette was you could practice just about anywhere, printing practice ammo to fit the situation.

From the corner of my eye I caught a slight movement, but didn't want to give away my position by reacting too quickly. I stayed completely still, scanning the area, but couldn't find anything. I thought someone could be up and to the right. Frak, maybe I was just hallucinating, too amped up on expectations.

The attack on the first holo player happened in the blink of an eye. A small, lithe figure, dressed entirely in black (imagine that), jumped silently from an upper level, rolled forward, extended a long black pole and thwacked the holo actor's head violently. I lowered my gun in her direction but before I could get a bead on her she'd vaulted back up over the alcove and disappeared.

She - I presumed it was a she based on her relative size - had been on the ground for no more than a couple of seconds and made no more noise than a slight scuffing. She might as well have been operating in zero-g as easily as she'd vaulted up and out of the way. I was starting to consider the openness of this encounter as a disadvantage to me.

I imagined she would make the same type of strike on the second alcove. No way had she seen me. I lowered my gun to try and fire at her, but her back was to me.

"Nice try, cheesecake." A rough whisper in my right ear, just before I felt the pressure of a soft object swipe across my throat. My helmet lit up blue. I looked over at the chiseled face of a man several centimeters taller than myself. He had bright blue eyes that were alight with amusement at taking me so easily.

I nodded, not wanting him to think me a poor sport. How he had so easily dropped in on me, I had no idea. I wondered if that had been the entire gambit. They'd discovered me the first time I'd spotted movement. Then the black-suited woman kept me distracted at the same time she took out another combatant. I vowed I wouldn't ignore a warning like that again.

"You still up?" Nick asked through the comm.

"No. I had a slight warning but really didn't stand a chance."

"I didn't see anything. My helmet just went blue right after I felt a thump on the back of my head."

"You get a look at 'em?" I asked.

"Yes. Guy about your height, really muscular, like Belcose."

"One who got me was tall, fairly muscular. I also got a good look at their third. I think a woman, small and incredibly fast."

"Marny still up?"

"Yup. She'd be on channel if she wasn't"

"I'm down, damn it." I was surprised. Marny wasn't prone to cussing. "Got suckered. I saw a big old boy and I wanted to get into it with him. Someone tapped me out right then and there with a thrown weapon."

"Sorry Marny. I'm about to re-enter."

"My fault, Cap, won't happen again."

The next few scenarios ran pretty much the same way. I got a couple of shots off but never came close to hitting anyone. It was always a misdirection. One of them would get my attention in one direction and then someone else would take me out from another. I needed a better approach.

The final scenario was set in a heavily wooded forest. Ugh, I had virtually no experience in the forest. The scenario map showed two buildings; a barn and a building next to a stream. I'd been pretty consistent in trying to set traps, waiting for someone to attack a holographic combatant. I wondered if they might be keying off my predictable choices. This team had probably run enough scenarios that they could easily figure out where the holo players would be set up. By now, they knew right where to find me based on how the holo players were reacting.

It was time to mix things up a bit. I felt like this team was relying on the predictability of the holo players too much. Maybe I could use that against them. Nothing else had worked, so it was worth a try.

My understanding of the holo players over the last few days was that they operated in a limited area. They would path around;

some using a linear path, some just a set of boundaries, like a room, hallway or small building. Marny had said that the holo players responded to us. If I had enough time, I was pretty sure I could make something work.

"Nick, on my six!" I said.

"Roger." Nick ran out from behind a tree and we sprinted down the road to the other side of a bridge and into one of the old wooden buildings we'd seen on the map. As I expected, there were four holo players in the building on the first level.

"You willing to be bait?" I asked.

"Can you take one out?"

"Better odds, I think."

"Let's do it," he said.

I explained my plan and we took our positions. Nick hid behind a large wooden cupboard. It was a good hiding spot and would give him a chance in a normal scenario. Of course, this wasn't normal.

I held my pistol as if I were pointing it at someone directly across from me. I'd seen holo players lining up like this a million times over the last few days. I picked my route and started pathing it faithfully. It was all about repetition. I kept my eyes alert but didn't move my head side to side, like someone who'd been thwacked a dozen times in the last couple of hours.

One moment I was walking up the stairs and the next I heard a slight scuffling below, near Nick's position. I spun around and fired just above Nick's position on full automatic. The figure who'd just thwacked Nick with a Bo Staff was launching themselves up the stairs at me. His helmet lit up blue.

"Frak!" He gave me a quick salute and sat down. My helmet lit up blue just after I felt a soft thud on the back of it. It had required sacrificing both Nick and myself to take out one of them, but I felt like we'd still achieved the impossible.

In the end, we'd played scenarios, not real life. Our opponents had been relying too much on the weaknesses and limitations of the holo players. For me, that was the crack in their armor.

"Come down. It's an impasse." I heard a woman's alto voice

call from outside the building. "You're past my weapon range and you'll never hit us."

I looked at the extremely muscular man who was seated on the wooden stairs. He shrugged at me as if to say, why not? I gave him my hand to help him up. He surely didn't need my help, but he accepted it. I have always liked a good sport. The three of us exited the building and walked toward the clearing.

"Mano a mano takes all," Marny called from a nearby tree.

"Accepted," the small woman said.

The woman had no sooner responded when Marny swung down easily from a lower branch of the tree and into the clearing. She landed in a three point stance with her eyes locked on the small figure. In her free hand, Marny held a long black Bo Staff. I had no idea where she'd come up with the weapon. It was the second time I'd seen her with this staff in a combat situation. The first had been on the pirate base near Baru Manush.

The small woman didn't hesitate and launched an attack at Marny. Her speed was difficult to follow, the staff she held spun around her body at angles that were visibly impossible to identify. It was mostly just a blur. A fourth figure joined us - the taller man who had taken me out so silently in the first scenario.

Marny gave ground to the woman who was less than half of her own mass. She was obviously trying to judge the enigma that approached. Making her decision, Marny stepped into the whirlwind. The staffs connected with a resounding crack. Having successfully stopped the maelstrom, Marny pushed her advantage and started methodically striking and trying to overpower her adversary.

The small woman made a surprising move and dropped her staff to the ground. She did this at the same time Marny swung through with a hard strike. Marny was pulled forward, off balance. Up to this point, Marny had been hammering the smaller woman, and with each blow, advancing.

The small woman jumped forward, placing one of her feet on the side of Marny's calf, using it as a step to bring her even with Marny. She unloaded a vicious blow into Marny's helmet with her fist. Helmet or not, I would have gone down. Marny staggered but didn't fall and had the presence of mind to use the smaller woman's momentum and her own over-commitment to allow her body to spin around.

The woman was thrown forward as Marny gave an extra push with the back of her staff. I recognized the next move as the woman, instead of landing, rolled over her shoulder and back up to a standing position. It was a basic Aikido maneuver that one of my own adversaries had taught me not so many weeks before.

Marny, seeing her opponent without a staff, threw her own aside. She gave the smaller woman the universal signal for 'bring it' and beckoned her forward.

The woman gave a small forward nod and brought her fists up in a classic boxing stance. It looked ridiculous. She was giving up forty kilos and twenty centimeters. Marny took it plenty seriously and adopted a wary martial artist stance. Apparently, the woman was bluffing since as soon as she saw Marny's stance, she also switched up.

She launched herself at Marny in a flurry of blows. Marny defended, moving at speeds that I thought were beyond her. For nearly a minute the two women traded strikes. The smaller trading two for Marny's every one. Their fatigue was evident, especially Marny's.

The bout finally ended when Marny slightly overplayed one of her strikes. The smaller woman ducked under and slithered up Marny like a snake in a tree, ending up behind her, with her legs wrapped around Marny's chest. One arm was hooked under Marny's jaw and the other levered it like a vice.

"Submit?" she asked breathily.

"Frak. I submit." The woman immediately let go and dropped to the ground, sitting unceremoniously. Marny fell back heavily and lay out on the ground next to her.

"Marny Bertrand." Marny held her hand over to the seated woman.

"Tali Liszt."

IT'S A SMALL WORLD

The heavily muscled man, whom I'd lured, using Nick as bait, turned to me with an easy smile and stuck his hand out to me. "Ben Rheel, friends call me Jammin."

"Liam Hoffen," I replied. "And this is Nick James."

"Jordy Kelti." The taller of the two joined us. At two meters tall, he was significantly taller than all of us. He was also well muscled but not to the extent of Ben. "Nice takedown on Jammin. Maybe we grab a beer and you tell us how you did that."

"Just got lucky." I definitely felt that way.

Jammin looked from Jordy Kelti back to me. "That wasn't luck." It was a statement of fact. There was no challenge or question, simply a statement. I didn't know how to respond, so I looked back toward the two women on the ground.

"That was quite a show," I said.

"Yeah, Tali's going to be pissed," Jordy said, chuckling.

"How's that?" Nick asked. "She came out on top."

"Tali's more of a one-shot, one-kill type of gal. The fact that it took her seventy-six seconds is going to really chafe her."

"I had seventy-eight," Jammin said.

We walked over to where the two women were recovering. Marny sat up as we approached.

"Everyone still whole over here?" Jordy asked.

This earned him a glare from the smaller woman, Tali.

"Aye," Marny said. "But I'm gonna need a patch for my jaw tonight." She nursed the side of her face.

"Are you sure? It felt like an iron plate to me." The woman smiled admiringly at Marny.

I held my hand out to Tali as Nick had already made it to Marny. She accepted the help and it only took the lightest pull on my part and she sprung to her feet.

"Liam Hoffen."

"Shite, no kidding. Tali Liszt," she answered. I looked at her, slightly confused, but pushed on. "And my buddy, Nick James."

"We got a thing going tonight, Captain. You guys join us for barbeque?" Tali asked. This caused me to do a double take. I quickly replayed the conversation and couldn't find a reference to my being a Captain. Tali obviously noticed my confused look. "You show up. I'll explain. Say, 0600?" She pinched an address and tossed it at me.

My HUD showed the location to be well south of Puskar Stellar in what appeared to be the middle of nowhere. Odder and odder. I looked at Nick and Marny, who both nodded their agreement.

"We'll be there," I said.

"Until then," She nodded to us and walked to the nearby exit, Jammin and Jordy following along in her wake.

"Well, that kinda spiked my weird-o-meter," I said.

When we exited the building we watched three grav-bikes flying away at high speed, all in different directions.

"You know her?" Marny asked.

"Not at all."

"Should make for an interesting night," Nick offered.

A familiar silver cab arrived and we loaded up.

"I've a tonne of things to get settled this afternoon," I said.

"Did you get investors lined up?" Nick asked.

"Contracts are in your queue. I sent Ordena the rough drafts yesterday. I think you just need to accept them. Sam's been pretty great. We should formalize some sort of arrangement with him in the future. I'd never have been able to put this together without him."

"Sam?" Nick asked.

"That's what Ada's dad goes by."

"Sure, if we could have someone putting together loads for the tug, that'd be worth something. I got a ping from the shipyard. *Sterra's Gift* will be ready by 0900 tomorrow. Have you finalized the load for Jeratorn?"

"I'll do that when we get to the hotel. I didn't want to commit until I knew when we'd have the ship. What about another crew?"

"I'm not sure about that yet," Marny said. "If there's a chance of a crap-storm I don't think we want someone we don't know."

"Yeah, frak. Makes sense." I felt like we were flying short-handed, but she was right. "How about the chandler? I'd like to go heavy on supplies."

"Thinking about staying out a while?" Marny asked.

"Not really, but I've got a weird feeling about this trip."

"Weird like you think it is going to go easy? 'Cause as far as I know you've never actually made it to a single destination without getting into it."

"Hah. No. It's just Qiu being tight-lipped about the mission and Belcose dropping Harry Flark's name."

"I wouldn't think the Navy would be quite so accommodating if they weren't expecting trouble. I'll bump up the supplies," Marny said.

We made it to the hotel and walked up to the room without saying much. I had a million things that I needed to get done and I imagined Marny and Nick felt the same.

"Ready to go about 1700?" Nick asked as I was ducking into my room.

"Think we need to bring anything?" I asked.

"I'll get the hotel to put together something for us," he said.

Open comm, Qiu Loo. I shut the door to my room.

"Loo."

I mentally bristled at her terse greeting. She had denied visual comm, which wasn't totally unexpected.

"Sunday, 1700 at Coolidge ship yard. Work for you?"

"I'll be there. Anything else?"

"Nope."

"Loo out." She terminated comm. At least I had that out of the way.

Open comm, Ada Chen.

"Hiyas, Liam." She opened the video channel. It was refreshing to see her cheery smile.

"Heya, Ada. Can you arrange to get the barge-string ready to go by Sunday, 1700 or so?"

"Sure. Am I soloing it?"

"Can you load solo and we'll meet you? We'll be leaving Coolidge shipyard at 1730, give or take."

"Any reason for me not to get rolling first thing Sunday? You'd be able to catch me by midday Monday."

"I guess it's up to you. I just don't want you too far out without an escort."

"You sound like Dad. Nothing's going to happen this close to Mars, especially since we aren't filing a plan with anyone."

"Jeratorn Co-Op knows we're coming."

"Pirates aren't interested in empty strings, we're safe on the way out."

"I suppose. Okay, sure. If you want to get rolling early, send us navigation data-stream and we'll catch up. For my sake, though, don't sail directly there. Make a couple of legs along the way."

"That's going to cost fuel," Ada waggled her virtual finger at me.

"That's a cost I'm willing to pay. I'll tell Marny you're disembarking early. She's taking care of the chandlery order."

"Great! Happy sailing, Liam. See you Monday."

"Roger that, Ada. Happy sailing." *Close comm.*

I shot a quick comm over to Marny about Ada taking off early. I didn't want to interrupt my work.

Open comm Sam Chen.

"Sam Chen," he answered.

"Hi, Sam. We should be in Jeratorn in sixteen days. You want to start firming up the load?"

"Not yet, Captain, but I'll have it done before you get there."

"Did you get the contracts back from Nick yet?"

"They just arrived. You guys must be working this afternoon."

"Finishing up a few last minute details."

"Captain, you take good care of my girl out there."

"I will, Sam. Let me know if you need anything. We'll be under hard burn by 1730 Sunday."

"Understood. Be safe."

"Roger that." *Close comm.*

Run TradeNet saved query for Jeratorn. Optimize for arrival on or before eighteen days from Sunday 1800. Order by profit, eliminate bond in excess of two hundred fifty thousand.

The returned list of loads was even longer than it had been two days ago when I had last checked. The available profit was even higher, but so were the required bonds. It wasn't a good sign. High bonds made me believe the shippers were building into their calculus that loads might not actually make it.

Open group comm Marny, Nick, Ada.

One by one they popped up into my vision, the AI placing their avatars next to mine.

"What's up, Cap?" Marny asked. All three were looking at me.

"I'm not sure. I guess I'm just having some second thoughts."

"What's bugging you?" Nick asked.

"Aren't we contracted to the Navy to do this?" Ada asked before I could respond to Nick.

"Nothing specific, Nick. It's things like Jeratorn paying really high and … well … just a bad feeling I've got. And, yes Ada, we're contracted, but I'd rather deal with that than push anyone into something we know is wrong."

"So, you're saying we're getting paid too much and that's got you spooked?" Marny said.

"Well, when you say it that way it sounds ridiculous."

"Aye," she replied.

"Equal votes. Anyone want out? No hard feelings if you do," I had to get this out in the open.

Ada was first to answer, "Liam, there might be something going on, but that's always the case. Listen to your feelings, but canceling the run isn't the right thing. Be prepared. Take precautions. Sailing is always a risk."

"I'm in," Nick said.

"Gotta agree with Ada and Nick on this," Marny said. "Cap, nothing ever goes as planned. You have to put yourself out there."

I sighed, kind of wishing someone would have bailed. But, at the same time, I would also have been disappointed.

"Roger that. Game on. Sorry for the last minute jitters." *Close comm.*

Select first load plan. Finalize contracts.

If everything went without a problem, we'd earn seventy-five thousand for this, more than we were going to make for the ore delivery. In actuality, there were three different loads and they all needed to be picked up in Puskar Stellar and delivered to Jeratorn. We could pick them up as soon as *Sterra's Gift* was ready to go.

Having finished my duties, I rejoined Nick and Marny in the living room. When we finally left, I was going to definitely miss this spacious suite. It had nearly the same number of square meters of floor space as all of *Sterra's Gift*, the main difference being every square meter in the suite was made for relaxation. I would miss that bed and shower, to be sure.

"Is there a time slot I can take *Sterra's Gift* down to Puskar Stellar tomorrow? Ideally, it'd be afternoon so I could bring Tabby along." Nick held up his hand to ward me off a minute.

"Explain replaced." Nick was clearly talking to someone virtually. I wasn't used to looking for whatever clues a person gave when they were using an earwig. I did notice, however, that the earwig cable running along his cheek was slowly pulsing green. It made me wonder if mine did that.

Nick listened for a while and finished up. "Include replicator specs? … Right … No, I get it, I'll take it up with my Captain. Thanks for the update. Yup, 0900." I watched Nick's earwig blink red and then back to its normal black color.

"What was all that about?" I asked.

"Shipyard. They decided to replace our turret," Nick said, frowning.

"I don't follow, it's not their ship."

"Right, their project engineer missed that."

"Did he look at it? Does it look like a Navy ship? Can they undo it?" I asked.

"Not in time and he didn't see the ship, he's planet-side. I think it confused him since the turret we had installed was Navy issue.

He said it's a pretty decent upgrade and doesn't require ammo "

"Oh, so maybe I shouldn't be complaining?" I asked.

"Marny?" Nick asked.

"I'd have to see the specs, but the general difference is laser blaster turrets are faster with less punch. No ammo, but they require an energy store and you can run that thing dry."

"How fast?"

"Like I said, I need to see the specs, but probably seven or eight minutes of continuous rapid fire and then you'll be down to a much slower rate of fire. You never truly run dry, since the ship is continuously charging it, but the fire rate is terrible at that point."

"Hah, dumb it down a little, good or bad?"

"For us, I think it's great. It eliminates the crow's nest. Almost all of these babies are operated remotely. You'd puke if you spun around inside one of those bad boys. That puts the gunner on the bridge, which is better armored. But, if we run into something big, the laser blasters have difficulty ripping through the armor."

"How big?"

"I wouldn't want to run into anything much bigger than *Sterra's Gift* without a full load of missiles."

"Okay, it sounds like they're doing us a favor, other than they probably took our ammo. Did they give us a load of missiles like we agreed?"

"It's an upgrade, Cap. Probably worth more than the ammo, and yes, six missiles."

I should have picked up on the fact that we could only hold four, but it'd escaped me for the moment. Later I would be very grateful that the shipyard had increased our capacity to hold two more missiles.

"Perfect. Nick, are they still ready to go at 0900 tomorrow?"

"Yup."

"Any problem if I take her out tomorrow afternoon to get loaded in Puskar Stellar?"

"I've got the chandlery loading at 1000, then I'll need some time to re-fit the armory." Marny said. "You should be good after 1400. That work?"

"Yes. I want to take Tabby with me, she frees up at 1200."

"I've got some work to do on the ship, but I don't mind if you're underway," Nick added.

"Can you think of anything else? Ada's going to take off sometime Sunday morning and we'll catch up with her."

"You contact Lieutenant Loo?" Nick asked.

"Told her 1700."

"I think we should take Ada with us tonight," Nick said. It caught me off guard.

"Really?"

"Yup. She's crew now and I think it'd help her to feel part of the team."

"Why not? I'll make the call."

Open comm Ada Chen.

"Miss me already?" Ada asked cheerfully.

"Hah, yes. Any chance you want to meet us for a get together tonight?"

"Formal or informal?"

"We'll be going informal and can pick you up. It's somewhere south of Puskar, say around 1745? Sorry for the late notice, just came up this morning."

"Part of being a spacer - plans are always changing. Sure, I'll send you my address. See you in a couple of hours."

On the way out of the hotel, Nick stopped by the concierge desk and signed for two large bags. The taxi he'd hired was larger and nicer than the ones we'd been using to get back and forth to the training facility.

"I hired it for the night - save us from all of the MAG-L connections," he explained.

"What's in the bags?" I asked once we were underway.

"Picnic food, whatever that is," Nick said.

The larger cab we were in was very comfortable and once we got out of town it sped up considerably. I estimated we were traveling at least one-hundred fifty meters per second. In space that wasn't very fast, but with all the atmosphere rushing by, it felt quite a bit different.

The cab slowed once we hit the outskirts of Puskar Stellar and finally set down on the street in front of a tall building. It looked like an apartment complex. Nick opened the door and Ada was already standing on the sidewalk waiting for us.

She was dressed in a white sun-dress with large yellow polka dots. She was such a nice looking girl, it made me feel off balance. Nick extended his hand and helped her into the cab. I felt a little jealous at his thoughtfulness, especially when she rewarded him with the bright flash of her petawatt smile.

I felt a little better, albeit no less confused, when she asked, "So you're my date tonight, Liam?"

I looked to Marny and Nick and couldn't come up with a good answer right away.

"Uh ... yeah ..." I finally recovered and committed myself to the conversation. "I sure am." I smiled back at her as convincingly as I could.

"Hey, Cap. I think she's just messin' with you," Marny said.

"How we fixed for time?" I asked, in an obvious attempt to change the conversation.

"Aww... Liam, I'm sorry. I've made you blush," Ada said kindly. I'd spent a good deal of time with her and knew she liked to joke around. I also knew she didn't have a mean bone in her body.

"Just caught me off guard a little," I said.

"We're really headed out of town," Nick said. We all looked out the windows.

"Where do you think we're going?" I asked.

"It's a house," Nick said. "Registered to Natalia Liszt, who happens to be a highly decorated, special-forces operative - retired. She runs a private investigation / security company."

"Where'd you dig all that up?"

"It's all out there if you're willing to look for it."

Several minutes later we'd completely left Puskar Stellar behind us and the cab accelerated back to its max cruising speed. When it finally slowed, we were approaching a lone house, sitting in a field of low growing grasses. There were two other outbuildings on the property, but other than that, nothing was visible for kilometers.

"Man, she's way out here," Nick said.

"I'm guessing she values her privacy," Marny suggested.

"Where'd you meet her?" Ada asked.

"Training exercise this morning. She and Marny duked it out. It was epic," I said.

"Oh, I hope you didn't hurt her too much." Ada looked a little shocked.

"She kicked my ass," Marny said.

"That's not what it looked like to us," Nick responded. "You gave up your staff when she dropped hers."

"She did that for me," Marny explained.

"What do you mean?" Nick asked.

"She was way faster than me. It was only a matter of time and we both knew it. She was giving me another chance by dropping her weapon. It was unnerving."

"Right. That reminds me, don't you need a med-patch for your jaw?" I said.

"Aye, already taken care of. It didn't take much time, most of my jaw was reconstructed out of alloy. When Tali said she thought she hit a steel plate, she wasn't really too far off. Then again, I'd bet she isn't made of all her original parts, either."

"No kidding," Nick said.

"Nope. Gross you out?" Marny looked at Nick with concern.

"Nah, makes me want to know what else isn't real though." Nick waggled his eyebrows at her suggestively. I'd never seen him respond like that before.

The vehicle chose that moment to come to a stop.

"Oh, man, just when it's getting good," I complained.

Nick opened the door and a warm, dry breeze blew into the cabin.

"I never get tired of the real atmo," Ada said, taking a deep breath.

"It's so weird," Nick said.

The cab had landed several meters away from a large, old,

white house. Tali exited the house and walked toward us. She was wearing form-fitting black pants with clunky boots and a white sleeveless shirt. Her long black hair blew freely in the wind. I, once again, mentally face-palmed myself as I seemed always to be surrounded by gorgeous women. She waved with a friendly smile.

Just behind Tali, a young girl, full of energy, bounded out of the house. She was dressed casually in jeans and a loose t-shirt. When she took notice of us approaching, she swerved in behind Tali and sidled up next to her. It felt like an unusual reaction to seeing expected guests, but she could just be shy.

"I hope you don't mind, but we brought our other crew member with us," I said when we got closer.

"Not at all. Tali Liszt." Tali held her hand out to Ada who shook it. "And this is Jenny. Jenny, this is Liam Hoffen, Nick James and Marny Bertrand."

"Oooooh." Jenny said. I guessed her age at fourteen, although I was terrible at guessing. The young girl didn't accept the hand I offered, which wasn't all that unusual, and stayed behind Tali. What surprised me was that Tali had remembered all of our names.

"Come on in," Tali said. "You can put your bags on the kitchen table. There're beers in the fridge. If you wait for me to grab it, you'll likely be thirsty for a long time, so make yourselves at home."

Jenny ran into the house in front of us. I didn't know her very well, but she was acting like something was up. I was already a little on guard with Tali's comfortable use of our names.

When I entered the kitchen there was a third woman standing there. She was taller than Tali. Initially, I thought it might be her mother due to the silvery hair. But, her body was wrong for that. She was also very attractive. All at once it hit me and my head snapped up to her face.

Her smile was incongruous with my memory, but it was absolutely her. "Celina?" I asked out loud, although I was mostly just processing.

"Captain Hoffen," she replied demurely.

I crossed the room to shake her hand but she wasn't having any of it. She grabbed me and pulled me in for a hug.

"I don't understand. How'd you get here?" I asked as she gave Nick a hug.

She didn't answer right away but gave a worried look at Marny. Last time they'd seen each other Celina had directed much of her distrust at Marny.

"Accept my apology for being a bitch?" Celina said.

Even I knew those were the right words. Marny, who'd been just a little rigid, melted and crossed the room with a huge smile. "You've got a story to tell, I'd say," Marny responded and gave Celina a big hug.

READY TO SAIL

Celina – or Lena as we learned she liked to be called - caught us up on how, after we'd left her on the cutter, she'd been able to locate and rescue her sister, Jenny, with Tali, Jordy and Ben's help.

I turned toward Tali, who was next to me. "So what I don't get is how you figured out who we were at the training facility."

We were all sitting around a large bonfire Tali had started. I'd never seen such a large open fire before and it made me nervous, but Tali assured me she did this all the time.

"Mostly it was the team makeup. A female pro with two competent rookies. Marny's training actually worked against her, we've been trained to pick apart Marine discipline. No offense, Marny."

Marny raised her beer and tilted it toward Tali. "None taken."

Tali continued. "You also have a slight bobble in your stride from your prosthetic. That mostly sealed the deal for me. Not to mention, Lena here gave us a pretty good description of your group when you were together on the Red Houzi base. So, I've got a question for you. How'd you take down Ben? We haven't lost a team member in over a year and certainly not to rookies."

"I didn't figure it out until the end," I said.

"You're killing me. What?"

"You guys are so good that you were using the computer players against us. One of you would show yourselves for a second, or take out a holo just to see what would happen next. Computer players would react predictably, real opponents wouldn't, giving their positions away. Once you identified us, you could focus on flushing out and lighting us up. So, I did the same thing," I said.

"You used the computer players against us?"

"No, I disarmed you by acting like a computer player. You had obviously caught on to the way we were setting traps – near groups of holos. I put Nick in a spot where you would expect him to be waiting and where Ben would be required to commit himself to make the kill. I was nearby, acting like a computer player. As soon as I heard Nick get hit by Jammin, I reacted. I'd never do that in real combat. Nick's too valuable, so it wasn't really fair."

"Thanks bud," Nick saluted me from his seated position.

"That's the point," Tali said. "That's combat. There are patterns to how people behave. And it's never fair. You picked up on our pattern in less than ninety minutes. You have to know how unsettling that is."

"Unsettling was watching you and Marny go at it," Nick said.

"I'd like to have seen that," Lena said.

"Your martial skills are superb, Marny," Tali gave her a warm smile.

"Nobody should move as fast as you do. Thanks for dropping the staff, by the way. If you hadn't, you'd have ended me pretty quickly." Marny conceded.

"Your defense was incredible. I couldn't leave without experiencing your hand-to-hand."

A male voice came from behind us. "Jammin says seventy-eight seconds."

"I counted seventy-six," Tali responded.

The taller team member who'd introduced himself as Jordy Kelti walked into the fire-light. We shook hands and introduced him to Ada.

"Ada. Such a pretty name." He had a friendly smile that showed way too many teeth for my taste. I felt a stab of jealousy when Ada returned it.

"Where's a guy get a drink around here?"

Jenny had jumped up when Jordy arrived, run over to the cooler and pulled a bottle out. She obviously had a crush on him. Having heard her story, it wasn't hard to imagine why.

"So where are you headed next?" Jordy asked. He'd taken a seat next to Ada.

"We just finished a week of shore leave, and we'll be outta here early next week," I said. "How about you guys?"

"We're between jobs. It's hard to get back to private investigations after… well you know…" Tali said. The thing was, I did know. We could have very easily turned down the Navy and taken a safe job. It was hard to turn away from an adventure.

"Any chance you're looking for a gig?" I asked. I'd need to clear it with Nick and Marny but I just had a feeling about this team.

"You lose something?"

"No, but we're headed into something that could get dicey."

"You're serious?"

"I think so."

"I don't think we're looking for work - I just don't see us as crew."

"This'd be a one-time gig. We've got a contract with the Navy for extra security."

Jordy stood up and walked over to where we were talking. Apparently, I had his attention.

"Why would the Navy pay for extra security for your run?" he asked.

"I can't tell you outside of an NDA (non-disclosure agreement). If you're interested in talking about it further, we'll be picking up a load in Puskar Stellar tomorrow afternoon. It's a serious offer."

"Hmm. I'll talk to the team and get back to you. Send me details about when you'll be loading tomorrow."

"I can do that," It felt good to reach out to someone I had respect for. Maybe they'd take the gig or maybe not, but at least I'd been proactive.

It was well after 0030 when Ada, Marny, Nick and I shuffled into the waiting car and started back for Puskar Stellar to drop Ada off.

"Talk about a change … I hardly recognized Lena," I said after we took off.

"She's probably gained ten kilos since we last saw her. That's a heck of a story about how they rescued Jenny," Marny said.

"Tali, Jammin and Jordy are the real deal," I said. "I hope they think about my offer."

"They will," Ada said.

"How do you know?"

"Like a moth to a candle. You guys are the real deal too and if you watched the non-verbal communication between them, you'd know it. They could no more walk away from a fight than you guys would."

"You really see us like that? Primed for a fight?" I asked. It wasn't how I saw myself.

"Not so much fight - more like not stepping away from doing the right thing. None of you have an ounce of back-down in you and I guarantee that Tali and Jordy saw that. It's who they are too. It's also why I want to be part of the team. I want my life to add up to something, just like you do."

It was a sobering thought and sat me back in my seat.

"You were getting pretty chummy with Jordy there," Marny teased Ada. "I'd be careful with that one."

"Oh he's nice enough, but I think I've got his number."

"A little pretty for me. I go for the dark, rugged ones." Marny gave Nick a wink.

We dropped Ada off and made it back to the resort without incident. Tomorrow would be busy, but at least Marny wasn't going to make us do combat exercises, for once.

When I woke up the next morning, I took a shower and put a suit-liner and vac-suit on for the first time in a week. My AI reminded me that I had an earwig on and asked if I wanted to remove it or simply integrate it. The earwig had significantly better resolution than my suit's HUD, so I opted to integrate. I'd collected a small pile of clothing from our different adventures and decided to send all of the new items to the recycler. I'd keep my dress clothes, but didn't see how I'd need a running outfit or swimming suit anytime soon. If I did, I'd simply replicate one.

I joined Nick and Marny in the living room. Breakfast was a simple affair and I chose a meal bar and orange juice. If we weren't working hard, I didn't want to get too filled up.

"What time are you picking up Tabby?" Nick asked.

"About 1200. I thought I'd show her *Sterra's Gift* and she could ride along when we picked up the load."

"Yup. I think Marny and I are headed there now. Navy still has a little work left, but it's all external and they're okay with us being on board while they finish up. Do you want the suite for tonight?"

Nick and Marny's bags, which had grown on this visit, were both sitting by the door to the hotel.

"I'm hoping to convince Tabby to spend the night on the ship."

"Okay, I'll get us checked out then."

"See you on board, Cap." Marny gave me a quick thump on the shoulder and the two of them grabbed their bags and left.

I sifted through my comms and responded to the numerous small details that seemed to make up my life. My AI was learning how to help me process the comms and I was spending time teaching it how I wanted to respond to most things. Business communication was a new thing for my AI. I really needed to look into an upgrade that would help with the process.

Initially, I looked at different legal plugins, but they all seemed too specific. I was conflicted. I really didn't want those kinds of details to take over my life. I'd be happy to pay Ordena to handle it for us. Nick, no doubt, would also keep a pretty good watch on things. I kept searching, but hadn't found a suitable plugin by the time I needed to pick Tabby up.

Just as I was climbing into the cab, I received a comm from Tali. She was interested in talking about our job and would meet us at the location I'd sent to her last night. If there was any way to get her on board, I'd do it. I still had a bad feeling about this mission and bringing in a heavyweight team would go a long way toward resolving that.

I showed up early and actually got to go into the visitor's center of the Naval Academy. It was more like a museum than anything else. There were two large replicas of ships. The Magellan class battleship got my attention. In addition to every conceivable type of turret and missile array, this ship showed something I hadn't expected. At the front of the ship it looked like most of the bow was solid. There were sensor arrays across it, but the normal seams where panels were connected didn't seem to be in evidence.

"It's cast in a single piece at the largest foundry ever built in space." The voice belonged to an older officer dressed in a crisply pressed uniform.

"That's hard to imagine. Must make it nearly impossible to stop."

"We'd like to think so. Captain Peltrain," He held his hand out as a greeting.

I accepted his hand and shook. "Liam Hoffen."

"Thinking about a career in the Navy, son?" He was apparently not interested in beating around the bush.

"No, sir. Not eligible. Just here picking up a friend."

"Well that's a shame. A cadet?"

I was a little uncomfortable. I knew they had rules against public display of affection, but I didn't know what else might be off limits. Not much I could do about it.

"Yes, sir. Tabitha Masters."

"Name doesn't ring a bell. First year?"

"Yes sir." I was relieved to see Tabby enter the room with a small pack. She raised her eyebrows on approach, but otherwise didn't say much. When Captain Peltrain turned to see her approach, she pulled up into attention.

"At ease, Miss …" He was clearly retrieving her information, "Masters. I was just talking to your friend, Mr. Hoffen, here."

"Yes, sir." He was still reading his HUD. It was generally considered rude when talking to someone in person, but we were in no position to point this out.

"Hate to keep you from leave. Nice meeting you, son." He nodded and walked off.

Tabby visibly relaxed. "Let's get out of here," she said. I had a cab standing by and we walked out wordlessly and jumped in.

"Nice guy," I said.

"He can be a pain in the ass, but I'm on leave and don't want to talk about it, so what's the plan?"

Coolidge Space Elevator, I directed the cab. "They're just finishing up *Sterra's Gift* and I need to pick up a shipment in Puskar Stellar and meet with someone about crewing for us. You okay with all that?"

"I'm in for anything."

When we'd left the space elevator a few days back, it was dark and rainy and we hadn't been able to see any details. Today the sun was shining brightly and the structure was an incredible sight. The ten-meter diameter tether stuck up through the blue tinted glass building. From our vantage point in the cab, we could see that the MAG-L had a few tracks that also entered the large terminal.

"How long does it take to get to orbit?" Tabby asked.

"Coolidge ship yard is 520 kilometers straight up. It takes ten minutes to get to the top, just like it does coming down."

Tabby switched out of her cadet uniform and into her old vac-suit while I bought us a couple of one-way rides to the top. We shared the elevator car up with four other naval personnel. They were all enlisted and working for the shipyard. Each talked freely about the work they'd been doing, but most of it was beyond me. We exited the elevator onto a large platform that was the central hub joining many hallways. The exits were set up like spokes on a wheel and went in every direction.

Locate Sterra's Gift. My HUD lit up with a long floating arrow that superimposed on the inhabitants of the station.

"This way."

We walked for twenty minutes and turned down a hallway with an airlock at its end. I imagined that *Sterra's Gift* was on the other side and that it was pressurized but SOP dictated the lock. We both automatically pulled our vac-suit hoods up upon seeing the universal indicator L-1, letting us know we were one level away from vacuum. For us it wasn't an exercise, we'd experienced decompression and didn't have any interest in a repeat.

I placed my hand on the airlock panel and it cycled immediately. If the other side had been vacuum, we'd have had to wait for the lock to fill with atmo. Immediate entry meant it was pressurized, as I'd expected. We cycled through the far door of the lock and walked across the gang plank. I was surprised to see that the outside airlock door to *Sterra's Gift* looked new. It made some sense. In the short time we'd been around the ship, the door had been removed or forcibly opened at least twice.

"We got some upgrades. She's been sitting here for the last week."

"I've never been on board," Tabby said.

The inside of the airlock was sparkling clean and freshly painted. I didn't recognize it in the least. We walked across the hallway toward the armory door, which sat directly opposite the airlock. The door was open and Marny had things lying in the doorway. Both hallways and the door were just as crisply painted as the airlock had been. Marny must've heard us and stuck her head out of the armory.

"Heya Cap, Tabby," she said. "Ship's clean as a whistle. Navy sicced their bots on the interior. You gotta look in here, too." Marny was excited.

I stuck my head into the armory. It was just as clean as the hallway. Where there had once been shelves full of projectile ammo, there were now cabinets with some blinking lights on them. Marny looked to be in the middle of organizing a rack full of blaster rifles, pistols, and different types of ordinance. On the other side of the room were several armored vac-suits. It was in disarray, but I knew Marny would be working on that.

"Weird without all the ammo," I said.

"That's what all those blinking lights are - capacitors and batteries for the turret. I looked at the specs, it's a big boy. Wish we'd had that before. Go find Nick in the engine room before you go forward, I think he wants to show you some changes."

"Looks good, Marny. Let me know when you're done with the chandlery."

"Aye. They'll be here in an hour or less."

I showed Tabby the galley and mess and then took her back to the engine room. Nick had a large vid-screen on the wall in front of him that was currently displaying different system statuses.

"Tabby, welcome aboard." Nick hopped out of his chair and gave her a quick hug. "Like my new station?"

"It's great. This chair wasn't here before was it?"

Nick chuckled. "No. I can tell which end of the ship you're interested in. You're going to want to see this, however."

Display exterior Sterra's Gift. Rotate slowly on vertical axis. Apparently, Nick's AI wasn't used to his new vid screen, so he had to pinch the display from his HUD and throw it up on the screen.

The ship he displayed resembled my knowledge of *Sterra's Gift* but there were significant exterior differences. My eye first jumped to the turret. It looked a lot different without the crow's nest. Instead of popping up so the gunner could get a clear view of the targets, it was flat and in-line with the spine of the ship.

The next major difference was that we no longer had missile racks, but instead there was a new missile tube running down the lower side of the ship. Probably the most significant change was some sort of an engine port that pointed forward, exiting just beneath the missile tubes.

"Is that a forward thrust engine?" I asked Nick.

"Yup. They gave us a heck of a deal on it."

"I can do a hot approach?" One of the things I disliked about *Sterra's Gift* in combat was the constant flipping over for deceleration, or at least accelerating on a new vector.

"It adds a lot of flexibility. Like it?" he asked. Pride showed on his face - this ship was important to him.

"It's incredible. How much did we spend?"

"We went in the red a little on this. The engineer approached me on Thursday, needed an additional seventy-five for it all. I probably should have asked you, but he needed an answer right away. So then I figured I'd wait until you got to see it."

"Like I'd have said no." I rolled my eyes and gave him a grin.

"Yup. They also added a bunch of armor too. Want to see the rest of it?" he asked.

"Sure do."

"Follow me." Nick led us forward past the armory and stepped in the door labelled BR-1 on the starboard side. It was the room I used since Marny and Nick had taken to using the captain's quarters.

"Marny and I talked about it and are moving over here," he said.

The room had been neatly upgraded. The original bunk beds had been removed. The far side of the room had a wider bed raised up to about a meter and a half off of the floor. Underneath were deep cabinets and lockers. On the near side was a small round table with two chairs next to it.

"You're moving out? This'd work fine for me."

"Doesn't make sense. The captain's quarters are a working room in a ship. It's where we should be having conferences and strategy meetings," Nick said.

"Hmm, I suppose. But you're just as much an owner of this as I am."

"It's not about that. We need to have no confusion about the pecking order on the ship."

"Well. It looks nice. I don't suppose it's a big step down."

"Nope. Better mattress than you have."

"Anything else?"

"Not really." Nick exited and headed aft.

I showed Tabby the captain's quarters. The door was right next to the closed door of the bridge. To say that nothing had been changed wasn't entirely true. It was true that no new features had been added, but carpet had been replaced, everything was spotlessly clean, and the couch and table had been updated.

"Want to sleep here tonight?" I asked Tabby.

"You sleeping on the couch?" she fired back.

"Whatever you want."

She slapped my shoulder playfully. "I'm sure we could work something out."

"Cap, chandlery delivery is here early, we'll be unloaded in less than ten." Marny's voice came over the sound system in the room.

"How're you talking over the speakers in the room?" I asked.

"Nick turned it on. Use the person's name first when you talk, AI figures out if it's a communication and pipes it to where the person is."

"That's handy." I purposefully didn't use her name, I wanted to see if it would be smart enough to recognize we were still in conversation.

"Some people don't like it, especially if they talk to themselves," Marny quipped.

I led Tabby out of my newly renovated quarters and forward to the bridge. Just like my quarters, the bridge didn't sport a new configuration but everything sparkled like it had just been manufactured. The carpet was either new or just cleaned and all of the paint was fresh.

"Pretty," Tabby said with genuine affection.

"Didn't always look this way. Navy really set us up nice on this."

"Cap, we're clear."

"Thanks Marny. Nick can you start a pre-sail check?"

"Yup. We're green."

"Grab a chair." Tabby was about to sit in one of the rear stations. "No, grab the starboard pilot's chair. Nick's most likely going to be hanging out in the engine room.

"Yup." Nick's voice offered over the room's sound system.

Set course for Puskar Stellar Terminal Five. Negotiate landing.

"You're not going to sail her?" Tabby asked, just a little offended.

"Trust me, you'll understand." We were currently pointed directly at the terminal. *Sterra's Gift* started slowly backing out of the slip and our view of the shipyard grew. We rotated and suddenly hundreds of ships came into our immediate view. The ships were travelling in all directions and at varying speeds.

"Frak. That's insane."

"Piloting through that is doable, but you've got to follow the navigation plan pretty strictly. Too much of a pain, in my opinion."

I'd also never entered the gravity of a planet before in a ship, so today was going to be a new experience. The terminal where we would load cargo was on the surface, in an un-enhanced area of gravity on Mars - which meant it was .38 gravity. I wasn't about to try my hand at a landing maneuver there either. The AI navigator neatly lined us up and set us down in a bay. We came to rest on our landing skids.

I sent a ping to Tali to let her know we'd landed. I immediately heard back that she was nearby and would be over within thirty minutes. I then popped the exterior ramp and lowered the cargo bay lifts. The loads I'd signed up for would fill both of our cargo holds, but leave the one remaining bunk room empty.

A ping from the stevedores told me we should be ready to load within the hour. Those guys could get their noses out of joint, so I'd been careful to inform them of our progress.

Tabby and I sat on the lower step of the ramp chatting while we waited. After about twenty minutes, a cab set down several meters off the bow of the ship. I immediately recognized the small black-suited figure of Tali emerge from the cab.

"That's my crew interview," I said.

"Her?" Tabby said as Tali pulled her long black hair out of her face. "What kind of crew do you need?"

"Security." I tried to play it straight. I could see where this was going.

"And she's what you think of when you look for security?"

Tali walked over toward us with a smile on her face. "Greetings, Captain." She held her hand out to shake. "Tell me this isn't Tabby Masters?"

"Uh, yes, sure is." I responded.

Tali held her hand out to Tabby. "Tali Liszt. Honored to meet you, Miss Masters. Quite a feat you pulled off on Colony 40."

"Uh, thanks." It wasn't very often that Tabby was caught off guard.

"Don't be so surprised. I'm in the business, what you all pulled off was big news in my circles. Liam says you're over at the Academy. Good memories over there for me."

"Are you an officer?"

"Special forces, retired."

"Oh, it's a pleasure to meet you, ma'am."

"I had that coming, but let's not do that? I know what they tell you, but just between us it's Tali, okay?"

Tabby smiled, "Gotcha, thanks."

"Nick, Marny, care to join us in my quarters? Tali's here."

I led Tali and Tabby up the stairs and back to my quarters. Nick and Marny were already seated on the couch.

Secure ship.

"I got your NDA, Tali, so we should be able to talk freely."

"Is it okay for me to be here?" Tabby asked.

"Yup," Nick didn't skip a beat.

Tali started right in. "You said you weren't really looking for crew and things might get dicey. What are you looking for?"

"Navy's being real tight lipped about this. The mission was explained to us very simply. Transportation to Jeratorn for one of their undercover operatives and then extraction of same operative with a package. Mission could require light fire support."

"What does light fire support mean?" she asked.

"Well we're getting mixed messages about that. The operative thinks there could be as many as fifty enemy agents on the station, but isn't particularly sure. The operative also believes she will either be successful or dead, no in-between."

"Cheery sort," Marny offered.

"Yeah, no kidding," I said.

"What else do you have?"

"A bunch of chatter that makes us believe something bigger is happening." I said.

"And his gut," Nick gave me a sideways glance.

"What kind of chatter?" She gave me a small nod. "And, I don't easily dismiss gut feelings. Our brains are pretty amazing at sorting out information."

"Getting loads to Jeratorn is ridiculously easy and the money is probably double what I'd expect. Everyone is looking for high bonds, like they don't expect us to come back. When I researched their ore storage, it looks like they're busting at the seams. Feels a lot like it did on Colony 40 right before M-Corp would show up with their giant freighter and buy up everything."

"You think the Navy is trying to head off an attack?"

"Colony 40's station administrator just transferred over to Jeratorn. Coincidence?"

"Is he the package?" Tali asked.

"Rather not say," I replied.

"What are you paying?"

Nick pinched at his vision and flicked something at her. "That's our crew budget. I'll throw in my personal share of the freighter's load." He pinched a second figure and tossed it to her.

"Nick ..." I tried to stop him.

"I got us into this and I want to give us the best shot I can."

Tali looked at Nick and then to me. "Ben's out, but Jordy's in. I don't mean to be condescending, but it's a little short."

"I was afraid of that," Nick said.

"What if I throw in my share of the freighter?" I asked.

"Let's be clear on what the roles are. Jordy and I will work with you. When it comes to field work we don't take orders from anyone. You can ask us to get something done and we'll do the best we can. I promise, our best is pretty good. On the ship, we'll respect your authority. I'm not saying this to be a prick, I just want to make sure we're clear."

"Crystal," I said. "So you'll take it?"

"We're in," Tali replied.

"We sail at 1700 tomorrow from Coolidge Shipyard."

"Jordy's in the cab with our gear."

CONVOY

"Tali, you and Jordy will be in BR-3 tonight. Sorry for the close quarters."

"Wouldn't have expected any different," Tali said.

"You can keep your gear in your room or if you want, I can give you access to the armory. If you wouldn't mind, I'd like to review our stock with you. I still have access to the Navy's quartermaster if we're missing anything." Marny stood up, clearly looking to get moving.

Tali stood with her. "If you want to help, we've got a pretty decent stack of gear."

"I'll help," Tabby offered.

I watched as the three of them disappeared from the room.

My HUD flashed an incoming comm request.

"Hoffen," I answered.

"Lou Buggentower, Stevedore's Union. We're outside ready to load. Are you good to go?"

"I'll be right out." I walked down the hallway quickly and passed through the airlock.

A stout man in a white uniform handed me his credentials. I scanned them with my HUD. They checked out.

"Love these little cutters. Don't take but a few minutes to load. Even faster to unload. Anything going in the bunk rooms?" He asked.

"No it should all fit in the cargo holds."

"That it will. Any special weight distribution?"

"We're pretty even. Ideally, heaviest on the inside about half way up. More forward than aft. Is that doable?"

"Whatever you like. It's not a very heavy load, so it won't matter a lot," he said.

I should have thought about that. I knew where I wanted the weight, but didn't think about the fact that the mass/volume ratio was low. He could load it any way he wanted and we wouldn't feel it on the ship. I felt like a newbie, which of course I was.

"You got a tablet you're crossing these off on?" he asked.

"Sorry, I'm pretty new to this, why would I do that?" He'd already outed me as a newbie, I might as well not add on.

"Heh, you are a greenie, then. Captains like to keep track of what they're loading and match it up with the manifest. That way if anyone says they didn't deliver a crate, you can prove if you got it all or not."

"Frak, that makes sense," I said.

"Record it with your HUD. Make sure you catch every crate's serial number. You can go over it once you're sailing."

"Thank you, Mr. Buggentower," I said.

"No problem. Everybody has a first day."

Sterra's Gift – 001, he said. "It'll come up right there." He pointed to what looked like a MAG-L track ten meters away from *Sterra's Gift*. A flatbed train, forty meters long, filled with crates of different sizes slid along the track and stopped in line with the ship.

Two squat robots rose up off the far end, flew up next to the crates, and slid long metallic fingers under them. In concert, the bots lifted, using arc-jets similar to what our suits used and flew to us at a break-neck pace. Lou looked at his tablet and over to the containers and checked off the two serial numbers. I recorded it. I could see how a tablet that was running the same software he was running would make this quite a bit easier. Half an hour after we started, the cargo holds were both completely loaded.

"That's it, Captain Hoffen. Thumbprint here?"

I pressed my thumb onto his tablet. "Thank you, Mr. Buggentower."

"Call me Lou." He offered his hand and we shook. "Safe passage to you," he said over his shoulder.

Retract, pressurize, and seal cargo holds. In tandem, the elevators lifted back into the ship.

"Nick, prepare for departure."

"Aye, Captain."

I smiled. Marny was rubbing off on him. I found Tabby on the ship helping reorganize the armory. I thought about asking what was up, but I really didn't care. I looked back to the galley and saw Jordy sitting on a chair drinking a cup of something.

I walked back to him with my hand out. "Welcome aboard, Mr. Kelti. I know I speak for the rest of the crew when I say we're glad to have you aboard."

"My pleasure, Captain. If you'd asked me on Friday morning if I'd be sitting on a cutter headed into space the next day, I'd have bet everything I had you were wrong. But here I sit. Where's Ada?"

"She's on our freighter. Accompany me to the bridge? We're about to get underway."

"Certainly."

"I recall Tali referred to you as a combat medic. Have you had a chance to look at our supplies?"

"Not yet."

"Would you mind checking it out? I think we've got a good supply, but we're no experts."

"Happy to."

"All sections, check in. Status for immediate departure."

Nick and Marny replied in turn. "Green."

All ship announcement. "We're about to get underway for a shakedown cruise. If anyone needs anything on Puskar Stellar, this'd be the time to mention it. Otherwise, you might consider grabbing a chair. We won't be exceeding 1.5 gravity, but sometimes the transition is a little rough."

"Mr. Kelti, if you'd like to join me in the co-pilot's chair we can talk while we get going."

"Can do, Captain," he said.

Plot course. Triangulate our current position with Coolidge shipyard, at a distance of one-hundred thousand kilometers. Four hour transit.

The course wasn't much to look at and I saw that the burn plan was well within our normal rate.

Execute plan.

I was enthralled with how the ship interacted with the planet. The arc-jets lifted us and we slowly accelerated forward while rotating the nose of the ship skyward. As a spacer, I had no real affinity to the idea of 'up.' The ship's gravity system was still pulling me to the floor, so to me, it didn't seem like anything had changed. I looked over to Jordy to continue our conversation and was surprised to see him with his head back in the seat and his fingers gripping the armrests with what appeared to be a death grip. He was obviously having trouble with the ship being perpendicular to the surface.

"If you close your eyes, it'll just feel like a heavy gravity environment." I was trying to be helpful.

"I'm not a big fan of takeoff," Jordy said. He willfully loosened his grip.

"I was thinking we need a second on Ada's freighter, *Adela Chen*. How do you and Tali work?"

"She does all of our tactical planning, but I can guarantee she'll want someone on both ships if she's got any hand in security."

"Marny does our security. You suppose they've already worked this out?"

"That's not the question, the question is when they're going to tell us."

We both laughed.

Ice vapor rolled off the outside of the ship as we pierced through the upper atmosphere. What a rush. Escaping the atmosphere of a planet was just something you didn't experience if you spent all of your time in space.

Jordy's discomfort seemed to lessen as the effects of the atmosphere stopped jostling the ship. It made me think that he'd spent a good deal of time in space and the black blanket around the ship was easing his anxieties.

"How does your team work? Do you have specialties?" I was hoping to take his mind off of the things that were bothering him.

"Tali's always the tip of the spear. She likes to be first in. Most of the time she just drops 'em and leaves 'em for me to patch up.

Jammin's all about the heavy stuff. If we need to blow it up, knock it down, or make a general mess, he's the guy. I'm the long range guy. Part of being special-forces is being good at all of it, though."

"You guys were pretty impressive at the training facility."

"Thanks. We've been doing it long enough, we better be. Jammin's still pissed you got him. I told him how you set him up and it pissed him off even more."

"Is that why he didn't come along?"

"Nah, he doesn't like to go off-planet."

"You boys playing nice up here?" I heard Tali's voice and looked around to see her standing at the door.

"Come on in," I said. "Just grab any seat. We're not real formal."

"Marny told me you'd say that but she's trying to instill more discipline. Permission to enter the bridge?"

"Permission granted," I responded. "I think, technically, I was okay with 'come on in,' though."

"Maybe." She looked amused. "Jordy pinged me and said you wanted to talk about assignments. What's up?"

I gave Jordy a single raised eyebrow. At least I knew where I stood.

"More a question. Let's find Marny and hash it out." I stood up and walked to the back of the bridge.

"You're just going to leave the helm?" Jordy asked, concern causing his voice to rise.

"If we're not in combat, you're a lot safer if I'm not holding that stick," I said.

He looked from me to the chair and back, still a little panicked. I held my hand up in surrender and walked back to the seat. "You had that coming," I said under my breath as I sat back in the chair. "You guys play cards?"

"If you're in the service, you play cards," Jordy said.

"We've got four hours and we'll clear out of this traffic fairly shortly." Already, the number of ships I could see through the armored glass had dropped significantly. "Nick hasn't had access to the ship for several days and the Navy's been poking around in our systems. He'll be busy for the foreseeable future. We'll stay on the ship overnight, a hundred thousand kilometers off of Coolidge. It's a nice random location so we don't have to worry about visitors."

"You're my kind of paranoid, Captain," Tali gave me an approving grin.

"Poker?"

"When's dinner?" Jordy asked.

"We'll set a schedule once we're underway, feel free to dig in whenever you need. We're overstocked for the trip. In the past, we've gotten together at 1200 and 1800 and we keep coffee going."

"Permission to enter, Cap?" Marny asked.

"Granted. Where's Tabby?"

"She's back talking with Nick. Should I be worried?"

"I sure hope not. Poker?" I wasn't sure why I was having so much trouble getting a game going.

"Sure, I'm in," Marny answered.

I pulled out a deck of cards and started dealing them. We talked as we played, hashing out any number of small details.

The ship was running better than it ever had. Acceleration was smooth and the heat signature was way down. When we'd taken off from Mars and switched from normal gravity to ship-based, I hadn't even noticed the transition.

Tali was an excellent card player. I thought I was catching on to her tells and then she switched up on me, almost like she figured out I was reading her. I liked the challenge. Most of the time I had a decent idea how Jordy was feeling about his cards and Marny was an open book.

We arrived at the destination I set around 1800. It was a good time for us to take a break and eat dinner. The galley-pro did a great job of reconstituting the compressed meals supplied by the chandler's shop. I wasn't overly hungry, so I stuck with a meal bar, but the food smelled good. I was happy that the mess table provided enough seats for the six of us. We could have squeezed in eight, in a pinch.

"We'll sit out here tonight and first thing in the morning we'll head back to the shipyard. We aren't scheduled to leave until 1700, but if I can get hold of Qiu, I'll want to get going before that."

I continued, "We'll catch up with Ada, who's piloting the *Adela Chen*, sometime on Monday night or Tuesday, depending on when we get going. She'll pick up a string of barges tomorrow morning and then set sail for Jeratorn. We've agreed on a navigational plan that she'll modify along the way. We'll have to catch her transmission so we can adjust accordingly. Anyone have anything they need to add? It doesn't matter how big or small, this is a good place to bring it."

"Why all the course changes? Are you expecting trouble on the way out?" Jordy asked.

"Not at all, it's just a precaution. Ada's ship was attacked by someone who knew their flight plan."

"Cap, we need to talk about locking the bridge during the night watch," Marny said.

"What's your thought?"

"It's not uncommon for the pilot to rest during that shift. They'd be easy to sneak up on."

My mind jumped right to Xie Mie-su, our last passenger who'd very nearly taken Nick and me out. It wasn't fair, but I probably projected some of my angst about her onto Qiu Loo. "Sounds like a good precaution. Do you have a proposed timetable?"

"Why not lock it all the time?" Tali asked.

I looked at her. It was a good test of the table. I'd invited everyone to participate and now I was getting an idea that I didn't like.

"What's your reasoning?"

"It's the heartbeat of the ship. Leaving that door open makes you too easy of a target. It's no different than requiring people to request entry, just makes it a little more formal."

"Would anyone be able to override it?"

"I'd think the three of you would have palm access and no one else."

What she was saying made sense, I looked to Marny and she

nodded affirmatively. "How about we try it for this trip? If we don't like it, we can adjust."

Later that night on the bridge with Tabby sitting on my lap, I felt a pang of guilt. In the rush to get everything going, I'd not done a great job of paying attention to her. She'd been good about it, but I still felt badly.

"Hey, I'm sorry. It gets hectic when we're heading out. I'm not being very attentive."

"Are you kidding? This is so much fun. You do this every day now?"

"Yeah, I suppose."

"Cool."

"We can sleep in the captain's quarters. We're not underway and the ship will do what's necessary if something comes up," I said.

She was obviously getting tired and nodded her approval. The bridge door automatically closed behind me.

The next morning I woke up at 0200 and slipped out of bed. I palmed my way onto the bridge and checked system statuses. I'd never seen so many green systems on the screen before. I engaged the return navigation plan. I wanted to be docked by the time everyone got up and rolling. I grabbed a cup of coffee from the galley.

At 0600 we docked in an open berth at the Coolidge shipyard. I informed the docking master that we'd be gone within twenty-four hours and he seemed satisfied. I sent a comm to Qiu and asked if she would like to get going early and let her know she could board at her leisure.

Tabby joined me at 0830. "Hey, you left me."

"Sorry, I had to bring us back."

"We're at Coolidge?"

"Yeah, Marny and Tali are off on a last minute supply run."

"You mind if I get going a little early today? You've got a lot going on and I could use some more time with the books."

"Am I running you off?"

"Only a little. It's great, Liam. You're really in your element here. I'm so proud of you."

At 1030 Tabby and I walked over to the elevator.

"Probably see you in a month or so?" I said.

"Send me messages. It's hard for me to find privacy to respond, but I sure love getting them."

"Give 'em hell, Tabby. I love you."

"I know Liam. I feel the same way about you."

She stepped into the elevator and just like that she was gone. It was a long walk back to the ship.

At 1145 Qiu pinged me to let me know she'd be on board by 1330. And finally by 1430 everyone was accounted for.

"All sections report status for immediate departure," I announced over ship wide communication.

Marny and Nick both replied immediately with a green status. By taking off five hours early, we would overtake Ada and *Adela Chen* by midday Monday. I didn't know what I would do with myself for the next two weeks while we were sailing. Nothing on the ship needed repair and getting a return load from Jeratorn was still ridiculously easy.

"Permission to enter the bridge." Nick's voice came through the comm next to the bridge door.

"Granted," I was still feeling moody from leaving Tabby behind.

"What are you thinking for bridge shifts?" he asked.

"I was thinking about integrating Marny and doing four hour shifts, but making every third shift a six hour shift. It'll break up the day."

"Yup. I'll pass it on to Marny. You doing okay?"

"Yeah, it's just hard," I said.

"She's worth it."

There it was. He was right, but it didn't make it any easier.

"I'll take the shift until 1800, then you and Marny can take the next two. That work?"

"Yup."

At 1800, Nick relieved me, carrying a plate with him. "I think they're holding dinner for you," he said.

My next shift would be at 0400. It'd be a hard one to stay awake for, but if I only had to go four hours I figured I could do it. I joined the rest of the crew at the table in the mess.

"Cap, any update on when we'll overtake Ada?" Marny asked.

"Just after 1315 tomorrow," I said. "Welcome aboard, Lieutenant Loo."

"Thank you, Captain Hoffen."

"I trust the accommodations are to your liking."

"More than satisfactory. Thank you."

"Great. Shall we eat?" I'd noticed no one was eating. I'd heard about the ritual of waiting for the captain before starting a meal and I'd even experienced it on the *Kuznetsov* with Commander Sterra. I didn't think it would apply to me. I appreciated the gesture.

"Don't have to tell me twice," Marny said.

"Marny, mind if I ask you something kind of personal?" Tali asked.

"Fire away."

"How much of your jaw got replaced?"

"Not sure that's good dinner conversation - anyone squeamish?" She looked around the table. I hadn't thought she was serious when it'd been brought up before.

"I know I'd like to hear about it," I said. I was also interested in the idea that a bone could be replaced and wondered if that was possible for my foot.

"On the left side, everything from the eye socket down and most of the top jaw as well as the entire lower jaw."

"Synthetic skin, sinuses, the works?" Tali was obviously enthralled.

"Aye. If you look real close you can see where skin is matched back in with my own." Marny ran her finger along her cheek, leaning toward Tali.

Tali whistled in appreciation. "That's nice work."

"Mind if I ask how much of your arm is your own?" Marny asked.

I interrupted. "How do you know about that?"

"Cap, she hit me hard enough to shatter her hand a dozen times over. Initially, I was more worried for her."

"Is that why you didn't bruise?" I asked.

"It actually does bruise but it's not anywhere near as noticeable. If I use the right kind of patch it heals most things overnight."

"Entire arm, shoulder, socket, clavicle, shoulder-blade, ribs and part of my spine," Tali said somberly.

"I'm sorry to hear that," Marny replied.

"It was tough for a while, but like everything else, you either let it get you or you don't. Right Liam?"

Tali's question caught me off guard. I finally answered, "Seriously. I'm done moping. It's just hard when I have to say good bye." I didn't think I was bringing everyone down.

"Uh, Cap, I think she's talking about your foot," Marny said.

"Oh …"

The next morning 0400 came unmercifully early. I palmed my way onto the bridge.

"Captain on the bridge," Marny's voice was subdued.

"It's mesmerizing, isn't it?" She was gazing out at the stars.

"Sure is."

"Thanks for taking a shift."

"Just part of the job, Cap."

"Well, get some sleep, we'll see you in the morning."

"Aye, aye."

The shift went without incident and Nick relieved me at 0800. I slept for a couple of hours and had my alarm set for 1200. I relieved Marny early so I could be piloting when we overtook Ada.

At 1323, and with a bridge full of spectators, I slid *Sterra's Gift* up alongside the *Adela Chen*. Normally under hard burn, we wouldn't be able to communicate, but I was close enough that we were able to punch through the interference.

Hail Adela Chen.

"You sure got here fast." Ada's always cheery voice played across the sound system of the bridge.

"You want to break from burn? We'd like to transfer a passenger."

"Are you joining me again, Captain?"

"Not this time and you're on a public comm."

"Hiyas, all!"

Everyone chuckled and returned her greeting. She had an infectious personality.

"Okay, burn off in 3... 2... 1..." She counted down and I adjusted so that we were sailing along together, no longer accelerating.

"Who am I getting?" Ada asked.

"Jordy Kelti. You okay with that?"

"He'd better be on his best behavior. I won't have anyone messing up my ship."

"You hear her, Jordy?" Marny asked.

"Yes, ma'am. Unlock your airlock and I'll be over in a jiffy."

He wasn't kidding either. No more than ten minutes later, he was safely aboard the *Adela Chen*.

"Well, there's one last thing," I said.

Broadcast on both ship's public address. I instructed. I caught Nick rolling his eyes at me.

"Breaker one-nine, Breaker one-nine." I said in the cheesiest voice I could muster. I had a larger audience than usual, but I'd be darned if I was going to miss this.

C.W. McCall, Convoy, I instructed the AI.

The song started out with someone talking on the radio and I really only remembered the chorus, but I had to join in once we got there, all the same.

Cause we got a little convoy
Rockin' through the night.

...

JERATORN HO!

It would take two weeks to arrive at Jeratorn. If it were just *Sterra's Gift*, we could easily shave off five of those days, but the *Adela Chen* wasn't designed for the same type of acceleration while pushing barges.

Life aboard the ship quickly fell into an easy rhythm. One of my favorite activities was watching Tali and Marny spar. It was obvious that Tali was significantly faster and had better technique than Marny. It didn't seem to bother Marny in the least and she accepted the smaller woman's advice easily.

Marny, in turn, pushed Nick and me to practice with her. If feeling tired and beat up were any indication of progress, then I was doing really well. Otherwise, I didn't see the progress that Marny insisted was there. At a minimum, it gave us something to do.

Midpoint in the journey, we stopped the hard burn in preparation to start decelerating. We decided to take a break for a couple of hours and have Ada and Jordy join us. It was mostly a celebration to break up the monotony, but I thought it would also be a good time for us to talk about how I wanted to approach Jeratorn.

The mess table was a tight squeeze for the eight of us, but we'd all become pretty comfortable with each other. Marny had a special treat for us in the form of chocolate chip cookies. I was pleased that Qiu had loosened up enough to join us. She was quiet, but it meant something to me that she made an effort.

"As you all know we're less than a week from Jeratorn," I started. I wanted to make sure I had everyone's attention. "Ada, how long do you think it will take to refuel and load the barges?"

"We'll drop the string at the co-op and then head over to the refueling station. Most of the time, strings get loaded within twenty-four hours, sometimes more quickly."

"How is Jeratorn set up? Refueling at the main station?"

"That's right. The co-op ore station is maybe fifty kilometers away from the main station. I imagine it's getting pretty full, with as little traffic as they've had."

"That's what concerns me. Makes 'em a big target."

"I say we sail in at the same time. I drop the string, while you fuel up and then you unload while I get fuel," Ada said.

"Lieutenant Loo, any way to predict how long you'll be on station?"

"Most likely case is four days or less. If I can't get the information I need by then, I will have blown any chance I had."

"I thought you were planning to bring a package back with you," I said.

"Depends on the information."

"Fine. Marny, you good with that plan?"

"Small tweaks. I'd prefer that we're not unloading while Ada's fueling. Maybe we heave-to off the station instead of docking overnight. That'd keep us close enough to communicate with the lieutenant, but far enough away that anyone approaching is suspicious."

"After a couple of weeks of sailing, I think we'd all like some shore leave. Any issues with that?" I asked.

"How about we play it by ear. If everything's quiet, then we tie up for the night at the station. If things are looking sketchy, we go back to plan A."

"Good. I like it. Anyone else have anything to add? Tali?"

"I agree, we can assess the risk once we get there, but it sounds like a plan. I think you want to let people know that the two ships are together. Strength in numbers 'n all. I wonder, though, what happens with the tug once the string is full?" Tali asked.

"If Lieutenant Loo is done in four days or less I'd like to hold Ada back so we can sail home together. If it takes a lot longer than that, we may need to consider sending Ada on her way, alone. I guess I'd like to play it by ear."

"Makes sense," Tali agreed.

"Any other business?" I asked.

"Did Sam finalize that ore contract yet?" Nick asked.

"Let me check, we may have received a comm by now." I looked at my comm queue and didn't see anything from Sam. I wasn't surprised, as we still had a week of sailing left. When we'd left Mars, the market for most ores was sinking. "Nothing yet. I'm sure he'll have it lined up by the time we arrive."

"He'd better," Ada said.

"I sincerely doubt he'd mess with you," Jordy added.

"Do I smell fear?" Tali asked.

"No. I'm just saying …" Jordy looked away.

"Bawk bawk bawk …" Tali quietly imitated a chicken.

"Meeting adjourned. Happy midway! Where'd those cookies go?" I said.

After an hour, we agreed it was time to get back underway.

"Liam, would you like to pilot the circumvolve? It'd be good experience for you," Ada said.

"Absolutely!"

Back on the tug, I slid down into the pilot's seat, with Ada in the seat to my right. Jordy was interested enough to stand behind us and watch.

"Do you remember the checklist?" Ada asked.

"Not all of it," I said.

"Okay, I'll run it, but you have to check 'em off." I appreciated that Ada wasn't giving me a hard time about this. I recorded her list so I could transcribe it to my own reminder list later.

"… release the glad-hands … "

"Check."

"Stow the tongue and wait for the green light."

"Check … we're green."

"Replace the dead-heads."

"Why not leave the dead-heads off, we're just going to release them when we get to the other side?" I asked.

"Technically you could, but if you always put them on you never have to question if you've done it."

"Check."

"We're free. Captain, bring us around."

I pulled the sticks out from beneath the arm rests and locked them into place. I felt a lot more comfortable with them this time. I slid the tug up and rotated in a slow cartwheel, stopping the rotation once we could look straight down on the barges.

"Ugh," I heard from Jordy. I turned to see him sit down on the floor. I'd heard of people who couldn't take orientation shifts, but I was surprised that someone with Jordy's background was one of them.

"Sorry man," I said. I'd wanted a good look at the barges, but they weren't anything more than large metallic platforms. I rotated the ship around so we were sailing in line with the string.

"Thank you Liam, that was very thoughtful," Ada said.

"Not everyone's born in space." I said. I could hear Jordy breathing hard.

I slid the ship around and lowered it to be in line with the barges. "Hit the big switch?"

"Nicely done, yes."

I flicked the switch and watched as tongues slid out of the barge toward the freighter.

"How are you doing back there, Jordy?" Ada asked.

"I'm fine ..." He sounded anything but fine.

"Ada, tell me why this ship sails so slowly when not attached to the string. It has significantly more power than *Sterra's Gift*." It was a problem that'd been bothering me since I first sailed it around.

"Inertial and gravity systems wouldn't be able to keep up. It's something I can override in an emergency, but normally it's best to leave that alone. It's also very easy to get out of control with those safeties off."

"You've done it?"

"All the time when I was younger. You'd have trouble keeping up with me in that lug of a ship you sail."

"Did you seriously just challenge me to tag?"

"Don't start something you can't finish, pal."

A final clunk was felt as the tongue finished seating itself into the frame of the freighter.

"Back to work then. Thanks for thinking of me," I said. I walked past Jordy who was still looking a little green. "Sorry, Jordy." I patted him on the back and slid down the railing.

"Never sail with a spacer …" He muttered above me.

I exited the airlock and arc-jetted back to *Sterra's Gift*. I took it slowly so I could see all the upgrades that had been made by the shipyard mechanics. Of all of the changes, I was most excited by the armor added to the belly of the ship. It made us a little slower, but would pay for itself in repairs alone if we kept getting shot at.

Back on board, Marny, Nick and Tali were still hanging out at the galley table. "Ready to get underway?"

"Let me run a check," Nick said.

"Can we skip the bad country music?" Marny asked.

"Hah … You never know." I didn't have anything planned, but I wasn't telling them that. I palmed my way onto the bridge and slid into the chair.

Open comm with Adela Chen. "Ada, we're about to start our burn."

"Okay, I've got the nav plan plugged in and we're ready to go."

"Happy Sailing! Over and out." I said. End comm.

"All sections, check in, status for departure." Nick and Marny reported green.

Engage deceleration burn plan.

The second leg of the trip was as uneventful as the first. I spent time working on my yoga with Tali and Marny, who both seemed to enjoy my pain, and Nick and I continued training with Marny in Krav Maga. We weren't getting drastically better, but at least I was starting to grasp some of the fundamentals.

We were three hours out from Jeratorn and I would be back at the helm in less than an hour. I found Marny and Tali talking at the galley table, so I grabbed a pouch of orange juice and joined them.

"I'd like to meet with Qiu today and discuss a communication plan while she's on the station. Would either of you like to join me?"

"We'd both like to be there for that. I tried to approach her about it, but she's a might bit reserved," Marny said.

"She in her cabin?" I asked. Bunk Room 2 (BR-2) was no more than five meters from where we were sitting.

"Aye," Marny said.

I walked up the hallway and knocked on her door.

"One moment, please."

After a few moments she opened the door and looked at me questioningly.

"Would you be available for a short meeting?"

"Give me five minutes?"

"In my quarters."

Qiu nodded and shut the door.

After several minutes Qiu knocked on the doorframe of my quarters. Tali, Marny and I were sitting on the L-shaped couch. "Come on in."

"What's up, Mr. Hoffen?"

"Captain," Marny corrected. If being corrected was annoying to Qiu, she didn't show it.

"Captain," she acknowledged.

I had no idea how to handle the tension so I pushed on. "Lieutenant, I would like to have an established communication protocol while you're on station."

"I'm not sure what you mean," she said.

I thought I'd said it so darn Navy-like I was disappointed to discover she didn't know what I was asking.

"Sure you do," Tali said without looking up from a reading pad she was gesturing to. "How about - no less than every six hours you will communicate with this ship or we'll come looking for you."

"It would destroy my mission if you did that," Qiu said.

"Do you have a reason why you wouldn't want to communicate with us?" I asked.

"I will do as you request and communicate every six hours."

"We'll give you as much leeway as possible, Lieutenant," Marny said.

"Thank you, is there anything else?"

"Once we've off-loaded the cargo and taken some shore leave, we'll be standing off several thousand kilometers, close enough for quick communication but far enough away not to cause problems."

"That will work fine." Qiu stood and left the room.

"Grab the door, Cap?" I was seated closest to the door and swung it closed.

"All good?" Marny asked. She was looking at Tali.

Tali placed a small device on the table and my ears popped, like they often did when pressurization occurred. "All good," Tali said.

I looked at the device that I suspected generated a sort of privacy field and asked, "What am I missing?" My voice sounded strange, like I was talking next to a fan.

"We've infested the reluctant Lieutenant Loo with nanite trackers. For the next twenty days, she'll be exhaling these little guys everywhere she goes."

"You get this from the Navy quartermaster?" I asked.

"No," Tali said.

"Is that what you were doing with the reading pad?"

"Yes, I was transferring them from the chair to her suit. They'll migrate into her respiratory system, where they can reproduce."

"Frak, that's disgusting. Won't she be pissed if she finds 'em."

"Not going to happen, Cap. These little buggers are biological and they don't show up on scans unless you know specifically what you're looking for. Even to bio-scans they look like bad breath. I've got a specially tuned sniffer that recognizes their signature. It'll tell us when any surface we're looking at had contact with her."

"So this junk's all over the ship and reproducing?"

"Paranoid much?" Tali asked. "No, I programmed them to target Loo. Here, look." Tali handed me her reading pad. It looked like I was seeing directly through the pad at the table in front of me. There was a small smudge of yellow on the table and when I lifted it up I could see a large cloud on the door.

"That's just the baseline data. Your AI will analyze the data for you," she said.

I hit the button and the smudges turned into more obvious shapes resembling chat balloons you might see in an old-school comic strip. There was a lot of information, including the time when the contact occurred. It also included more invasive information, like blood pressure, respiration rate and body temperature.

"This stuff's a little scary," I pushed Tali's reading pad back toward her.

"Yes, it's also on loan and would cause problems if anyone found out we were using it," Tali said.

"No worries there. Pretty sure I don't need you or Marny pissed at me." We all laughed, but I was at least partially serious.

I excused myself and grabbed a large cup of coffee from the galley. It was brewed from synthetic beans, but was pretty close to the real thing and I appreciated that Marny was saving us the significant difference in cost.

I palmed my way onto the bridge. "Captain on the bridge." I said it to save Nick the trouble. "I'd like to bring us in, if you're okay with that."

"Yup. I've a few things to tend to so that'd be good," Nick said. We exchanged the ritual words of transferring the bridge watch and I sat in the chair.

We were still sailing backward towards Jeratorn on the decelerating burn plan and would be for the next two hours. We would only flip over for the last half hour of our trip.

Calculate when the bow thruster will have enough thrust to complete our deceleration plan.

The ship's AI replied. *That point was crossed fifteen hours ago.*

I rubbed my hands together in excitement. *Roll ship and engage bow thruster to continue current burn plan.* The ship slowly disengaged the rear engines and used the arc-jets to rotate us in a graceful tumble.

Incoming hail from Adela Chen.

Accept.

Spooling down the rear engines had caused us to sail right past Ada's position. She hadn't missed it.

"What's up Liam?" she asked.

"Trying out my new bow thrusters. I'll slide right back."

"Okay, a little warning might be a good idea next time."

"Right, sorry."

"No biggie, glad everything's okay."

I coaxed the bow thrusters to pull us back in line with Ada's ship. I lined us up momentarily so we could see each other through our armor-glassed cockpits. Ada waved back at me. It wasn't a particularly safe place to stay, so I moved back to the formation we'd been sailing in for the last couple of weeks.

I felt a little nostalgic when I looked out into the deep dark. In the distance and with the help of my HUD, I could make out many of the outlying large asteroids in this part of the main asteroid belt. It felt both familiar and foreign. My mind tried to locate markers I was used to seeing, but of course they weren't there.

I wondered what my parents, Big Pete and Silver, were doing at this moment. I suppose they were working their claim. I hadn't heard from them for a while, but the last I had, Big Pete was onto a spot he thought was really showing a lot of promise. I'd, of course, heard this from him for as long as I could remember. He was the eternal optimist and had eked out a life where many had failed before him. It seemed to me to be a hopeless life, but Dad was thrilled by it every morning when he woke up.

Display layout of Jeratorn on forward holo, include nearby asteroids and outposts.

Jeratorn was three independent towers, each with a spread-out cluster of habitats linked together to form a rough cylindrical shape. These three main structures were laid out in a loose triangular configuration and connected via multiple catwalks. It defied the normal logic of building one dense structure that would be easier to defend against random asteroids and space junk. A long finger-like structure stuck out from one of the buildings. This was apparently a pier for ships to dock at, as the HUD showed several ships at rest, on top and in berths.

Only a few asteroids showed on the vid screen, a lot less than I'd expected given my experience on Colony 40. The AI showed several long range, asteroid-mounted turrets that covered the wide corridor between the co-op's ore station and Jeratorn. They were significantly heavier weapons than we had at Colony 40 and some of my original concern about safety dissipated.

The AI alerted me to a new comm from Sam Chen. *Play Sam's comm on main holo.*

Sam Chen was sitting at his desk in his apartment.

"Captain Hoffen, we've cleared a full load for the strings. Price has been holding steady for a couple of days now. We're priced nice and low, so get that load hooked up and sailing and we'll clear a hefty profit. I just heard a rumor of tensions between the PDC and the North Americans. Somebody's trying to redraw some borders. Hate to be too much of a capitalist, but they'll need good old fashioned steel if they want to beat on their war drums too much. Send me a ping when you're headed home. Oh, and tell Ada to listen to her comm once in a while."

Record response.

"Got it Sam. Thanks for setting that up. We have a layover here, but I'll send Ada packing in four to five days no matter what. Hoffen, out."

End comm.

When you're sailing long distances, time can get away from you. I think a lot of it has to do with the fact that for days on end you're simply looking forward to your point of arrival. It seemed like I had barely sat down when the AI started spooling down the forward thrusters as it was programmed to do when we were thirty minutes out. I thought I might be able to make out the station, unaided, through the armor glass.

Hail Jeratorn control tower. I didn't know what they called it out here, but my AI would be able to translate that just fine.

"Jeratorn control. What's up?" It was a significantly less formal response than I'd expected. Even on Colony 40, we used more formality than that.

"I've got two ships on approach. We should be at the ore station in thirty minutes. Any protocol you need us to follow?"

"Nah, we're pretty laid back here. I'll give 'em a shout and let them know you're inbound. Are you tying up here?"

"We're planning on refueling and taking some shore leave. We'll need two medium berths, one of those needs to be a bay for unloading."

"Total will be six hundred for each twenty-four hour period. How long're you staying?"

"Put us down for twenty-four, we're on a tight schedule. Any problem if we need to extend that?"

"We don't get that busy, I've got you down, Captain ..." He was obviously fishing for my name.

"Liam. Thank you. Over and out." *Terminate Comm.*

All ship announcement. "We'll be arriving at the ore station in thirty minutes. Prepare for arrival."

Incoming hail from Adela Chen.

"Hey there Ada, what's up?"

"Have you called in our arrival to Jeratorn?"

"Just did."

"Stay on the comm. I'm going to talk to the co-op ore station."

"Roger that," I said.

"Jeratorn Ore Control, this is *Adela Chen* arriving with an empty string. Please provide instructions."

"Say again? That sounds like my girl from the *Baux*. That you Ada?" The man's voice was pretty high and his inflections made him sound like he would be able to sing my old earth country music pretty well.

"Yes, hello Elvard. How have you been?"

"Can't complain. Well, I suppose that's not true, but good enough. Hey, I heard an awful rumor about your momma. Tell me it ain't true."

I winced. I suppose he felt like he was on a private communication but what a thing to ask.

"Mom and I got attacked on our way back from Delta. She didn't make it."

"Sure sorry to hear about that. Is that the reason you're sailing with a gun ship?"

"Yes, at least partly."

"You'll have to tell me all about it. You gonna be at the Welded Tongue later? I get off in a couple hours. You still owe me a date."

"Don't make me hurt you. Tell you what though, I'll buy you a beer."

"It's a date." Elvard's voice was triumphant. "You have your pick of bays today, but we won't have a shift until tomorrow that can load it. Things have been real slow."

"Tell me about it tonight?" Ada asked.

"Talking sure is a thirsty business."

"See you tonight, Elvard."

"Count on it."

BUSINESS AS USUAL

The Jeratorn Cooperative ore station sounded more impressive than it was. There was a total of three buildings sitting on a large, conveniently flat, asteroid. In this case, 'large' was a general description and did not indicate size on a solar system scale. This rock was only one kilometer long by five-hundred meters wide – nothing particularly spectacular. But from a 'really great place to sift and stack a few hundred million tonnes of refinery grade ore' perspective, this was one of the coolest asteroids and largest rocks I'd ever seen. I suspected someone had located it and paid to have it towed into its current location. Or possibly, Jeratorn station had been moved nearby because of this rock's particular utility.

The power plant, machine shop, and control tower were located on the narrow side of the asteroid. Blinking blue lights marked the location of the gravity generators placed every twenty meters along the circumference. The generators were connected by thick power cables to each in series, finally ending back at the power plant.

There were massive piles of ore on both sides of the rock and I estimated they were close to sixty percent full. It would take an empty M-Corp freighter with a whole lot of cargo sections to haul that much ore off. Our three strings were capable of hauling seven point five kilo tonnes back to Mars. We wouldn't be making much of a dent in the pile.

I was still on the comm with Ada when we got close. Nick, Marny and Tali had joined me on the bridge to get a good look at our new surroundings.

"That's a whole lotta ore, Ada," I said.

"Never seen it so full before. Most of the times we've been here they're scraping up a pile for us."

"That's gotta be hard on the miners," I said. On Colony 40 we'd go four to six months between pickups from M-Corp and we'd always be running short of funds when they finally arrived. We knew a lot of the less fortunate miners who would be well on their way to broke, hanging on by a thread, waiting for the freighter to arrive. If what Ada was saying was true, people here might be getting fairly desperate.

Ada slid her freighter's barge string neatly up to a large buoy that was flashing red. Her orientation was perpendicular with the asteroid. A handler would come along later and connect the barge's gravity generators to hold the loads down. While sailing, the freighter was able to feed most of its energy, caused by acceleration, back into the barge's gravity system and keep the loads in place.

Once in position, Ada dropped the tongue and slipped the tug away from the barges.

"Let's get some go-go juice," she said.

"Go-go juice? Hah. I'm on your six," I said.

"Try to keep up…"

Ada spun the now freed tug in place and rocketed away from our position. I thought about chasing her for a moment when I heard …

"Full load of passengers, Cap," Marny warned.

Frak. I dutifully rolled *Sterra's Gift* around in a slow arc and followed after the fleeing *Adela Chen*.

"Roger that," I said. "This one goes to you, Ada Chen."

"Aww, don't be a sore loser."

The closer we got to the main station of Jeratorn, the more obvious its design, or lack thereof. The three large cylindrical structures were obviously patched together sections, having been built up over the years. I'd received a berth assignment that was several spots away from where the *Adela Chen* would be docked. I wondered why they'd split us up like that and hoped it wasn't due to poor maintenance.

"Marny, would you see if Lieutenant Loo needs any help getting off the ship?"

"Aye."

"Ada, are you topping off with O2 crystals also?"

"I'm in pretty good shape, only about twenty percent down. You might want to check prices."

I punched up the station's price list and discovered she was right. O2 was outrageously priced, as was fuel. I felt fortunate that Nick had negotiated to have the Navy pay our fuel bill, although our account would get hit pretty hard in the meanwhile.

"You're right Ada, thanks for pointing that out. Let's hold off on the O2 for now."

"Okay, give me another twenty minutes."

"Cap." Marny's voice came over the bridge's speakers.

"What's up, Marny?"

"Loo's gone. I knocked on her door and when she didn't answer, I opened it and she'd cleared out."

"That's strange. Any ideas on how she left?"

"No, let me see what I can find out."

"Let's leave it alone for the moment. We should probably talk about how we want to do shore leave first."

"Aye. I'll be right there." Marny must have already been in the hallway because she requested entry a moment later.

"How do you want to do this?" I asked. Tali and Nick were both on the bridge, but this was clearly Marny's responsibility and I wasn't about to undermine her authority.

"We'll have to do this in shifts. It's a pretty easy split. Two from *Sterra's Gift* and one from *Adela Chen*. And ... Since everyone's on comm right now, I'll go over the rules. First, stay out of confrontations, I don't need to be getting anyone out of the brig. Second, first names only and no titles. There're no rules about weapons here, but be discrete about it. A flechette is a good choice if you're going to carry, since killing a local is generally a good way to get locked up. Remember, in the eyes of the local law, locals never start anything ..."

"Good info. You have shift rosters picked out?" I asked.

"Nope, that's your job."

"Four hour shifts?" I asked.

"I'd go three hours for tonight. That'd put us on a shift change about 1900 so everyone can have a chance at the local cuisine."

"Let me see about lining up the stevedores and I'll get you a shift roster."

"Aye."

"Anyone have any questions? Nick, how're we doing on O2 crystals?"

"Completely full. The algae system, if anything, is over producing."

"Any chance you want to sell some of it?" I asked. "The O2 prices are sky high here."

"I'll look at it," he said.

"On my way to the dock, Liam," Ada said over the still open comm.

"Roger that. We'll head over and get fueled up now."

Display navigation to Jeratorn fuel station. I pulled *Sterra's Gift* out of the berth slowly and navigated there. It was on one end of the largest of the three habitation complexes. I was shocked by the fuel prices and made a mental note to make sure to take that into consideration on any deal that, in the future, looked too good to be true.

The excitement of the station approach had dwindled and I found myself on the bridge, alone, once again. People were getting ready for shore leave.

I had three different receivers for the load aboard the ship. *Send notification to shipping recipients of our arrival in station. Request windows of when they'd like to receive delivery.*

The fuel hadn't even been completely transferred to the ship when the first response arrived.

Captain Liam. We'd like to arrange for immediate delivery. Will you accept? Beth Anne Hollise.

Before I could respond, I had an incoming hail.

"I'm going to have to drop our comm, Ada."

"Okay, ping me when you figure out shore leave."

"I will, I'll try to get it going soon."

"No worries." Ada terminated communication.

Accept hail.

"Captain. Gerald Beutler, and I just received your notification. I've got the local stevedores standing by, are you in a position to offload now?"

"Just taking on some fuel. We're in berth fourteen and should be back in twenty minutes, give or take."

"Great. See you there."

"Marny, can you join me on the bridge?"

"Be right there, Cap." It took her a little longer this time, but she joined me just as I was signing off on the fuel bill. We'd never paid anywhere near that price for fuel.

"How can I help?" Marny asked.

"We have stevedores waiting for us back in the berth for an immediate offload. I think we'll be getting to this right away."

"Aye, aye. I'll suit up."

I sailed *Sterra's Gift* slowly up toward the berth and returned the first call. *Establish communication with Beth Anne Hollise.*

"Captain, great, you got my message. We've been waiting for your arrival and we'd like to offload right away. Can you help with that?"

"Stevedores are already on their way. If you clear it with them, we can deliver your load too."

"Thank you, Captain. I'll give them a buzz right now."

I almost expected the third shipper to ping me before I slipped back into our berth, since the first two had been so quick on the draw. Generally, protocol called for a prompt receipt of goods, but I'd been told that a two or three hour window was pretty common.

The berth we were in had no working bay door which meant we'd be in vacuum. The bay was set to .6 gravity which was standard for most space stations. Any less than that was harmful to the human body over long periods of time.

Marny met me at the airlock wearing her armored vac-suit and carrying a heavy blaster rifle. She handed me a holster with a blaster in it.

"I thought you said flechettes."

"Not when we're offloading cargo. Never know who might be lurking around."

We stepped out of the ship and I noticed that Marny had the lights up all around the ship. *Sterra's Gift* gleamed in the light, having just received fresh paint. I almost choked up looking at her - I was so proud of our ship.

A man stepped out from next to the airlock and walked up to me.

"Ready to get going, Captain?" he asked.

"Mind if I scan your ident?"

"Not how we do it out here," he said.

"It is today." Marny looked as intimidating as always.

"You really want to do this?" he asked. "I can make this go fast or slow."

"Hey look, we're not trying to be pricks here. We just don't know you. How about first round's on me?"

The man looked at Marny then over to me. "Okay, top-shelf though." I wondered if he shook everyone down like this. It wasn't strictly legal to gift a stevedore, but I figured a friendly drink could be considered a social gesture. He held his identity up for me to scan. Richard Horten. It was legit enough.

"Who do you have first?" I asked.

"Gerald Buetler," he said. "He's all fired up, too."

I'd found the program that linked to the stevedore's inventory checklists and had loaded it on my tablet. I chose Buetler's shipment and the list of crates displayed on my tablet. I sent the information over to Horten's tablet and instructed the ship to lower the two cargo bay elevators. Thirty minutes later Buetler's load had been removed from the ship.

"Have you heard from Hollise?" I asked Horten.

"She's coming through the airlock now," he said. "We'll deliver the crates to her right here and she'll have her staff move them out."

I loaded Beth Anne Hollise's manifest onto the tablet. There were forty-two crates, all listed as restaurant supplies.

Marny intercepted the approaching female figure and scanned

the ident in her outstretched hand. I was accustomed to seeing women in tight vac-suits but Beth Anne momentarily distracted me with her generous curves. Extra body weight was a personal decision and easily removed with med patches. Beth Anne had clearly made some personal choices.

"Beth Anne." She held her hand out to me, knuckles up.

"Liam." I took her limp hand and shook it the best I could. She smiled accommodatingly, as if we were sharing an inside joke.

"If you'll allow it, I'd like to offload next to the airlock and have my boys move the crates on down to the bar. Would that be okay with y'all?"

"How long will it take to clear the bay?" Marny asked.

Without looking to Marny, Beth Anne answered with a reassuring smile, "No more than forty minutes or an hour."

It was difficult to not be drawn in by her. I wasn't excited about tying up the bay like that, but as long as they stayed away from the ship we'd be okay.

"I don't see why that'd be a problem. Marny?"

"That's fine, Cap. Just need to stay away from the ship."

"Oh, certainly," Beth Anne answered.

"Let's get this done," Stevedore Horten broke in.

An annoyed look passed over Beth Anne's face for a moment, then her smile returned, causing me to question what I'd seen. I suspected that she had to deal with Richard Horten regularly.

I flicked my fingers across the top of my reading pad, sending the manifest to Horten's tablet.

"Where do you want 'em?" I looked to Beth Anne.

"Mr. Horten knows where. Isn't that right, Dick?"

"It's Richard and yes, I know where."

Even with the constant heat provided by my vac-suit, it felt chilly in the docking bay all of a sudden. I was relieved to see the now familiar shape of the unloading robot arrive between Richard and me.

"I'll leave you boys to it. Liam … until we meet again." She gave me a generous smile and sauntered off.

"Word of advice," Morten said. "Stay clear of that one."

"Just here for a delivery, Mr. Morten. We don't need any drama."

"Just saying."

"Appreciate it. I've got R-201 on that one, you good?" I made a slightly exaggerated press on my reading pad showing I'd marked off the crate being patiently carried by the forklift robot. Richard shook his head with knowing disapproval and also checked off the crate. The unloading went very quickly since the robots only had to fly a short distance.

When the last of Beth Anne's forty-two crates were finally unloaded, I turned to Horten. "I've got one more load for T. Merrish, but I haven't heard from them yet. I imagine we'll see you later."

"Hang on, I can get him on the comm. I don't want to have to come back."

I could see him talking behind his face shield and then I received a ping. I pulled up my comm and saw that Horten had been successful and T. Merrish had given permission to have his load delivered to a secure bay nearby. In the end, we were at it for a total of ninety minutes, but all the deliveries were complete and money transfers were in progress.

"Thank you, Mr. Horten. I appreciate you expediting that last load for us."

"Don't forget about that round," he said.

"I'll ping you when we get our schedule figured out." I answered. Horten stalked off without saying anything else.

Beth Anne's crew had reduced the pile of crates to about half and it was clear they'd be done within half an hour.

"Any reason not to start shore leave now?" I asked.

"No, I've got the sensor strips watching the bay. We should be fine." Marny patted the ship.

We walked up the ramp to the airlock and cycled through.

Send message to both ships, public address. "First leave is Nick, Marny and Jordy - and you're free to go. Please be back by 1930."

Unloading had taken longer (of course) than I'd planned for and leave was only going to be two and a half hours. It would give each shift time to have dinner at one of the two restaurant / bars in the station. Once we had regular crew I'd need to get better at this or I'd have a mutiny to deal with.

I might as well see about return loads for *Sterra's Gift*. I wasn't sure when we'd be taking off, but I'd give myself some leeway.

Open TradeNet search, Jeratorn to Mars, target arrival twenty to thirty days from today.

There was a long list of possible return loads. The most profitable being more than a dozen people who were looking to relocate. We weren't set up for passengers, so I filtered them out. The cargo transfers weren't as profitable as we'd seen coming here, but I could easily fill the hold if I was willing to put up a three hundred thousand credit bond.

I eliminated the most egregious late delivery penalties and finally settled on a single shipper. Qiu had given me a four to ten day window for departure and it was a two week trip if we kept company with the *Adela Chen*. On the outside, it would take us twenty five days. We'd start picking up penalties on day twenty-eight, giving us an additional three days of buffer. By day forty, we'd lose all profit on the deal.

I signed it and arranged to load at 0800 tomorrow. What's the worst that could happen?

THE WELDED TONGUE

Nick and Marny were in high spirits when they returned. Apparently, the two of them and Jordy had enjoyed themselves at Patrick's Pub.

"You might try the other place," Marny said. "The beer was good but the food was all rehydrated ration packs."

Open comm with Ada. "You want to join me?"

"Wouldn't miss it. Meet in the hallway in five?"

"Roger that."

I found Tali sitting at the table in the galley. "Join me and Ada for dinner?"

"I thought you'd never ask." Tali stood up and walked out with me. I'd grabbed a hip holster and put one of the flechette pistols in it. It felt provocative, but I'd had enough problems in the past to warrant being prepared.

Tali and I met Ada in the hallway.

"Any recommendations on dinner?" I asked.

"Welded Tongue is probably the best," Ada answered.

"That's a weird name," I said.

"You'll see."

We walked down the hallway about a hundred meters to an air lock and cycled through it. We were in an L-2 space so I relaxed the rigid helmet from around my head. Tali and Ada followed suit.

Ada led us through a few more airlocks. The general condition of the station wasn't excellent, but it looked better than I'd expected from the exterior. The hallways were clean and the airlocks mostly free of grime. It seemed like a good sign that upkeep was occurring.

The name of the bar became obvious when we arrived. Above

the doorway to the entry was the metal replica of a human tongue as if it had been sticking out of someone's mouth. It was indeed welded to the station above the wide double doors.

Being the middle of the week, I didn't expect any place to be too lively. The noise coming through the doors made me question if that was a reasonable assessment. If the room was capable of holding a hundred and fifty people I'd have guessed that at last a hundred of them were here right now. We had to push our way through the crowd to find a table in the back.

There was a live performance on the stage and we were as far away from it as you could get in this fairly small bar. They were playing an odd assortment of instruments, most of which I didn't recognize, and they didn't sound too bad.

I was about to send a ping to Richard Horten when I noticed he was sitting at the bar staring at me.

"I'll be right back, I need to do something," I said to Tali and Ada.

Headed toward the bar, I caught a sweet smell, seconds before a hand brushed across my lower back and pulled me in the direction of its owner. I turned to see the marginally familiar face of Beth Anne Hollise. She had changed from the dark, tight fitting vac-suit to a really tight dress, deeply cut in the back and a little too sheer in the front for my comfort.

I turned to her and attempted to skillfully extract her arm from around my waist. My skills and her own were in two different leagues. She used my momentum to step in and I ended up brushing closely to her body, becoming very aware of her all at once.

"Captain. Welcome to my humble establishment. I wanted to personally thank you for delivering my supplies. I was starting to get worried that chivalry might be dead."

I pushed her arm down. If I was honest, I'd have to admit that I found her to be extremely attractive. I hadn't been around such a shapely woman before. I knew my ability to resist her would be sorely tested if I allowed us to stay close together. I wasn't about to betray Tabby, but there was a small part of me that sincerely regretted that decision. I was a dog.

"Quite happy to help," I said. "You're the owner here? It looks like you're doing very well for the middle of the week." I felt like I needed to shout, although my own earwig was already limiting the noise I was receiving in my ear and amplifying Beth Anne's speech.

"Yes, I am. And ... they're here because of you, Liam. They all heard that I got a shipment in and knew we'd be flush with supplies. Join me for a late dinner?"

"It will have to be another time. My friends and I just arrived and I don't want to leave them hanging."

"A loyal companion. Such a wonderful characteristic. Mind if I join you all a little later?"

"It'd be our pleasure," I said.

"Very well." I started to leave and she turned, perhaps a little too quickly. She stumbled, causing her well-apportioned body to brush against me once again, as she grabbed me and I helped to steady her.

"Oh, pardon me," she said as unconvincingly as I could imagine.

I smiled, despite my desire not to acknowledge the contact. I looked over to see the stevedore, Richard Horten, sitting at the bar, watching the entire interaction. He shook his head at me disapprovingly.

"I told you to stay clear of her," he said as I approached.

"She seems nice enough."

"Wait until you owe her something, then tell me what you think," he said.

"I hope it never gets to that," I gestured at the bar. "What're you drinking? I'd like to make good on my word."

"A double of Macallan." Horten licked his lips as he said this to the bartender who'd walked up. "My new friend here is buying."

The bartender, a skinny kid who was several years younger than me, looked at me for approval. I nodded affirmative. The kid pulled down a bottle that didn't look like it got used very often and poured a measured amount into the bottom of a wide bottomed glass. He handed the glass to Richard Horten who smelled it before taking a long drink.

The kid held a swipe pad up to me. I was shocked at the price - sixty five m-creds. I didn't want to give the little troll, Richard, any satisfaction, so I swiped it and then laid my hand on his shoulder. "Have a good evening," I said.

As I walked back to the table I noticed that both Tali and Ada were staring at me as I approached.

"What?" I asked as I sat down.

"Do you know that woman?" Ada asked.

"Beth Ann Hollise. She owns the bar and was one of our deliveries today," I wasn't about to admit to knowing why they were asking.

Ada ignored my nonchalance. "You seemed very chummy with her."

I felt my cheeks flush. "That's not how it was happening. I didn't even know she'd be here. She got chummy with me."

"Yeah, you were just fighting her off with a stick," Tali added.

I rolled my eyes at them both as they were now giggling at my discomfort.

"Who was the guy at the bar?" Ada asked.

"Stevedore. He wouldn't show me his ident without me offering to buy him a drink. A very expensive drink."

"Oh. I hate guys like that. There's nothing you can do about 'em either," Ada said, suddenly serious. "Speaking of …" I followed her eyes over to a gawky looking man who was making his way through the crowd, clearly headed toward us.

"Who's that?" I asked just before he arrived at our table.

"Hi, Elvard," Ada said.

"Mind if I join you?" he asked. "I think you promised me a drink. And please, you know better. Call me E.V."

Ada looked at Tali and me apologetically, "Uh, sure E.V., we were just getting ready to order dinner."

"Oh, that'd be great. I'm starving," he said.

I was starting to realize why spacers kept to themselves when they'd visited Colony 40. So far, we'd talked to four or five people and at least three of them wanted something from us.

"How about instead of a drink, I'll buy you a protein burger, just like I'm getting," Ada said.

"Add a couple of beers to that and we're even."

Ada was about to say something, but I cut her off. "Beers are on me, Mr. ...?"

"It's Rastikle, but everyone just calls me E.V. Didn't catch your name."

"I'm Liam and this is Tali. We're sailing with Ada."

"Oh, you must be in that cutter. Anything in those missile tubes?"

"You sure don't beat around the bush. But no, missiles are out of my budget. If we can't scare them off with the laser blasters, we can most likely outrun 'em."

"Yeah, makes sense. Lotta folks out here wish they had some missiles, though."

"What do you mean?"

"Three out of the last ten loads outta here got jacked on their way back to Mars. Two of them just completely disappeared."

"Who do you think was behind it?" I asked.

"Who else? Red Houzi, of course," he said.

"Seems pretty organized for them. How are they intercepting the ships? They'd need to have deep scanners."

"There's rumors that one of the big boys are backing them."

"Big boys?" Tali's interest was now piqued.

"Yeah, like EEC, PDC, NAGeK. My bet's on the Chinese." E.V. was referring to the different Earth coalitions who'd come together for space exploration and exploitation.

"To what end?" Tali asked.

"Expansion. PDC has the fastest growing fleet and they need the materials. It's the simplest answer," he said.

PDC referred to the People's Democracy of China.

The beer and burgers arrived and we set aside conversation for the time. Fried potatoes, protein burgers and beer. It was a great combination.

"You all look so serious." I recognized Beth Anne's voice

before I turned to see her. "You should be celebrating. E.V., what're you doing here?"

"Uh, nothing much, ma'am. I was just catching up with an old friend," Elvard answered, his voice hesitating in nearly a stammer.

Beth Anne grabbed an empty chair and pulled it up to the table. "Perhaps you'd excuse us?" E.V. got up and left without so much as saying goodbye.

"I think he's afraid of you," Tali said.

"Strange little fella," Beth Anne said. "That's more likely his guilty conscious; he owes me money. So, Captain Liam, when will you all be heading out?"

"I imagine that will have something to do with when we can get loaded up. We're a little concerned with all of the pirate activity we've been hearing about around here."

"Aww, don't pay attention to Elvard. That kind of talk can ruin a station and it's just not true."

"It didn't stop us, but still, I don't think we should be tempting fate either."

"You settled on your return load? Maybe you have a little room for a few off manifest crates? I could make it worth your while."

"If you're going to Mars, you can get anything into Puskar Stellar. There's no customs inspection," I said naively.

"Manifest is still checked. I'd be looking to send some things without necessarily having my name attached to them - if you get my meaning."

I really didn't understand what she could hope to gain by this.

"I'm thinking a couple thousand a crate?" She was using her sweet voice.

"We're pretty full on this run."

"Well, you think about it and give me a shout before you get going. Like I said, I'd make it worth your while."

Beth Anne patted my leg uncomfortably high on my thigh under the table and then stood up, giving us a broad, welcoming smile. "Enjoy your dinner."

Once she was out of earshot, Ada offered, "That was creepy."

"Not sure what to think of either of our visitors," I said.

"I'd trust E.V. a whole lot further than I'd trust that woman," Tali said.

"What could she possibly want to ship off-manifest?"

"I don't think that's important," Tali said. "Once she gets you to do something illegal, she can use it as leverage."

"I suppose." It wasn't overly important to me. We weren't currently looking for help with loads and money was moving fairly easily. I didn't need to add legal problems, especially since Mars Protectorate had by far the most liberal laws related to free trade when compared to any other space faring nation.

"Well kids, I think I've had enough fun for one night," Tali said. "I'm going to head back to the ship."

"Ada, we've got another hour to party. What's your pleasure?"

"I think I've had enough for the evening also."

"Well, let's get rolling then. We've got cargo to load tomorrow morning."

Tali and I saw Ada to her berth and returned to the ship, where I found Nick and Marny on the bridge.

"You're back early," Marny said.

"The bar had a weird vibe," I said. "Oh, we're putting on a load for Mars tomorrow morning at 0800."

"How many days do we have to deliver it?" Nick asked.

"Twenty eight days, starting tomorrow. Then we get into penalties."

"That should be easy enough."

"So … what if Red Houzi's getting help from a government?" I said.

"Where'd you come up with that?" Marny asked.

"Just something someone said tonight."

"I hope you're wrong, Cap." Marny said.

"At dinner, a friend of Ada's was saying that three of the last ten freighters from Jeratorn have been intercepted."

"How's that even possible?" Nick asked. "I can see getting lucky and intercepting one, but three?"

"What about military grade scanners?"

"Let's not even go there. Pirates are one thing, but we don't want to get mixed up with military," Marny said.

"Have to wonder why the Navy'd want to drop a MINT agent way out here," Nick said.

"You can drive yourself nuts with speculation," Marny answered.

"Agreed. So tomorrow 0800. I'd like to accompany Ada out to the co-op to pick up the barges too," I said.

"You hear from Qiu yet? It's got to have been six hours by now," Marny said.

"Not yet."

"Hope she's not going to test us on that."

"I just hope nothing's happened to her."

I SMELL A RAT

I'd excused Marny and Nick from watch that night. I knew I wouldn't sleep much, since I still hadn't received a comm from Qiu. At 0400, I heard a request to enter the bridge. It was Tali's voice.

"You up, Liam?"

"Yes. Come on in."

"Any word on Qiu?" she asked.

"Nothing yet. I'm thinking about sending a comm off to the Navy."

"She's more than six hours late, and as much as she didn't want to communicate with us, she wouldn't jeopardize her mission by ignoring the communication protocol. I'd be careful about sending off a comm, it could be intercepted."

I wasn't thrilled to share with Tali that we had special Navy issued communication equipment. But it seemed like she needed to know, as it could possibly change the way we moved forward.

"I'd like to show you something in my quarters," I said.

"Not sure we're that good of friends yet," she quipped. I didn't initially catch it and then snapped my head around to look at her. A single raised eyebrow and a slight grin clued me in. "Am I really so old you didn't see that coming?"

Confusion coursed through my brain as I tried to come up with a face-saving response. Tali was an incredibly attractive woman, but she was also very intimidating, especially after working out with her. Her lithe body had caught my attention more than once, but I didn't consider myself to be in her league. So many cluttered thoughts left me incapable of answering her with any speed.

"I'm hurt." Tali pouted her lips.

"Oh, no … that's not … no … I don't …"

"Just frakking with you, Liam. Let's go to your quarters to see your thing," Her smile was almost predatory.

I sighed, exasperated, and gave up. "This way." I knew I was outmatched as I pushed the bridge door open and walked into the captain's quarters, Tali following close behind. Indicating to her to close the door, I pulled out the chair locked in beneath the desk and sat and palmed the unremarkable panel on the wall next to the hull of the ship. The panel retracted and I pulled out the keyboard.

"What's that?" Tali asked.

"Encrypted Naval comm. It's coded to a single recipient."

"I see that," Tali said. "I'm familiar with the model. Instant comm within 2 AUs. Very nice, very discrete. Who's it coded to?"

"My contact in the Navy and it always takes him some time to get back to me."

"Well, he's holding out on you. Not that it matters, but when I said instant, I meant it. I'd let him know what's going on either way," Tali said.

I typed in, *Agent missed check in, six hours late. Please advise.* I palmed the screen closed.

"Did Marny talk to you about the fact that Qiu got off the ship without us knowing about it?"

This got Tali's attention. "What do you mean?"

"Sometime before we made it to our berth, she got off the ship."

"You don't know how she got off? What about the video?"

"Haven't looked yet, she was due to get off anyway, so what did it matter?"

"Don't know. I just don't like mysteries."

"Easy enough to look through the video, although it'll be easier on the bridge."

"Do you mind?"

"I'm gonna need some coffee …"

I started a fresh batch, disappointed that I'd let it run dry. We went back to the bridge to use the holo-projectors.

Show Lieutenant Qiu leaving the captain's quarters, yesterday.

The soft male voice of the ship's AI replied, *No holographic playback available for requested subject.*

Track backwards from our docking at Jeratorn berth to first recording of Lieutenant Qiu Loo.

No information available for requested subject.

"Try the mid-point dinner, she was there," Tali suggested.

Show seven days ago when the crew of Adela Chen boarded this ship.

The AI chose to start outside the ship where Ada and Jordy were arc-jetting from the tug over to *Sterra's Gift*. They cycled through the airlocks and walked down the hallway. Just as they were turning the corner the scene froze.

No source of data for continued playback.

"How'd she do that?" I asked aloud.

"I think we have some idea what Qiu was doing in her room on the way out. Removing that much data is darn near impossible. It must have taken quite a lot of effort."

"Do you suppose that's just how MINT operatives work?"

"Maybe, but what if it wasn't her? What if someone else wanted to wipe out the record of her trip?"

"Who'd want to do that? Moreover who'd have access?"

"Governments have been denying the existence of covert intelligence operatives for centuries. It's just a lot harder nowadays. It's the same reason the Navy contracted you to deliver her. They didn't want people to know where she came from. So far, I'd say they're doing a pretty good job."

"So they can just bust into my ship and wipe my records? Doesn't that put Qiu at a lot of risk?"

"Probably less than if you had it. Right now if the bad guys, whoever they might be, captured your ship, they wouldn't be able to learn anything about her."

"I suppose. Kinda pisses me off," I said.

"Sure. That makes sense."

"So, you think we should just drop it?"

"Think you can?

It was 0600 and I rationalized that Nick and Marny would want to be informed more than they would want additional sleep.

Hail Marny.

"What's up, Cap?" She sounded like she was wide awake even though I knew I must have just woken her.

"Nothing imminent, but we have a situation I think you should look at."

"Permission to enter bridge."

One thing was certain, nobody was ever going to get the drop on Marny. I wondered how she kept herself at the ready all of the time.

"Granted."

Nick followed closely on Marny's heels and once again he looked like you'd expect from someone who'd just jumped out of bed. Marny, of course, looked like she'd been up for hours.

I explained the missing video data to them and that I'd sent a request for instructions to Lieutenant Belcose on the *Kuznetsov*.

"We might have a response by now," I said. "I'll check. See if you can find anything I missed."

As I left, I heard Nick providing instructions to the ship's AI. He wouldn't easily accept that the data was lost. In my quarters, I opened the panel in my desk, once again revealing the communication equipment.

A message was waiting for me.

Hold action for eighteen hours and then return to Mars if no further communication is received. Belcose Out.

My stomach sank as I read the words. Belcose would simply have us abandon her. I wasn't a MINT agent, but I couldn't imagine just giving up on Qiu. I sent a reply.

Will hold position until 2400 and reassess.

I rejoined the crew on the bridge. Nick was fast forwarding through the recordings. By the look on his face, he hadn't found anything yet.

"Any word from Belcose?" Marny asked.

"Yes. We're to wait for eighteen hours and if we don't hear anything we're to leave."

"That's pretty cold," she said.

"Not really," Tali interjected. "That would put her out of

communication for twenty-four hours. If she doesn't have an exfiltration team then she'll have to find her own way out. Not much you can do."

Nick hadn't been paying a lot of attention to the conversation up to this point.

"You know how hard it would be to remove all of this data? We're talking tens of thousands of micro nodes that had to be wiped. She couldn't possibly have had enough access to do all that."

"Anything in the logs?" I asked. I had no idea what I was talking about, but when Nick went on a hunt for something, he always ended up talking about log files.

"No. It's crazy. They're clean too. I couldn't do what she did even if I wanted to. Even with all my access. Wish I knew how she did that," Nick's frustration came out in his words.

"How bad do you want to know?" Tali asked.

"What do you mean? Do you know what's going on?" he asked her.

Tali pulled out the small object she'd placed on the table when we'd talked to Qiu in my quarters. She thumbed it on and placed it on the console next to where Nick was sitting. My ears popped again and I could feel a weird pressure against my ear drums.

"No, but I know someone who could figure it out ... for a price."

"How much?" I asked

"Normally she gets three hundred an hour. I'd guess she could find it in three or less."

Nick looked at Tali skeptically but didn't say anything.

"Let's send her a message and see if she's willing to poke around. It's a big deal that someone can wipe systems on our ship," Nick said.

"I'll send it right away. Marny, I bet with a little detective work and the nanite tracker we can figure out how she got off the ship. Want to help?"

"Aye. That I do."

Nick continued to sift through images from different sources and I heard him growling with dissatisfaction. I decided my efforts would be best used on a navigation plan back to Mars. When we finally left for Mars, I didn't want any delays for lack of planning. At 0700 Marny and Tali re-entered the bridge.

"Hold on to your seat Cap, you're not going to believe what we found," Marny said. She definitely had my attention. I noticed that Tali was holding several objects.

"What do you have?"

"She exited the ship using the secondary airlock."

"Under the bridge? That's crazy, how'd she get down there?"

"There's a hatch in her bunk room that looks newly installed. She dropped down below decks and gained entry to the airlock."

"Shouldn't that be locked out by security?"

"It is, and as you might expect, there's no record of her using it. The nanite trail is very clear, though. We sent the timestamps to the ship, so we should have been able to watch her walk through the ship virtually. Except, when we tried that, all those records were missing, too. You can't actually see those locations at the times when she's there."

"Hang on, I'll superimpose them onto a different time sequence. We won't see her, but we can at least see where she went," Nick said. He started typing into a reading pad.

"She stashed a few things in a compartment - also newly installed. They aren't important, just items that could identify her as Navy; an ident bracelet and her wedding ring, along with a few other personal items."

"She's married?" It was hard for me to think of Qiu Loo as being friendly enough to hook up with someone. It struck a chord with me, finally humanizing the enigmatic woman.

"So someone has taken control of your ship, installed secret compartments, and broken your security and the big revelation for you is that she's married?" Tali asked wryly.

I looked back and smiled sheepishly, "No, sorry, it was just the most surprising thing. I guess I'd already started to suspect the other stuff."

"Got it," Nick pushed his hand across the reading tablet with a flourish and projected a gray mono-chrome woman's figure in the doorway of my cabin.

We watched her walk back from the cabin to BR-2. She entered and moved around the cabin. The AI did a reasonable job of inferring what direction she was pointing, but without understanding what she was doing with her hands, the movement didn't always make sense.

"Hey, that's not supposed to be there," I said, when a compartment popped open on the exterior wall of the room while she stood next to it.

"It looks like that was installed while the ship was at the shipyard," Marny said.

"You think they did something to the AI core that gave Qiu the ability to mess with the ship's recordings?" Nick asked.

"It's a reasonable guess, but it'd just be speculation."

We watched Qiu's image lie down for a period of time. Nick sped the time sequence up and finally she got up, opened a small hatch beneath the bunk and made her way through the emergency airlock. The time sequence lined up with when we docked at Jeratorn.

"Well, mystery solved. It seems like that was a lot of work to go through instead of just exiting through the normal airlock," I said.

"Can you think of a reason why she'd want to hide the fact that she'd been on this ship?"

"I see no advantage in us sharing that information," I said.

"I don't think Belcose was very straightforward with us about what is really going on here. What if one of us was taken hostage? Perhaps Qiu had to take precautions in case one of us was made to talk," Marny said.

"Agreed. Now I hate to sound like a mercenary, but we have a load to put on in twenty minutes, so this will have to sit for now."

"Aye, Cap. Not much more we can do anyway. I'll get changed."

Hail Adela Chen. The AI didn't respond.

"Hold on a sec," Tali said. She grabbed the small device and turned it off. The weird pressure dissipated and my ears popped again.

Hail Adela Chen. This time we were successful.

"Hiyas, Liam. What's up?" I always enjoyed hearing Ada's cheerful voice.

"Any word from the co-op on our ore?"

"Yes. They're loading the string right now and it'll be ready shortly."

"I'd like you to grab it and head to our first heave-to position. We're picking up a shipment at 0800, but are having some issues with our first package. We need to look into things."

"What kind of problems?"

"We're not really sure, but I need you to follow the plan. If for some reason you don't hear from us, make your way back to Mars. I want you to build your own nav-plan. I'm concerned our original might not be secure."

"Oh, that sounds ominous."

"I think I'm just being paranoid, but just in case, you know what to do."

"Sure do, Liam. Be careful, okay?"

"Roger that. You too, Ada." *End comm.*

Tali once again deployed the small device. I started to find the ear popping to be annoying.

"Liam, before you leave, I've got a message back from the person I was telling you about. She's willing to do a diagnostic, but wants to know about your comm gear. Are you willing to let her know about the Navy transceiver in your cabin?"

"Why would she care about that?"

"Full disclosure. I might have intimated at its existence - no details. She and I have a long history, so I hinted."

"Why would she care?"

"That device isn't what you think it is. The Navy's long had quantum comm devices that can instantly communicate over extreme distances. For whatever reason, your contact – Belcose, I presume, from the conversations on the bridge - didn't want you to know of its capabilities. Point is, there's a good chance that Bit could hook up to it if I told her about it."

"Frak, yah. I'm okay with that. Nick?"

"How much do you trust this Bit?" he asked.

"I've trusted Bit Coffman with my life more times than I can count. She's odd, but you'll not find a greater technical genius."

"That's a lot. I'm in," Nick said.

"I'll send the comm right now," Tali said.

OBJECT LESSONS SUCK

Marny insisted that I switch to an armored vac-suit for loading the shipment. In her mind, we were past the point of pretending that everything was okay. If Stevedore Horten found it odd, he sure didn't say anything. I didn't ask for his ident today, since I recognized him, and he was his normal unhappy self. The load I'd selected didn't completely fill our holds, but pretty closely maxed out our available bond. The barges and ore had eaten up the rest of the bond we had on loan from the Navy.

Back on the ship, Tali waved us over to the door of my quarters. Marny and I followed her in and I relaxed the helmet of my suit. Nick was already there and I felt the now familiar push of the privacy device that Tali kept deploying.

Projected against the hull, next to my desk, was a live stream image of an unusual looking woman. She had a red-blond buzz cut and a proportionally larger than usual head. She appeared to be slightly heavier than most, with bright blue eyes and it didn't look like she sat still very well. Apparently, the conference call had been underway for a few minutes. The woman saw me enter and pointed at me from the wall.

"That must be the Mac-Daddy himself. You guys want to tell him or should I?"

The woman was speaking at a high rate of speed and it took me a moment to parse all of her words. I looked over to Tali, who was chuckling to herself.

"It's your show, sister. Give it to him," Tali said. Clearly, Bit Coffman put her in a good mood.

"Well, good news first. I don't think the Navy did anything too nasty. All flight control systems, O2 handling, septic, navigation, etcetera, etcetera, etcetera are functioning like they should."

"Bad news?"

"They're in deep. This thing is crawling with covert tech. Your buddy's been spying on you, hardcore. He sees you when you're sleeping ... type of thing."

"Knows when we're awake?" I couldn't resist.

"HAH! Bingo. Tali, where you been hiding these boys? I like 'em, even if they are wet behind the ears."

"Any way to get rid of it?" Nick asked.

"Not practically. Sure, if you were back here on Mars, I could get my grad students to crawl all over it and take the good stuff."

"What would that cost?"

"Probably twenty liters of Fizzy Cola and a couple of bushels of jalapeño flavored popcorn."

"Bushels?"

"Spacers ... A bushel is a whole lot. Point is, with some bribery, a couple of weeks and you let me keep what we remove, we'd do it for free."

"So we don't have to worry about losing control of the ship?"

"Nah. If you really want that video back, I could get it, too - it's still around. They've just done a good job of hiding it - not a great job."

"I don't think that's necessary," Nick said.

"Can't tell you how much we appreciate the help, Bit," I said. I felt relieved to have an idea of the scope of the navy's invasion of our privacy.

"One more thing," Tali said.

"What's that, Talisman?"

"No nicknames, Bit."

"Sorry." The large woman had an impish grin on her face as opposed to Tali's disapproving schoolmarm scowl. I suspected this was a repeating theme in their relationship.

"We're short on time, Bit. I'll catch up with you when I'm back on Mars." Tali flicked off the transceiver and also turned off her scrambling device. Apparently, the quantum communication device wasn't affected by her scrambler.

Establish comm Adela Chen.

"Hiyas, Liam."

"Any word on your barges?"

"Yes. They're all done. I was about to hail you and let you know we were headed over there. Jordy wants to know if we want to do any personnel transfers."

"I don't think so. We're planning to meet you at the rendezvous later on today and we can transfer then if we need to."

"Okay, we're just pulling away now. Stay safe," Ada said.

"Roger that, Ada. You too. Ping me when you're clear of Jeratorn, okay?" It was a load off my mind to get Ada underway. I was torn between sending her on without an escort and having her stay in this area. Either way had risks.

"Will do." She terminated the comm.

"I think Tali and I should make a sweep of the station and see if we can get an idea of where Qiu might have gone," I said.

"Are you thinking rescue mission?" Tali asked.

"Not at all, more like getting the lay of the land. She may just be ignoring us."

"How do you suppose we'd figure that out? And, for the record, I think it should be me and Tali," Marny said.

"I know. I'm not expecting any action, but if something goes bad, I need a fully functioning ship. Same reason I want Jordy to be with Ada. I'm trying to keep someone with real skills with each of the squishier members of the crew." Marny pursed her lips. I felt like I had her agreement at least for the moment.

"I'm thinking we keep it simple. We'll just take a tour of the main corridors on the main level and see where it leads us. How are we set for encrypted communication if we find something?"

"We checked out a few Navy comm encryption upgrades from the armory for the suits, so we should be fine. I'd also prefer you were both in armor," Marny said.

"I think we'd stand out too much. This is just a friendly walk around the station - two crew members taking a stroll while on leave."

"Young lovers?" Tali asked. This caused everyone to laugh.

"Seriously?"

"I wasn't really, but now that it's out there, it is a really good way to get around. People are generally put off by public displays of affection."

"Let's see if that's necessary," I said.

"Aww, don't be such a prude, I won't bite ... hard." Marny and Nick snickered again. It didn't help that she was both beautiful and deadly.

"Flechette or blaster?" I asked.

"I put some new flechettes in the armory. Let me grab one for you." Marny got up and walked out of the room.

"Come up with three locations that we could be headed to. If we get stopped for some reason it's best to have an answer."

Display map of station. Highlight businesses that are currently open.

The projection on the forward wall of my quarters showed a dozen businesses.

"There's a breakfast diner near the top and a replicator on the lower level. Nick, can you queue up something on that one?"

"Sure, make sure you bring me something from the diner."

Marny came back in and handed me a substantial looking flechette pistol.

"Ruger F0C. It's got a full suit interface, guided shot if you're fast enough, and a hell of a punch. I'll key it to you so the bad guys can't pick it up and shoot you with it."

It was heavier than any of the flechette pistols I'd held in the past.

"What kind of loads do I have in here?"

"Basic loads. They'll have a substantial punch - nothing fancy though."

Tali pinched the air in front of her eyes and flicked a virtual object at me. The interface for the nanite tracker popped up a request on my HUD. I accepted.

"Let's take a little walkabout," Tali said.

"Are you going to carry a weapon?" I asked. She didn't have a holster on and was dressed in the same tight black vac-suit she'd been wearing the entire trip.

"Oh, don't worry, I'm packing."

The nanites had an interface that could be set to narrow our search. I adjusted the range so I wouldn't have to see all of the trackers inside the ship. We would start at the timestamp where Qiu had left the ship.

Tali and I cycled through the airlock and walked down the ramp of the ship. Scanning the bay, I didn't see any of the telltales of Qiu's trackers. It wasn't a big surprise. She'd actually left the ship before we pulled into the bay and her suit wouldn't have vented any trackers, even if she had come this way.

We passed through the airlock at the back of the bay and found ourselves in a long concourse that joined the docking bays with the main station. The faded and chipped label L-1 was stenciled at eye-level, providing a reminder that we were in a pressurized environment adjacent to vacuum. It was both common practice, and in most places, the law that vac-suits were worn in these areas. Technically, you could live in the station without a suit, but depressurization was very possible. Most people kept them on just to be safe. I wouldn't expect to find any trackers here either.

Our bay was only a hundred and fifty meters from the A tower of the Jeratorn station. We'd learned that the three main sections were referred to as towers and were creatively named A, B and C. Jeratorn station was home to twenty-five hundred people. Each of the towers were mainly residential with businesses haphazardly sprinkled around.

Our first destination was The Oval Plate toward the top of tower B. It was a breakfast diner that was open from 0500 to 1300 each day. The short hours and specific cuisine seemed odd on a station like this.

Our route was planned to take us past the station administrator's office. It was a little out of the way, but if anyone asked, we could simply say that we took a wrong turn. According to Belcose, the current station administrator was one Harry Flark, the administrator of Colony 40 when it had been attacked a couple of months previous. The Navy was very interested in why he might have moved between stations and I believed that Qiu's mission was ultimately to arrest the man. His office was an obvious, possible destination for her.

Cycling the airlock between the docking bay concourse and the main thoroughfare of Tower A was quick since there was pressure on both sides. The thoroughfare was L-2 space and we were able to relax the helmets of our vac-suits. I was grateful for having purchased the earwig on Puskar Stellar as it gave me great access to my HUD, even when I didn't have my helmet on.

We immediately saw evidence of Qiu having passed through this area. We'd programmed the AI to optimize the color of the nanites through our HUDS so more recent activity was a bright glowing green and less recent was red. The program would continually adjust this spectrum upon running into new nanites. Bottom line - green was good.

"Follow the trail or get some breakfast?" I didn't want to be too obvious in what we were talking about.

"I'd like breakfast," Tali said. I jumped a little when she took hold of my hand.

"Easy there, big fella. Your blood pressure's headed north. We're just a happy couple out looking for something to eat."

I nodded. She was right. Seeing the trail was causing my heart rate to accelerate. It was mostly excitement. Her steady hand calmed me.

"Suppose they have cinnamon rolls?" I said, mostly to play along.

"I'm counting on it."

We walked down a wide hallway that was both well-lit and in good repair, if not somewhat worn. There were several retail spaces with glass panels overlooking the hallway. Only two of them were currently open and both of them looked to cater to the needs of asteroid miners, which made sense. It reminded me of where I had been only a few months before.

"Want to stop in and browse?" Tali asked.

"Maybe on the way back. I might pick up something for Dad."

So far, I was familiar with the route we'd taken. The Welded Tongue was four levels below us. This trip, we'd taken the elevator up seven levels instead. The Oval Plate was actually on the eighth level of Tower B, but the station administration was on the seventh level of Tower A. We'd be able to cross over to Tower B on a small cat-walk on level seven after a small detour past the station administrator's office.

We hadn't seen more than a dozen people in the station, so far. I'd expected it to be busier. On approach to the Station Administrator's office, a knot of people next to the entry door were discussing something in earnest. I saw, with concern, that one of the people was none other than Harry Flark. I broke out in a cold sweat. I didn't want him to recognize me.

"… you can explain that to Ms. Tracy once they've arrived. Tell 'em to get their asses up there right now, got it?" Flark's face was red with exertion. Too late, I realized I was staring at him. He looked over at us. He was going to recognize me and I couldn't think of anything …

My head felt like it had exploded and my cheek was on fire. I turned toward the pain and realized that Tali had slapped me hard with her open hand. She was saying something to me in an angry voice, grabbing the hair on the back of my neck and pushing me down the hallway away from Flark. I was having a difficult time gaining my equilibrium and stumbled.

I actually heard Flark guffaw. He had obviously witnessed the exchange between Tali and me. We made it back to the elevators before my head cleared sufficiently to say anything.

"I thought we were supposed to be lovers!"

"You'll learn not to talk to me that way," Tali said in a stage whisper.

Once on the elevator Tali raised her helmet and I followed suit. She obviously wanted to talk privately.

"Did you see that? He had green trackers all over him. He's seen her very recently and her blood pressure and respiration were sky high when he did."

I wanted to rub my jaw some more, as it was still throbbing. She hadn't spared me much on her strike. "Uh, sorry, I kind of froze up when I saw him."

"Situational awareness, Liam. You need to anticipate what might happen so you can prepare for it. You knew there was a possibility of seeing him. Next time, you need to visualize a plan for what you'll do."

"Did you visualize slapping me?" I asked, just a little annoyed.

"I certainly did. I also considered grabbing your ass and kissing you, as well as a few other options."

"That would have been nicer," I complained.

"Wouldn't have worked there, what with you staring at him."

"Sorry."

"I think we're even on that," Tali said with a chuckle.

We traversed the hallway on the eighth level of Tower A. The hallway was adjacent to the exterior of the station and had armored glass panels, giving us a nice view of the center of the three Towers. Under different circumstances, I'd have liked to have been able to stand in the hallway and take it all in. We passed through the airlocks to a small catwalk that joined Tower A and B.

Once in Tower B, we relaxed our helmets. I appreciated the ability to rub my cheek and I'd be willing to bet I had a red mark where she'd struck me. The Oval Plate was only ten meters from the airlock. It was a busy place with at least fifteen booths and tables, half of which were occupied. There were more people in the restaurant than we'd seen in our entire walk to get here.

"Would you like a booth or a table?" a kid, who couldn't be more than ten years old, asked. It wasn't uncommon for the kids of miners to take jobs to help out with the family income.

"Table'd be nice," Tali said.

We sat down and browsed the menu. It was limited, but held the breakfast essentials; eggs, waffles, bacon, etc. I found cinnamon rolls on the menu and couldn't wait to order. Marny had introduced me to that delicacy at the resort and I loved 'em.

I ordered half a dozen rolls to go and a cup of coffee and another roll to stay. Tali ordered a large breakfast that appeared to be mostly protein based, although she also ordered a cinnamon roll.

When the food came, I dug in. It was every bit as good as those we'd had at the resort on Coolidge.

"Let's run by The Welded Tongue on our way back," Tali said.

"Sure, if we go through Tower C, we can pass the security station too. And before you ask, I've a plan that doesn't involve getting slapped."

I looked up to see two station security personnel arrive at the diner. They scanned the restaurant and headed straight toward us. They were wearing armored vac-suits and carrying long blaster rifles.

Tali immediate opened a comm channel with Marny, "We're about to be taken into custody, if we don't resolve it within two hours, come looking for us."

Two more security personnel arrived and were standing guard at the entrance to the restaurant. All talking around us stopped as everyone watched the two armed men approached us.

"Don't do anything crazy, Liam," Tali warned.

"I'd listen to your girlfriend," the smaller of the two said. He was a scruffy looking man with a poorly grown red beard. "Get up, you're coming with us."

I stood up …

"Gun!" The red haired leader shouted. He snapped his gun level with my head. His companion leveled his gun at Tali. The two in the hallway aimed into the restaurant at us. The fifteen or twenty people who had been nervously watching us to that point, scrambled chaotically for the entrance.

I held my arms up to show that I wasn't a threat and the little bastard slammed the stock of his weapon into my kidney. I fell to my knees and felt his foot push me down into the floor.

"Keep your hands above your head," he instructed. I felt him roughly remove the flechette pistol from its holster. "You won't be needing that." He pulled my arms around and slid cuffs over my wrists. "Search the woman."

"Yeah, got it," his taller dark-haired companion agreed. I was able to see him roughly frisking Tali over her vac-suit. He paused inappropriately, groping and nudging her. She didn't say a word.

I wondered if she was going to go off on him or not. Finally, he finished and slid cuffs over her wrists.

"Get up." The red haired man jabbed me with the barrel of his rifle, of course, right where he'd hit me before.

"Gimme that," he demanded and pulled my earwig off of my face. He didn't bother releasing the earwig and it ripped some of the skin along my cheek before it let go. I appreciated that the taller man was gentler with Tali, although he pulled it off all the same.

They escorted us out of the restaurant and pushed us down the hallway back toward Tower C. I thought about asking them what was going on, but I already knew. Flark had recognized me.

DOUBLED-EDGED SWORD

To say I was surprised to see Lieutenant Qiu Loo in the cell next to us would have been a stretch. To say she was in bad shape, wasn't. Qiu had been beaten badly and she lay motionless on the lower bunk of her cell. They'd taken the time to remove her vac-suit and her suit-liner was torn. Her breathing was shallow, which led me to believe there were serious injuries.

The room we'd been placed in looked like it belonged in an old western vid. The three cells took up most of the rectangular room, each cell separated from the other by round iron bars. There were bunk beds welded to the back wall in each room.

"Qiu," I whispered hoarsely through the bars. "How bad are you hurt?"

"You should've left," she said between shallow breaths.

"Help is coming," I said.

"It's too late. Get out if you can."

"How'd they catch you?" I asked.

"They were waiting for me. You've got to get word to Belcose. There's a mole on our side. You also have to tell him they've set up a base in the neutral territory." She was in tremendous pain, struggling between each word for breath.

"Who? Where?"

The door swung open and none other than Harry Flark strode through. "Oh, how touching."

"What do you want?" I couldn't help myself.

"Want? Hah! Nothing from you … now. If someone had told me that I'd wake up today and find Liam Hoffen strolling around my station, I'd have shot 'em for bringing up your name. You want to know the crazy thing?"

I just looked dumbly at him. What could I possibly say?

"No? I'll tell you. I don't even have time for you. Imagine that. Asshole number one flies onto *my* station with *my* ship and the best I can do is lock him up 'cause I've got bigger fish to fry."

"We've already notified Mars Protectorate. They're on the way. You won't get away with it this time either." That caught him off guard.

"Seriously? We took Colony 40 for almost fifty million in ingots and all you got was a cutter that was ready for the scrap heap. And you think you won? No, finding you is just the icing on the cake. Once we're on the way, I'll send my boy, Ivan, up to take care of you. I'm sure Ivan will have a special treat for your girlfriend. No, by this time tomorrow, even the mighty Mars Navy won't be able to touch us. Colony 40 was just a warmup. A way to get enough money for the real haul. I'd officially like to thank you and your family for their contribution."

"You'll never get outta here in time. You can't load all that ore before they get here," I said and then it dawned on me.

Flark's smile grew as he saw that I understood.

"Where would you get a big enough ship to move that asteroid?" I asked, momentarily drawn in.

"It's amazing what you can buy for fifty million nowadays, especially if you're willing to make a good deal on several hundred million kilograms of refinery grade ore."

There was a knock at the door where Flark had entered. "Commander Flark, I have news," a voice carried through the door.

"What?" Flark snapped.

The door opened and the dark haired man who'd groped Tali looked over at us, obviously not wanting to share this information with a room full.

"I just ..."

"Out with it. You're looking at so many corpses."

"Yes sir. The frigate and hauler have arrived."

"Perfect. Bring the spy along, she may yet have some value." Flark's lackey unlocked the door to Qiu's cage and pulled her off of the bunk. She could barely walk.

"You'll get yours, Flark." It was the best I could come up with.

"No doubt I will, Hoffen, but not before you get yours. Enjoy your visit with Ivan."

Flark walked out of the room with the dark haired soldier and Qiu following behind. It was hard to watch. If I could have killed Flark at that moment, I would have.

"You'd have saved us all a lot of time if you'd resisted earlier," the red-haired soldier from the restaurant said, entering the room.

Tali took this moment to finally say something. "Ivan?"

A second slightly taller man had entered the room. They both had the unmistakable air of mercenaries.

"Nah, that'd be this guy."

A third very large, heavily muscled man entered the room. He was larger than either Marny or Gregor Belcose and had a deeply scarred face and long greasy black hair that flowed down his back. I wondered how well that worked with his helmet.

"I hate to be impatient, but we're in a bit of a hurry," Tali said. I'd been staring at the three, trying to figure out our best strategy. Even with Tali's skills, we were in trouble. What was she thinking? Her words seemed completely incongruous with our situation.

Her comment, though, caused Ivan's shoulders to shake as a deep rumble emanated from him. I realized it was what he passed off as a laugh. It was terrifying, as it only enhanced my perception of him as a monster.

"Bet that smart mouth will be singing a new song in a couple of minutes," Red said.

"Only one way to find out." Tali took a step forward. She hit a nerve with Red as he lunged forward to grab her through the bars.

"Bitch," he said as he came up short.

"Open it," Ivan growled.

Red pulled keys from a pocket. His hands were shaking. I suspect it was some combination of rage and excitement. He fumbled the key in the door's lock, but finally opened it.

I looked to Tali who stood relaxed, staring down Ivan. I had to give it to her, if she wanted to weird him out, she was doing an excellent job. I wasn't handling it quite so well. I really had no idea where to stand or what to do with myself so I mostly fidgeted, looking between Red and Ivan.

"Relax, Liam, Ivan won't come in first, he'll want to draw this out," Tali said. "If he simply wanted to kill us, he'd have shot us from the door. Ivan's looking for a fight. He'll send his weakest in first to see what we've got."

"Right, big boy?" she taunted. This elicited a growl and a sloppy sort of grin from Ivan. "To be fair, you should take contestant number one, Liam."

Ivan shoved the taller soldier toward the door. I didn't know who was crazier, Ivan or Tali. They seemed to have some sort of strange ritual going on and the rest of us were just props.

I shook my head to help me focus and remove the distractions, which were now plentiful. I pulled my arms into the relaxed, natural stance I'd been working on for the last several weeks. My heart hammered and I heard blood pounding in my ears.

The dark-haired man rushed into the room as if to tackle me. We were in very close quarters and there wasn't much I could do to step out of his way. With more room, I'd be tempted to try to use his momentum by accepting it and rolling onto the floor and trying to throw him. It was more of an Aikido move.

In the end, I decided to keep it simple. I stepped into his lunge and brought my elbow around and smashed it into his face. It was a simple technique Marny had taught me for close-in combat. This didn't have the immediate impact I'd hoped for, other than to cause him to roar. Worse, I hadn't done anything to counteract his momentum and my back struck the top bunk violently at the same time my legs hit the lower bunk.

Had he hit me just a little lower I'd have been sandwiched between the two bunks with him on top. As it was, my chest and back took the brunt of his impact. We recoiled away from the bunks, still entwined. With my less than spectacular elbow strike, my arms were both over the top of his bent back. He started to pull away and I recognized a setup to a move I felt more comfortable with. I grabbed the back of his neck and pulled down.

At the same time, I brought my knee up as hard as I could into his mid-section.

I felt his vac-suit stiffen, which reduced some of the effectiveness of my blow. He started to drive his legs forward in order to push me back into the metal bunks. It was a panic move and I brought my elbow back viciously into his ear. With no vac-suit to absorb it there, he received the full force of my adrenaline-fueled blow. He staggered to the side, releasing me.

I knew better than to allow him to recover and followed with a hand-heel strike into his nose. Now that was a feeling I hoped to never experience again. My hand shattered his nose and I felt the cartilage and bone breaking as I pushed forward. He screamed in pain, but I didn't know if I could safely let up, so I grabbed his neck again with my hands and brought my knee up into his face. This time, I knew it was enough, as he fell limply away from me.

"I'd say round one goes to the underdogs," Tali said. "Round two?" She was still staring at Ivan. "How about we skip to the finale? I'm bored."

Quicker than I could imagine, Tali grabbed her left wrist with her right hand, extracted a narrow knife from her cuff and flicked it at Red. The knife struck him just under the chin and buried itself into his throat. He reached up and pulled the knife out, then turned and ran out of the room.

"Don't …" Tali said, too late. "Frak. Why do they always pull 'em out!?"

Ivan's eyes hadn't left Tali.

"I don't suppose you'd call it a draw?" she asked wistfully.

Ivan didn't respond other than to advance on the cell's open door. His eyes were burning holes in Tali.

"Try not to get in the middle of this," Tali said. Those words were obviously for me.

I'd sparred with the woman. She had never fought me with any of the ruthlessness I'd seen the first time she and Marny had faced off. She didn't need to, as she'd been able to handle me as easily as a cat handles a mouse.

I wasn't, however, about to let her face this mountain on her own. I understood that it was possible I would get in her way, but I also understood that I was just as likely to get in Ivan's. What I needed to avoid was the one punch knock-out I presumed he had in him. I pulled my vac-suit helmet up - it should be able to absorb something.

I wished I'd left my AGBs (Arc-jet Gloves and Boots) on, although they probably would have been confiscated along with our comms, when we'd been put in the brig. I ran at Ivan, mimicking the rush my dark-haired assailant had used on me. I mentally braced myself for the blow, but was still rocked by its ferocity. Ivan smashed his clasped fists into my back. I crumpled to the floor, gasping like a fish out of water, unable to find enough oxygen in what I was sucking in (which wasn't much).

I could barely hear the slaps, grunts and strikes through the pain, but after half a minute my mind started to clear. I sat up and scooted backwards, away from the ballet of two excellent martial artists. It struck me that the fight wasn't a lot different than what I'd witnessed between Marny and Tali. An impossibly fast assailant against an impenetrable rock.

It wasn't as if Ivan were slow, either. He just didn't have the same sort of speed as Tali. He was very smart in using the cell and bunk to restrict her movements and deliver several of his massive blows. I'd received just one of these and found it difficult to move. I couldn't imagine how she was able to continue to dance around him after receiving even one.

My head finally cleared enough for me to realize that Tali had completely occupied Ivan's attention. It was as if I didn't exist. More importantly, there was nothing between me and the open door. There were two possible approaches; slink away slowly or scamper quickly. I chose scamper. If Ivan was going to see me, there wasn't much I could do about it. If Tali failed, I could guarantee we were lost. At a minimum, he would have to turn his back on her to come after me.

I rolled over to my knees and crawled, despite the pain in my body. I got to my feet and stumbled through the door, moving as quickly as I could. I made it out of the room and into the next. It wasn't a large room and was split down the center by an armored glass partition with a door on one side and a counter that separated the public from the station security personnel on duty.

The armored glass door was ajar, the body of Red propping it open. He lay face down with his hands on his neck. Under other circumstances, I would have run over to try and provide some assistance, but I could hear the fight continuing in the room behind me.

I looked around and couldn't find any weapons, so I started pulling on cabinet doors. They were all locked. An idea I hated floated through my mind. Unfortunately, I wasn't in a position to be picky. I ran over to Red and felt his neck to see if he might be alive. He didn't seem to be, but that didn't make the next task any less gruesome.

I dragged his body over to the cabinets and laid his palm on the first security panel I came to. It's an awful business, moving a body. First, Red was heavier than he looked and second, I felt like a ghoul. Thing is, it worked. The panel turned green and I unceremoniously dumped the body back onto the floor. I pulled the door open and found several heavy blaster rifles on the shelf. I also saw our confiscated earwigs and weapons.

I dropped my face shield, which I'd completely forgotten I had on, grabbed my earwig and stuffed it into my ear. The thing about combat that most people might not know is that, under pressure, lots of things seem like a good idea. Adrenaline does a fabulous job of helping you forget what parts of your body are in pain or broken.

Somewhere along the line, my ear had come into contact with something sharp, causing major damage. I realized this because it felt like I'd just jammed a knife into my ear. The pain escalated as the earwig automatically reattached itself to my cheek, where Red had ripped a good amount of skin off. In the long list of regrets for that day, this had jumped to the top, at least momentarily.

Wincing through the pain, I grabbed a heavy blaster rifle and saw with satisfaction that it interfaced with my HUD immediately. I swung around and re-entered the room where Tali and Ivan had been battling. The room was deathly quiet and I hoped I wasn't too late.

I was thrilled to see Ivan lying on the floor, not moving. Tali had taken a knee, apparently to catch her breath.

"Let's move," She said. "We should be able to catch Qiu."

"Your comm is in the cabinet," I said. I'd seen hers sitting on the same shelf where mine had been.

"Don't forget your flechette," she reminded me. "I doubt Marny wants to replace those all the time."

She made a good point, although, I suspected she was messing with me. I grabbed the flechette and holstered it. I wasn't going to give up the heavy blaster rifle at this point and if Tali thought that I should, she kept it to herself.

Hail Sterra's Gift. Stream visual.

"Liam, status," Marny said.

"We're both up. Flark's got Qiu and is trying to get off the station. We're going after them."

Tali had re-established the nanite trace program and we had an easy green line that gave us the path to follow.

"Be careful. A big old frigate just rolled into the system," Nick warned.

"They're taking the co-op," I said.

"What? Why would they attack the co-op? It's just ore," Marny asked.

"No. According to Flark, they've got a giant hauler and are taking the entire asteroid."

"Holy shite," Marny said.

"Chat later. Let's go," Tali prompted. "Stay on my six."

I knew from training with Marny at the warehouse on Coolidge that my job was to make sure we weren't overtaken from behind. I followed her down the hallway to the catwalk that joined us back to Tower A. Fortunately, an elevator was waiting. Unfortunately, we could see this was the car that had carried Qui. They were quite a ways ahead of us.

"Move," Tali urged, as the door opened on the main concourse. The green trail of nanites led to the airlock of the docking bay concourse. We moved through as quickly as possible - the nanite trackers indicating we were now less than four minutes behind.

We sprinted down the concourse past the turn to *Sterra's Gift*. At the end was another airlock. The nanite trackers were all over it. Qiu had been breathing hard and spewing them vociferously.

I peered through the glass and saw the catwalk automatically being reeled back in. The frigate was pulling away and Harry Flark's face was in the airlock on the other side. For the second time that day I realized, too late, that people's instinct when being stared at was to look back.

Flark looked right at me and started shouting. I couldn't hear what he was saying, but I was pretty sure I knew what it was.

"We've got to get out of here!"

Tali must have figured out what was happening because she spun with me and we both raced back down the fifty meters to the airlock that led us to *Sterra's Gift*.

"Nick. We've got incoming!"

The airlock seemed to take its sweet time cycling. The first salvo from the frigate hit the end of the concourse at the same time we entered the airlock that was now a vacuum, equalized with space. We pulled the door closed just in time to see all of the debris of the concourse rush down the hallway and get sucked out into space.

We weren't in the clear yet, though. The bay-side door opened easily and we ran for the ramp. Fortunately, Marny had been thoughtful enough to have the space side of *Sterra's Gift's* airlock already open and we piled in, pulling the door closed behind us.

I mashed my palm onto the panel that would cause the lock to cycle and waited with frustration while it filled with atmo.

"Liam! We've got trouble!" Nick's voice was as excited as I'd ever heard it. I rushed down the hallway to the bridge and saw through the armored glass that the frigate, fully five hundred tonnes of muscle, sat broadside to the docking bay.

OUT OF THE FRYING PAN

I jumped into my empty pilot's chair, pulled the combat harness over my body and clipped it in, then pulled the flight control stick back from the forward bulkhead.

"I'll be in engineering," Nick said, heading for the door of the bridge.

"Not yet. Just hold on to something. Marny, do you have weapons online?"

"Roger that, Cap."

"Fire both missile tubes now. Everybody hold on."

Engage combat thrust controls.

I pushed the thrust control hard and we rocketed forward, just as the frigate started firing a broadside salvo at the station's docking bay, at which we were dead center. I doubted that initially they knew exactly which bay we were coming out, but I also knew they out-gunned us by an outrageous margin. We were the proverbial duck in a barrel once they figured out which bay we were in. The rounds weren't specifically aimed at us yet, but we were taking hits, nonetheless.

The frigate was so close to the station that the missiles couldn't be dodged. Unfortunately, the ship also had a countermeasures package that deployed flawlessly. Both our missiles hit scraps and exploded fifty meters before making contact with the ship.

It was devastating that the missiles hadn't done any damage, but at least the explosions had temporarily disrupted the bombardment lane between the frigate and the station. We desperately needed the extra few seconds. *Sterra's Gift's* inertial system was absorbing and redistributing as much g-force as possible. I couldn't push her any harder. We had to get clear. We wouldn't last ten seconds once the frigate locked on our position.

"Marny, put as much fire on that frigate as you can." My voice strained with exertion.

"Aye Cap, blasters are firing full and three seconds to missile ready."

"I'm rabbiting."

The design of a frigate is much different than that of a cutter like *Sterra's Gift* or even a much larger corvette like the *Kuznetsov*. Cutter and corvette tactics are primarily hit and run, but a frigate is designed to stand and deliver. The worst possible place to be is at a frigate's broadside. If I wanted us to survive this round, I had to change the geometry.

The disruption from our missiles and the frigate's general lack of knowledge of our location were working in our favor. The problem was, that only bought us enough time to launch *Sterra's Gift* out of the docking bay. The frigate would resolve both issues well before I could get out of its deadly reach.

I pulled hard left on the flight stick and twisted the handle, turning us broadside to the frigate. By itself that was a suicidal maneuver, but the twist on the handle was just enough to roll the belly of the ship up toward the frigate. I sure hoped the new armor we'd added at Coolidge was worth the hefty price we'd paid. I only needed a couple of seconds of grace. We were pointed in the opposite direction of our foe and the engines were running at near peak.

"Cap, I can't get any weapons on 'em upside down," Marny reminded me.

"Roger that." I didn't have time to explain what I was doing. I just hoped she'd figure it out.

Sterra's Gift was being buffeted by the increasingly focused fire of the frigate, but we were alive and surviving so far.

"Nick, armor status?"

"Can't take much more, but it's holding."

My HUD displayed the orientation of the frigate and I watched it rotate slowly to try to keep its guns tracking on us. We were quickly accelerating away from its effective range.

"Marny, do they have any missiles?"

"Don't know yet."

Our ship lurched to the left. With its inertial system, it would take a considerable contact to rock us like that. That hit hadn't come from the frigate.

"Station defensive guns are firing on us," Nick said.

"Frak! Roger that." I recognized Flark's signature from his attack on Colony 40. Take over the station's defenses, then roll in the pirates.

"Get close to the station. The guns are made to repel invaders, not shoot close in at the station," Nick said.

I really didn't want to do that, since that could endanger the population, but then again they had a frigate broadsiding them at the moment.

We'd already cleared the station so I pulled back on the stick to angle back toward it. I twisted again to reorient our armored belly to the frigate. I hadn't let up on the thrust since I'd jumped into the seat. The shift in direction caught the frigate off guard and interrupted their salvos, which we'd almost escaped. I felt sick having to head back toward the heavily gunned and armored ship.

The ship lurched again and a loud explosion rocked us. My vac-suit's helmet automatically deployed which meant we'd lost pressure somewhere on the ship. As soon as we'd taken off, the bridge door had closed, so my best guess, based on the sound, was one of the cargo bays. Frak, we had a full load.

"Can't take another one of those," Nick said. "Station gun penetrated the hull and we just lost the septic system and a portion of BR-2."

"Shite! Did we reseal?"

"Yup."

I'd aligned us to sail up close to the station. It was a desperate gambit. I decelerated hard once we came up next to it. I'd positioned the station between us and the frigate and I'd also snuggled in as closely as I could. I waited for impact from the station's guns. It never came.

I watched the course of the frigate. Unless it was willing to shoot the station apart, there was no chance for it to line up on us again.

"Marny, can you scan for other ships? I've got the frigate."

"Aye, Cap. I'll also keep an eye out for station inhabitants with attitude problems."

We were in the unenviable position of being the rodent in a high stakes game of cat and mouse. For the moment, the conflict had reached equilibrium, but I knew from experience that wouldn't last long. With the station perimeter defense guns online and tracking us as an enemy, we could neither run nor could we engage the frigate.

"We've got to get those guns offline," I said.

"Agreed," Tali answered.

"Nick, can you find where they're controlling those guns from?"

"Working on it. It's not on their public info."

"Tali, do you think your friend Bit Coffman could help?"

"Good chance."

"Nick, take over the helm."

"No need, I've bridged the Navy's equipment. I suspect Belcose won't like it, but the secure Navy comm is now available on bridge."

He didn't need to tell me twice.

Establish comm with Bit Coffman.

"Heya, Bitches. What's shaking?" Bit's voice came over the comm.

"Bit, thanks for answering. We're in a pinch here."

"Give it to me," she said.

"We're pinned down by Jeratorn's perimeter guns and we need to shut 'em down. Can you help us locate the control room?"

"That's hard. I'd probably have to eliminate all the residential spaces, cross that with all the power and sewer, take away the businesses, find the new construction and add-ons …"

"How long?" Tali cut her off in mid-sentence.

"Look, if I just do it, then you all think it's easy."

"Bit," Tali's voice was firm.

"Already working on it, probably take five minutes."

"Nick, can you take the helm?"

"Yup."

"What are you thinking, Cap?" Marny asked.

"I need my armored vac-suit and AGBs."

"Aye. That's what I was thinking, too."

I jumped up and pushed my way through the bridge door, thankful to discover that the hallway was still holding atmo. The bridge door closed behind me and sealed shut. Apparently the ship's AI wasn't taking any chances. I took this to heart and pulled the door to my quarters closed, I'd be in trouble if we depressurized while I was between suits.

Once changed, I pushed the large flechette pistol into the chest holster that I preferred for combat situations. Marny had shown me the value of being able to un-holster my weapon by reaching across my chest instead of trying to pull it off my leg or from my waist.

"Cap, Bit's got it, info's loading into our tactical displays." Marny's voice came through my earwig.

"Which tower? We need an entrance. What's the frigate doing?"

"Bit, any chance you can hack those guns?"

"Not in the amount of time you have available. I can, however, tell you they're trying to override the safety protocols on them so they can shoot you."

"Think they'll be successful?"

"Not sure, but I wouldn't bet against it."

"Look here," Nick said.

The rear holo projector displayed the three towers with the frigate and *Sterra's Gift* shown in their relative positions. Toward the top of one of the three towers a red box highlighted the position of the control station.

"Frak!" I said. Now I understood why the frigate was sitting in the location that it was. It wasn't just holding us in place, it was also guarding the control station.

"Buckle up kids, this is going to get bumpy," I said and pulled the combat harness back over my shoulders.

As if in direct response to my statement, we felt the whump of contact on the rear quarter of the ship.

"Damage to starboard engine," Nick warned.

I jammed the accelerator forward. The ship lurched with the sudden change in acceleration. I was relieved we hadn't lost much power. I ran directly between the three towers. There were random wires and cables that I couldn't dodge and the ship jostled as we ripped through. The noise on the bridge was horrendous. I was probably peeling off sensor strips and other less armored, but no less expensive, components. If we weren't running for our lives I might have been concerned about what I was doing to the ship.

Just as we were about to come free of the towers and provide the frigate with a clean shot, I swooped back hard, staying within the safety of the towers. I needed the longest, safest run I could manage before clearing the towers. There wouldn't be much time once I was in the open.

Another round from the station's defensive guns tore through the middle of the towers and ripped into the structure of Tower A. Whoever was manning the guns had absolutely no issues with killing civilians. I had to get out of here and not compound their danger.

We squirted out from between the towers and headed toward the aft section of the frigate. It was the one part of the giant beast that wasn't heavily armored and didn't have a plethora of guns they could utilize.

"Hang on," I said, as we ran out and accelerated away from the frigate. I'd exited the towers at a shallow angle and was directly in line with its rear engines. "Marny, get ready to drop two in his pipes."

"Aye, Cap."

I snapped the flight stick back and lined up on the frigate's engines. We were in the open – prime target for the station's guns. I hoped we could take another hit.

"Missiles away!" Marny exclaimed.

The frigate automatically launched its countermeasures, but one of the missiles made it through and exploded. I wanted to cheer, we'd finally hit the damn thing. Unfortunately, it still had two more operational engines.

Predictably, the frigate started to turn so it could line its weapons up on us. I decelerated so that I stayed aft, keeping in its blind spot at the rear.

Sterra's Gift lurched again.

"We've lost atmo in the main section of the ship. Those guns are tearing us apart," Nick said. It was as excited as he ever got.

"Marny, target that control room, I'm going to rabbit."

She'd been pouring blaster fire into the rear end of the frigate, but its armor was more than sufficient to fend us off. Sure. Give us a couple of hours and she'd break something, but we weren't going to last minutes, much less hours.

"Aye, Cap. I'm ready."

I punched the thruster forward and flew over the top spine of the narrow ship, our heavily armored belly once again between us and the beast.

"Bird's away," Marny exclaimed. I said a silent prayer for any innocents that might be close to that control station. The schematic showed the entire top side of the tower was for industrial use, but you never knew for sure on a station.

The bridge was quiet as we accelerated past the nose of the frigate. I could imagine Harry Flark watching us through the armored glass below.

"Status?" It was all I could manage, if I didn't get us out of the way of this frigate we'd be ripped to shreds.

"It was a hit. Those guns should be down, Cap."

I banked hard, using the towers as a shield from the frigate. *Sterra's Gift* was limping away, but at least we were going to survive this round. We'd taken away the frigate's ability to chase us and I'd like to say we'd handed out as much as we'd taken, but that simply wasn't the case.

"That went well," Tali said dryly.

LIPSTICK ON A BULLDOG

I set in a navigation plan to take us to the rally point where we would have met Ada and Jordy. They were long gone, but we needed a safe spot where we could heave-to and look over the damage to *Sterra's Gift*.

I didn't know if Tali was being serious or ironic, but I certainly didn't feel like anything had gone well since we'd run into Flark in the hallway. "We just got our asses handed to us back there, how could you say that?"

"I totally didn't take you as a glass-half-empty type of guy. You need to get your head on straight. What do you think the odds were of a lone cutter surviving against a frigate and half a dozen stationary turrets? Oh, and let's remember we started out by being trapped in a hole and broadsided by the frigate."

"He got away with Qiu and we're so full of holes I'm not sure we'll make it back to Mars," I wasn't ready to concede her point, but the way she said it had me reconsidering my point of view.

"You don't get to set the rules of combat. All you can do is react to the cards you're dealt. What you and your team pulled off just now was brilliant. I bet there aren't ten pilots in the solar system who could've pulled that rabbit out of that hat."

I desperately wanted to believe her, but it felt like a loss to me. The ship was beat to crap, quite literally, since when they'd holed *Sterra's Gift*, they'd destroyed the septic system. Qiu had been battered and taken and Flark had gotten away with it.

"I get where you're head's at, Liam. I don't know if I'm cut out for this either, but we're here and we have a job to do." Nick said. "Tell us about Qiu and Flark."

"Tali and I found Qiu in the brig when they locked us up. She was in terrible shape. I don't know how much longer she'll last without medical attention."

"Did she say anything?" Marny asked.

"Something about a base being set up in neutral territory."

"Not just neutral territory, THE Neutral Territory," Marny corrected. "Mars and PDC observe a no-fly, no commerce zone. I guess they figure space is big enough that they don't need to be bumping into each other."

"What do you think that means?" I asked

"It sounds like maybe the PDC is setting up a base," Nick said.

"Why does it need to be the PDC? The Chinese are business people first. There's no profit in war," Tali said.

"I thought they were trying to expand their fleets," I said.

"Everyone is expanding their fleets. I'm just saying; don't be too quick to blame the Chinese just because they're neighbors. It would take more than ten days of sailing to get into their space," Tali said.

"Who else would work with someone like Flark?" I asked.

"I think that's pretty obvious," Marny said. "He's Red Houzi."

It wasn't as though we didn't know Harry Flark was Red Houzi. But, implications became clear as we all combined the two conversations. The bridge became very quiet for a few moments, no one wanting to say the obvious out loud.

Nick broke the silence. "What if someone other than Mars Protectorate or People's Democracy of China set up in The Neutral Territory?"

"Frak. Red Houzi has a base? That's why Qiu's out here. She was looking for that base," Marny said.

"No. She said she wanted Flark. She said she was meeting with a contact who'd give her information on Flark. What if that was just a trap?" I asked.

"To what end?" Marny asked.

"I don't know. Delay?"

The lights of the bridge dimmed and the red warning lights pulsed around the top of the room. I'd set a proximity warning when I'd engaged the auto navigation system.

Identify ship. I jumped back into the pilot's seat and my HUD popped up an outline around a ship that was dead ahead.

It's the Adela Chen. The outline was easy to identify with the string of barges hanging off the front of it.

Incoming hail from Ada Chen, the ship announced.

Accept hail to bridge comm.

"Fancy meeting you out here," Ada said. Her cheerful voice was discordant with the mood of the ship and the tension we were still carrying.

"I thought you were headed for home," I said.

"We thought we might give it a few more hours, make sure you all got out of there. Glad you made it, are you ready to get going?" she asked.

"Things have changed and we've taken a lot of damage. We were hoping to hide out here and patch things up."

"What kind of damage, Liam? Is anyone hurt?"

"We couldn't get Qiu. She's alive, but I don't know for how long. Everyone else is fine."

I pulled *Sterra's Gift* up next to the *Adela Chen.*

"Liam … your ship. You're venting atmo from more than one spot. Do you have enough hull patch?" Ada said.

"We're maintaining pressure, but we're burning O2 crystals at an unsustainable rate," Nick said. "If you and Jordy would help us out with your hull-patch material it would save us from replicating it."

"Nick, what are your priorities?" I asked.

"Engine and hull first. We can worry about the secondary systems after that," he said.

"Marny, would you get on the comm with Belcose and let him know what happened? Ada, when you get over here, can you meet me outside with your hull-patch? Tali, could you and Marny coordinate a watch to make sure we're not getting snuck up on? Everyone should treat the entire ship as L-1 until further notice."

I pulled my helmet up and sealed the face shield. I was used to working this way day to day, so it wouldn't bother me. Planet-born people sometimes talked about how uncomfortable constantly being in their vac-suit was, but at this point it didn't really make much of a difference. We were no longer in a predictable environment.

I was sure I was missing something, but the hull venting atmo was all I really needed to know. I followed Nick back through the hallway. The door to BR-2 showed a red status indicating the room wasn't holding pressure. I wanted to look inside but that wasn't a good idea.

Prioritize hull breaches. My HUD showed a list of eight locations. Frak, but they'd done a lot of damage in a short time. I wondered, wryly if this was what 'light fire support' referred to.

I followed Nick back to the engine room. The first thing that struck me were the scorch marks on the walls of the hallway, just past the galley on the starboard side. The large cargo bays flanked the hallway on both sides. The access panel for the starboard cargo bay wasn't functioning, even to show a red status. The cargo bay wasn't on my list and that was a bigger concern to me.

Status of starboard cargo bay.

No status available, the ship's AI responded. That couldn't be good.

The engine room was a mess. Nick's tidy, organized space was in disarray. Cabinet panels had been jarred open and tools and supplies littered the floor. Ordinarily, that would have been my cue to dig in and help him pick up.

Locate hull-patch kits. The kits were a last-minute addition. I'd initially argued that they were relatively easy to replicate. Nick had pointed out that they were also very resource intensive, chewing up both time and raw materials which, if we had an emergency, would be in short supply. If I wasn't so concerned for the safety of the crew at the moment, I would have hugged him for his foresight.

My HUD finally showed an outline of the corner of one of the kits. It was under a pile of parts and tools. I slogged my way through the room, trying to not damage anything important as I pushed debris out of the way.

I located two of the half-meter square kits and one of the hand plasma welders. It was more than I could carry out, so I moved each item to the galley one at a time. Once I got outside the ship, the lack of gravity would make moving the awkward equipment and cases much easier.

"Drink something before you go out." Marny was blocking my path.

"I don't have time."

"That wasn't a suggestion. We're in combat, Cap. I know it feels like we're out of it, but we both know that could change in an instant. Don't make the mistake of taking care of your ship better than yourself." Marny handed a pouch to me.

I sighed inwardly. She made sense, but I had a million things that needed to get done. I also knew she wasn't going to be ignored. I plugged the pouch into a small receptacle in my helmet and was surprised at how much I appreciated the slightly sweet tasting liquid.

"Thanks."

I grabbed a hull-patch kit and walked to the airlock. Marny followed behind, holding a second kit and the plasma welder. For some reason, I was a little annoyed and wanted to ask who was keeping watch for approaching ships, but I bit it off. Marny was more than competent in this situation and I needed to trust her.

We cycled through the airlock. It crossed my mind that it was the first time this particular door had survived a combat encounter since I'd been around the ship. I exited on the port side and placed the hull-patch kit next to the airlock, knowing the hull had a small gravity field next to it, holding it in place.

I jetted out from the ship and surveyed the port side. There were no obvious issues, although atmo was venting from the belly. I needed a full understanding of all the damage before repairs began. Those atmo leaks would be my first priority, but they could wait a few more minutes while I finished the survey.

"Marny, I'll check out the starboard side first, then we'll get to patching."

"Aye."

My stomach sank as I arced over the top of the ship. The damage was astounding. By my count we'd taken four hits from

Jeratorn's large stationary guns. One of those strikes had shut down the starboard engine. It looked like a giant hammer had swung through the ship, digging out a large trench through the side. Part of the trench included the forward third of the starboard engine. Most of the starboard cargo bay was simply missing.

A second round had hit eight meters forward of that, grazing the side of the ship, leaving a rent that started on the topside and plowed downward, angling toward the center of *Sterra's Gift*. I pushed my arc-jets and flew around the side toward the belly, I had to see where the round exited the ship.

Predictably, it had exited the ship on the bottom almost at the centerline. It was a perfectly round, one point five meter diameter hole. I wondered at the difference between this nice clean, through-shot and the hammer-like rip that had taken out the engine and the cargo bay.

I put them both out of my mind for a moment and flew away from the ship to gain a larger perspective on the belly. Ada and Marny had followed me around the outside and were inspecting the damage.

The frigate's guns had done a thorough job of ripping up our new armor and a few comparably small holes were exhausting atmo. Under normal circumstances, I'd have considered the holes alone to be extensive. But at this point, they seemed almost trivial.

"Marny, Ada, do you want to start plugging the smaller leaks?" I figured they all needed to be fixed and I would have to spend more time thinking my way through the bigger issues.

"Aye, aye."

I moved off of the belly and to the front of the ship. We'd taken a substantial amount of fire when escaping the docking bay into the frigate's broadside. If I hadn't already seen the giant gash in the side of the ship I might have been shocked. As it was, my disappointment simply deepened. The nose and everything back had been stripped clean of all non-armor components and much of the armor was buckled and in some cases, shredded.

"Nick. Talk to me, what are you finding in there?"

"Starboard engine is a complete wreck. I can't get any response from it. Septic system is unrepairable. BR 2 and starboard cargo bay are both showing exposure to space. I can't get into the catwalk without decompressing the main part of the ship."

"Roger that. That lines up with what we're seeing out here. The front third of the starboard engine and cargo bay are completely missing. It'll take some creative thinking to figure out how to seal all that. There's a large, clean hole punched through from topside of BR-2. Looks like it exits just to the starboard of the keel. I think I can patch that. I've got Marny and Ada patching the smaller holes in the belly. I'm going to have to salvage some material to close the through-hole."

"Okay, I'm coming out to work on the engine and cargo bay. We're mostly stable inside."

I jetted over to Ada and Marny. They were making quick work of the holes in the belly. The patch kits had a large pouch of expansive foam, but it wouldn't take long before we ran out.

"You mind if I grab the welder?" I asked.

"All yours," Marny said.

I took the plasma welder that doubled as a cutting tool. Nick was, by far, the better welder, but I had plenty of experience fixing mining machinery. It wouldn't be pretty, but it'd be strong.

"Frak!" Nick said. I suspected he'd just cleared the starboard side of the ship and was surveying the damage to the engine and cargo bay.

I jetted over to the damaged section and met him. He was trying to get a good gauge of how a repair might be applied. With the amount of missing material and the limited tools we had, our goal was simply to restore some level of safety and function. That level was yet to be determined.

"Do the best you can. Like I said, you'll need to be creative," I said.

"How is this anything but a total loss?" he asked.

"Baby steps, buddy. Let's get her safe to sail."

"Cargo's lost." He was still processing the implications.

"Bond will cover that. I need you to focus on getting us back in sailing shape."

Nick sighed audibly over the comm. I knew him well enough to know that he was doing the math of how bad a loss we'd just taken. I wasn't going to think about it. We were all alive and that mattered to me the most. I knew that was the case for Nick too, but it was a lot to take in.

I needed a couple pieces of armor that I could cut out and make patches for the through-hole. I'd have to scavenge the armor that was hanging uselessly around the shredded engine. I instructed my AI to project an outline of the top-side hole onto a piece of the hanging armor. The plasma cutter had to work hard to slice through, but in the end I had two decent looking, mostly perfect, four centimeter thick patches.

I grabbed the patches and jetted over to the top side. It turns out that perfectly fitting pieces are really hard to apply since they want to simply slip through the hole. I resolved this by jetting back to the ruined cargo bay and cutting off a thin strap to tack across the opening. This held everything in place while I welded the seams. Pleased with the first patch, I was considerably faster at applying the second to the belly of the ship.

I caught up with Ada and Marny who were working hard to plug the hundreds of small holes in the armor. To me, it looked like they'd taken care of all of the atmosphere leaks and had moved on to the less critical, albeit uglier scars.

"I think Nick's going to need our help in that cargo bay," I said. "When you feel like you're in good shape, come on up and join us."

"Lipstick on a bulldog, Cap."

"What's that?"

"Oh, at this point we're just putting lipstick on a bulldog."

"I don't follow," It wasn't a term I was familiar with.

"I think she's saying we can help him now," Ada said.

I didn't have time to argue, or maybe I just didn't have the energy. We'd been at it for a couple of hours and between the adrenaline leaving my system and the sheer physical effort, I was tired. I was sure that was true for everyone at this point.

In the end, we did the best we could for the cargo bay and

shredded engine, overlapping our scavenged pieces carefully until we were confident the new walls of the cargo bay would hold atmo. We found large enough pieces to patch every possible weak spot, including the hatches and doors. Hopefully, the fixes would keep the ship from blowing a seam if we had to put her under more stress. I didn't think I'd be trusting *Sterra's Gift's* hull integrity anytime soon, however.

Finally, Nick was satisfied with the job we'd done and it was time to head back in.

"Lipstick on a bulldog?" I asked, the phrase had finally sunk in far enough that I could ponder it. "Why would anyone put lipstick on a dog?

INTO THE FIRE

It was hard to express how grateful I felt when Tali and Jordy greeted us on the bridge with a banquet of rehydrated and heated meals. They'd thoughtfully brought enough supplies forward for a crew twice our size, or so I thought.

"What's next, Liam?" Tali asked, once she'd given us a chance to work through the food for a while. I hadn't been this hungry for a very long time and was enjoying the process of simply sitting and eating with nothing crazy happening.

"I haven't really thought that through yet," I said. I knew people were looking for me to provide leadership, but I'd been running on instinct and urgency for so long I hadn't been thinking about the big picture.

"It's a problem common to junior officers," Marny said. It sounded like a jab, but that wasn't really like Marny.

"Oh?" I asked, not ready to take the bait just yet.

"Yeah, your mind is overwhelmed by all of the details and you're carrying too much of the load, Cap. Take it from someone who's been there. You've got several amazing strategic minds within arm's length. Use them." I was glad that I hadn't snapped at her like I'd wanted to.

I turned to Tali who was watching me intently. This was a woman who'd seen more combat in her thirty years of life than I ever would - at least I hoped that would be the case.

"Tali, Jordy, surely you've been contemplating our situation. What do you see as our options?"

"As far back as the Roman Empire there's been an understanding about the nature of combat and bold action. This crew is the living embodiment of the simple phrase 'fortune favors the bold.' Honestly, it doesn't work for everyone. It takes a disciplined, focused group to take advantage of the slim line between insanity and acceptable risk."

"I'm not really following. How does that apply here?"

"Let me try a different tack. What if I could wave a magic wand and we all got transported to a bar on Puskar Stellar?"

"Sounds pretty good at the moment," I said.

"You'd hate yourself," Nick interjected. I looked at him. I was missing something, of that I was certain. Nick wasn't just my business partner and best friend, he was very often my conscience.

It dawned on me, "Frak. Qiu." Nick nodded sagely at me.

"Give me some options," I said. I was coming up with nothing on my own.

"We've got to stop that ship," Tali said.

"What then?" I asked.

Jordy almost always let Tali do the heavy lifting when it came to strategic conversations. I didn't think it was for lack of good ideas. I just expected it was because they were so in-tune with each other that he didn't mind letting her run with the conversation. So it came as a surprise when he answered.

Jordy's voice was quiet, almost a whisper. "Get us on that ship with a four-man team and we'll take it." Jordy so often presented himself as the light-hearted playboy that it felt like we were talking to a completely different person.

"I count three real soldiers," I said. It wasn't false modesty. I knew darn well I wasn't in their league.

"You're right, of course," Tali said. It hurt a little to hear her say it, but it was the truth. "But Jordy already did that math. Would we rather have our whole team here right now? Absolutely. Guess what, though? Combat is all about making do with what you have. It's time to soldier up."

"How are we going to stop that ship?" Nick asked.

That was the moment I got it – the feeling of dead certainty. I knew what the right thing to do was. The plan formed in my mind like concrete. Nick was going to hate it, but I was committed to it.

I explained my plan to the group.

"That's suicide," Nick said.

"Not even close. It's the only way. Qiu's dead if we don't do this. You didn't see her Nick, somebody used her for a punching bag."

"There's no guarantee she's still alive." As predicted, Nick hated the plan. I knew him well enough that I could see him working through it.

"Does that really matter?"

We stared at each other for what felt like several minutes.

"Fine. No. Frak." Nick finally relented.

"Marny, what'd you hear from Belcose? When will Mars Protectorate be here?"

"They're still a day out."

"Jupiter. You'd think with all their ships, they'd have something a little closer."

"I think most of their efforts are focused within the Mars ecliptic. Jeratorn's a station of a few thousand. There are fifteen billion Mars citizens to protect. Bottom line is, they just don't hang around out here."

Marny and I walked Nick and Ada back to the airlock. I knew Nick felt like he'd drawn the short straw. He was probably already having second thoughts.

"I hate this," Nick said.

"I know, buddy, but it's the right thing and you know it."

"I don't have to like it."

Nick and Ada exited the airlock and jetted back toward the waiting *Adela Chen*. If this didn't work out, he'd never forgive me.

I entered the bridge.

"Captain on the bridge," Marny announced. We'd dropped that formality recently and I was a startled to hear her use it again.

Sterra's Gift shuddered as we started our burn. I didn't know exactly where we'd find the frigate, but it had to still be close to the co-op's asteroid. Even with a giant hauler, the convoy couldn't have gone very far in the last six hours. Especially since they had to come up with some sort of way to fasten the asteroid to their hauler.

My HUD outlined the triangularly shaped frigate while we were still well out of its weapons range. The hauler Flark had procured was indeed massive and almost entirely engines. There would be sizeable living quarters and likely more than one bridge, but the engines were so large it was hard to see anything else.

Hail the frigate.

I waited a few minutes.

Hail the frigate, tell them we're requesting a Parley.

I was a little surprised when this got me a response.

"Parley? You little shite. I already ran you off once, I won't be so nice next time." Flark's red face appeared on the forward HUD.

"Give us Lieutenant Loo and we'll be on our way."

"Or what?"

"Or I'll end you."

"Ha ha ha … you'll end me? Go home to momma while you still can."

"Liam, we've got company," Marny said.

Four dart-sized ships had launched from the hauler and were headed straight toward us.

End comm.

"Well, we have our answer," I said. In our current shape, four darts were going to be a problem.

I pushed forward on the thrust control stick. I couldn't out-accelerate the darts, but I might be able to spread them out a little if I was moving fast enough. Their damage would come from the forward guns. The problem was, once you got past a dart, they'd just flip over and come right back at you.

Marny was strapped into the gunnery chair and fire lanced over the armored cockpit toward the darts.

"Any missiles left?" I asked. I wasn't hopeful.

"None, Cap." Marny was concentrating, as her voice was tense.

"Get ready for a change up," I said.

The darts had split into two teams. One team would fly below, another above. They wanted to flank us and fly up on our tail, where we'd be more vulnerable. With two teams, one could always be behind us.

The first team was set to pass above us and I knew they would flip over and accelerate hard so that they could catch up to us. Just as they passed over, I pulled back on my stick and partially rolled over, putting us on a collision course with the two darts. One of them was able to roll out of the way but I caught the other one with the back end of my ship. The noise was horrendous but no new red statuses popped up. No sane pilot would have made that maneuver, but we'd already taken so much damage, I was willing to trade for a little more. The dart I'd contacted cartwheeled away.

I hit the forward thruster hard and pulled back harder, so I would be facing the remaining three. We were once again taking heavy fire. A red status popped up in my HUD. We'd lost atmo in the main portion of the ship.

Normally, in a fight, I'd be doing my best to keep my heavily armored belly to the adversary. Here, our only chance was if Marny could finish the other three off before they shredded us.

"Got one!" she exclaimed.

Another red status popped up and we lost a significant amount of thrust. It was the top-side engine. We were now sailing on a third of our normal power. That might have been okay against something large, but against darts it would be fatal.

Right in front of us a large explosion lit up one of the darts, vaporizing it. A quarter of a second later the *Adela Chen* flew through the debris at high speed. I watched on the HUD as Ada spun the freighter like a top and accelerated like a fighter pilot. The remaining dart dodged Ada, but Marny was waiting for the miscalculation and blasted it with *Sterra's Gift's* turret.

"Nice job!"

"Finish it, Cap."

I turned *Sterra's Gift* toward the frigate and pushed the thruster stick forward. I was used to a lot more acceleration, but this would do just fine. We'd passed over the frigate like this once before and no doubt their gunners were looking forward to another shot at redemption.

The frigate was not without some capability to fire from its stern. In good shape, the hits would have been insignificant, but the plinks and plunks we received were doing real damage and I was concerned for the integrity of the bridge.

The captain of the frigate was trying to position it into a broadside turn, but Flark had apparently been embellishing a little when he suggested they were in good shape. It was clear that the damage we'd done affected the frigate's ability to maneuver. What I wouldn't have given at that moment, for just one missile - although I suspected Harry Flark had a similar sentiment.

Finally, I found the opening I was looking for. I positioned the ship just below the frigate and well behind its engines. I was in their blind spot from a gunner's perspective and traveling at the same speed they were.

"Prepare for impact!"

I mashed the throttle forward. On our current course we would pass directly beneath the ship. At the last moment I snapped the flight stick backwards and brought the nose of *Sterra's Gift* up ninety degrees. The bright flash of the frigate's engines boiled all around the bridge as we passed through their wash. Our momentum, however, carried us into the actual engine housing and *Sterra's Gift* ground into the rear of the ship. The inertial system attempted to absorb the impact, but it was too much and we all flew into our flight harnesses. It felt like I would snap out of mine and then through the armored glass in front of us.

The bridge of *Sterra's Gift* went dark, emergency lighting snapping on, providing an eerie glow.

"Everyone okay?" I asked.

I heard some pained breathing, but eventually they all replied. I had to cut my harness off with the knife Marny had required I strap to my leg.

"That went well," Tali said when we were all finally standing in the middle of the darkened bridge.

A DEAL'S A DEAL

"I'll check the airlock," I said.

"No power, Liam, we'll have to pop the glass," Tali said.

"I've got it," Jordy pulled a thin cord from a pouch on his waist. The cord stuck to the glass and he ran it around the entire outline. It was hard to watch. Sure, I'd been the one to drive *Sterra's Gift* into the engines of the frigate, but blowing the glass seemed to just add insult to injury.

"Fire in the hole ..." Jordy warned. I had no idea how strong the explosion would be, so I jetted over next to Marny. We'd lost the artificial gravity with the power.

"Hold on to something ..." Jordy jetted back with the rest of us and held onto the back of a chair. The cord simply turned from gray to black and a second later the glass popped out and tumbled away from the ship, propelled by the atmosphere that desperately wanted out. A few seconds later we were in vacuum.

Full crew on this Russian-made frigate is forty-two," Tali said. "I've uploaded the deck plans to your AIs. I don't think we're talking more than half that. That's the good news. The bad news is the best point of entry is on deck five - the bottom of the ship."

The plan we'd devised was to have Marny provide the tactical walk-through and set the objectives. We'd spent nearly half an hour talking through our approach and I felt good about having delivered on my end of it. Losing *Sterra's Gift* would be worth it if we could get Qiu back. Getting Flark would be icing on the cake.

"First through the glass is Tali followed by Jordy. You'll take these defensive positions," Marny said. My HUD showed two blinking indicators on the three dimensional rendering of the frigate projected in my vision. Jordy would set up high on the engine cowl on the starboard side. Tali, low on the port. "Liam, you and I will set the charges on the engine."

The first part of the plan was to make sure the engines wouldn't start up again. We couldn't be sure that the damage we'd caused with *Sterra's Gift* would be permanent. The frigate had been trailing behind the hauler as it slowly accelerated the asteroid it was pushing. We strongly believed the hauler wouldn't disengage from the asteroid to come to the frigate's aid. If it did, there would be no time to reengage and begin its slow push before Mars Protectorate showed up on the scene. Sending its darts had been the only help the hauler could give at this distance.

Marny handed me a large blaster rifle. I strapped it to my back and pulled the flechette from its holster.

"You're going to want some firepower if we get into it out there," Marny said, noticing my weapon choice.

"I won't have time to aim it, I need something fast." I said.

Marny looked at me for a moment and made a decision. "Put the gun away. Normally, space marines hunker down and try to blow holes in things. But you're fast enough that you may very well get into close quarters combat."

She pulled a five centimeter flat handle out of my belt and handed it to me. She'd explained its use once already, but it was one of five new weapons that I was carrying. I had no plan to be experimenting with them in combat. She'd insisted that it wouldn't hurt me to have them available, just in case.

"Hold that. See? It expands into your hand. Flick it outward but away from everyone."

I'd seen nano blades on vids and had always wanted use one. I flicked outward and a thin blue glowing line appeared at the end of the handle. I knew from her previous description that the blue glow was only on my HUD and invisible to non-friendlies.

"Use that for up close and personal. Otherwise, be using that blaster rifle," Marny explained. I retracted the blade and reattached it to my belt.

"We've gotta get going," Tali said.

"Go."

Tali jetted through the blown-out section of armor glass,

followed by Jordy. They appeared to be more comfortable with arc-jets than Marny, but both had clearly been born planet-side.

Marny handed me a sack. "Your HUD has the locations to plant these. Just like we talked about before, your HUD arms them once you plant 'em. I'll blow 'em all at once."

"Roger that." My HUD presented a path to my first objective and I darted out of the glass. I couldn't help but look back over *Sterra's Gift*. We'd ground into the engines of the frigate and it looked like the spine of *Sterra's Gift* was bent. We'd rolled slightly on impact and torn off the newly added missile launchers. I felt sick looking at it.

"Suck it up, Cap," Marny reprimanded. She was right, I was starting to wallow again.

I had six charges to plant, all within thirty meters of each other. On the way to the first, I pulled one of the charges from the sack. The charge I held was an unimpressive container with very little that indicated its purpose. My HUD warned of extreme radiant heat on the engine's surface.

"What's the operating temp of these charges? I've got seven hundred degrees over here." The HUD had given me the exact temperature but I knew from experience that you didn't want to come in contact with metal which was a dull red color.

"They're good over a thousand," Marny reassured.

I ratcheted up my courage and gently pushed the charge onto the surface, being careful not to allow my gloves to touch the extremely hot metal. The gloves could handle it for a couple of seconds, but I didn't want to test them. The top of the charge flashed a green symbol that I didn't recognize, but my HUD confirmed that the charge was armed and synced.

I flitted over to the remaining five locations, each in turn and armed them. I had to work my way around *Sterra's Gift* and the more I did, the more I realized that this had been her last passage. I couldn't process it right now, but the sick feeling in my stomach grew that much more.

"Cap, you need to get those charges planted," Marny said as I caught up with her.

"All done."

Marny hesitated and I saw through her face shield that she was viewing her HUD, no doubt checking my work. "That's impossible, I've only planted two."

"Give me your bag and do that strategy thing you enjoy so much," I said lightly. Marny reluctantly handed me her bag and four new locations illuminated.

"We've got company," Jordy said. His voice was even, like he'd just asked for a cup of coffee. "They're tagged on tactical." Four red icons appeared on my HUD. The holographic model of the frigate showed them on the starboard side of the ship.

"I've got a pair over here," Tali said.

"Don't give away your positions. Let us get these charges set," Marny said.

I pushed my arc-jets hard and set the final four charges, barely pausing as I jetted across the surface of the ruined engine compartment.

"Charges deployed," I tried to keep my voice even and slow, mimicking Jordy, but it sounded higher than I was used to. Marny had moved to where Tali was tracking two figures jetting toward us.

"Three, two …" Marny counted down. The two icons on the port side of the frigate blinked out.

"That woke 'em up," Jordy said. "I don't have a shot."

"Form up on me," Marny said. She jetted down the port side of the frigate, staying close in. I jetted along the surface and caught up with her. According to my HUD, Jordy was just clearing the engine.

"Fire in the hole …" Marny said. Since I wasn't touching the ship, the only indication I got that the charges had fired was watching *Sterra's Gift* tumble slowly away from the back of the frigate. Up to this point, I hadn't had much time to think about it, but for some reason the image of my ship tumbling away was almost too much to take

"Tali, you're on point. We need to take that airlock. Jordy, you have her back. Liam, take a position on the keel, watching aft. We may have dusted those other four, but don't count on it."

I jetted down beneath the frigate, careful to stay close in. The guns of the frigate would be able to find us if we got more than twenty meters off its surface. Peering down, I was surprised by two figures jetting directly at me. Somehow they had my position. Both were armed with pistols and started firing.

"Contact!" I'd been jetting along in a fairly straight line, but a sensor strip on the frigate must have tracked me and was feeding info to the two attackers.

I fired my glove jets against the hull to divert my direction and pushed my boots to max thrust. It was a move I used all of the time in pod-ball when I needed to dramatically change direction. Blaster fire lit up all around me. It momentarily registered that I might have gotten nicked, but the armored vac-suit could absorb near misses all day.

A turret loomed in front of me. The guns weren't going to be a factor in this but a perpendicular object to the hull surface certainly would. I grabbed for a handhold and used my momentum to swing around the turret. My shoulder screamed, but I bet my pursuers wouldn't see it coming. With my free hand, I pulled the nano blade from my belt and gave it a hard flick.

Fifty percent isn't too bad in some circumstances, but in combat it can be a bitch when you're outnumbered. I'd caught one of the two pirates completely off guard and he continued to fly directly at my old position. To his credit, he tried to adjust at the last moment. Blaster fire stitched the space where I'd been and closed in on my current position. My plan was simple - put the nano-blade into his path and try not to catch too much of what happened next.

A nano-blade is a simple object, with an electrically stimulated filament that is impossibly narrow, but relatively rigid for its otherwise small structure. According to Marny, special armor exists that resists nano-blades easily - but it's expensive. More importantly, this guy didn't have that armor. I immediately discovered that I much preferred guns to blades.

I didn't have much time to think about it because the second attacker was clearly spacer born. He'd seen my gambit and had adjusted at the last minute. I let go of the nano-blade and focused on jetting away. I was in the unenviable position of running and dodging in the open. Further down the keel, I aimed for another structure, one where I could hopefully gain some cover.

Before I made it to the structure Marny spoke over the comm, "You're clear, Cap." It was surprising, since not more than a second before I'd seen the pursuing pirate's red blip on my HUD. Sure enough, it was gone. I turned back to see the narrow body of the spacer sail past me. I directed my AI to replay the shot and watched Jordy float out from his position next to the airlock and take the sixty-meter shot. It was one thing to hit a long distance target, but we'd both been juking and jiving back and forth. It felt like an impossible shot to me - apparently not to Jordy.

"Thank you, Jordy," I said, taking a position closer to the airlock, still covering the aft position.

"Nice flying," he said.

"Cut the chatter, Cap," I smiled, Marny was in focus mode and there was nothing but business - until there wasn't.

"Door's jammed, going to blow it," Tali said. "Three, two ..." She'd wasted no time in setting it up.

"Wait one," Marny said. "I've got a manual winch." I couldn't look back, but I'd seen her pack the device.

"We're through," Tali said finally.

The airlock was big enough for the entire team, but Marny didn't want to trap us all at the same time. She and Tali loaded in first.

"Clear," she said after a few minutes, I suspected the inside door had been stuck also.

Jordy and I cycled through the manual lock.

"It's safe to say they know where we're at," Marny said once we were through. Two bodies lay in the hallway - the walls behind them blackened.

I pulled the blaster rifle from my shoulder and locked it up under my chin like Marny had been drilling into Nick and me. For a moment, I was back in the simulator, even though I knew we were in real danger this time.

My HUD showed the deck we were on was the fifth and lowest deck. It was also the smallest. From the side, the frigate was roughly a triangular shape, pointed downward. Deck five occupied the bottom of that triangle.

The bridge and command were all on deck two. The only direct way there was up the elevator at the end of the hallway. Jordy was in the process of attaching explosives to the exterior door of the elevator.

"We'll clear forward, then aft. Form up on Tali," Marny instructed. "Go."

Marny swung around behind Tali and applied a perfect slicing-the-pie swivel. I took my position just behind Marny, and Jordy fell in behind me. It was my responsibility to make sure he didn't lose contact with us as we moved forward since he'd be facing the opposite direction.

Our target was a maintenance shaft running from this deck all the way up to deck one. We'd have to fight our way back down to the command deck, but we wouldn't be relying on the elevator controlled by those in command of the ship.

"Clear," Tali announced. The two rooms off the short hallway were devoid of personnel.

"Blow the elevator," Marny said. I heard the whump of small explosives detonating back in the hallway we'd just left. Tali led us back across the hallway and through another door. A man, no older than myself, cowered in a corner of the room. His pistol lay on the floor well away from him.

"Cuff him, Cap." I didn't hesitate and pulled a sturdy tie from my belt.

"On your stomach," I said. "Hands behind your back." He complied. I wondered what kind of bad decisions had led up to this point in his life. I pulled the cuffs tight, binding his wrists behind his back. I also cuffed his feet. I helped him roll over and pushed him into a seated position. "You get one chance with us. I see you out of these cuffs and there will be no quarter given. Read me?" He nodded affirmative. I released his helmet and detached it from his suit. He looked up at me in panic. "I'd recommend staying quiet. I doubt your buddies will appreciate you getting captured."

Marny looked at the young pirate. "How many on the ship?"

"... I ... I'm not sure," he said.

"Tell me," She was holding her gun menacingly.

"Twenty maybe, twenty-five. I'm nobody - they don't tell me," he said. Marny must have believed him.

"Let's move," Marny said. I stepped back into position. There weren't any other rooms to clear, just the maintenance hatch to be opened. It was possible they'd have a nasty surprise in it for us.

"Let Jordy and me take this," Tali said. Marny stepped out of the way, silent. "Liam, pull the panel and back off quickly."

Jordy stood directly behind Tali and they both gave me enough room to maneuver around them. I took out the multi-tool Marny insisted I bring along. The bolts were easy to remove and I pulled the panel back as fast as I could and moved out of the way.

Tali tossed an object through the hole and then ducked through very quickly, disappearing up and out of sight. Jordy followed her but instead of disappearing, lay on his back with his weapon pointed up the shaft. He fired twice and rolled back into the hallway. A moment later three bodies fell, one on top of the other.

Marny and I grabbed the bodies and dragged them back to where we'd left the bound pirate. He looked up at us with concern. I rolled each unconscious body onto their stomachs, not sure if they were dead or just stunned, but I wasn't taking any chances. I cuffed their hands and legs.

"We're clear," Tali said. "Probably won't be for long, though."

"Up the ladder, Liam. Go! Go!" Marny said.

I ducked into the narrow maintenance shaft. Tali was up about twenty meters, which was two thirds of the height of the shaft. I wasn't sure how Jordy'd shot around her without hitting her. Perhaps the pirates had entered from below her position.

I slung the blaster rifle over my shoulder and started to climb as fast as I could. My prosthetic leg was a significant hindrance and I felt Marny behind me, willing me to go faster. Tali continued her climb, above me.

"Fire in the hole…" Tali stopped near the top of the shaft.

"Keep going, Cap," Marny urged.

I wasn't sure why I was in second position until I heard blaster fire below me. Someone had ducked their head into the shaft. Marny and Jordy fired on them but I had no idea how effective they'd been.

"On my six, Liam." Tali kicked at the wall of the shaft and light flooded in as the panel fell into whatever was on the other side. She followed the kick by tossing what appeared to be three grenades. I didn't hear any noise, however. Without hesitation she jumped through the opening.

I was breathing hard from the exertion and had to grab the hand rail above the opening and swing through. My blaster rifle caught on the doorway and it broke off of my back as the strap was designed to do.

"Look out," I warned. There was nothing else I could do.

I tried to catch my breath and get in behind Tali. We were in a large storage room where crates lay haphazardly. Tali had taken position behind a crate. The entry door to the room blew inward and I was momentarily knocked back into the wall by the impact of the explosion. My vac-suit stiffened to absorb most of the blow.

Tali fired into the breach. A hand reached across the opening from the other side and tossed a grenade into the room. It froze in mid-air, one meter from the entrance and then exploded. Tali responded by throwing a grenade back through the hole.

"How did …" I started to ask.

"Remember what I told you, always be thinking about what you're doing next," Tali said. "I set up a stasis web before we jumped into the room. It wasn't hard to predict they'd blow the door and throw grenades through."

Marny jumped through the hole and handed me my blaster rifle. I pushed my flechette pistol back into its holster and accepted the rifle. "Sorry," I said.

"No time for that. Focus, Cap," I felt like she was always saying that to me - what a newbie. "We're in. Go," she said.

Tali rolled from her position and came up in a crouch. She moved fluidly to the doorframe and tossed a small puck-shaped device into the hallway. My HUD immediately updated the view. There was a pirate rolling in pain on the floor, but the hallway was otherwise clear. By my count we'd taken out thirteen crew members.

"Jordy, rig the shaft," Tali said. "Serpentine formation."

I finally felt like I had some idea of what we were doing. It was one of the two room-clearing formations we'd drilled on. Tali in the center of the hallway with Marny on her left and me just behind Marny on her right. Jordy would follow us backwards. I stepped forward and pulled my blaster rifle to my shoulder.

"Cuff him, Jordy," Marny instructed as we passed the pirate on the floor. "There's a stairway at the end of this hallway. Clear on the way."

There were several doorways between us and the stairwell. We'd cleared two of them when a man rabbited from a doorway at the end of the hall. Tali pivoted quickly and brought him down.

We'd just come even with the elevator. It presented a risk. If we left it open, our opponents could come from behind us. Even now, it made me nervous. The door could open at any time, allowing armed men to pour out into the hallway.

"They're watching us," Marny said. "We've probably reduced their number by more than fifty percent. The rest will hunker down."

"Can we hold up a minute?" I asked.

"What do you have in mind?"

"Let me talk to Flark," I said. "He has to know this isn't going well for him."

"Tali, pull back. Let's give the Cap a run at this."

Tali said nothing, but started backing her way down the hall. We all moved backward together until we reached one of the rooms we'd cleared.

"Liam, duck inside. We'll hold the hallway," Tali said.

Establish comm with bridge of frigate, request parley.

"What do you want?" It was a male voice, not Flark's.

"With whom am I speaking?"

"Captain Vilstrup. I repeat, what do you want?"

"I want the female hostage Qiu Loo, and Harry Flark."

"They're not here," he replied.

"Not possible. I just talked to him forty minutes ago."

"A small ship picked him up no more than ten minutes ago."

"We've blown your engines and the Navy is on the way. What's your exit strategy?" I asked.

"Currently, we're trying to repel boarders. I haven't worked things out much past that."

"Look, Captain, I've got no taste for blood. I'm after Lieutenant Loo and Flark. We've got no beef with you. That said, in my opinion, this is Flark's ship and I'm taking it. If you want to stand between me and this ship, then we can end this parley now."

"What's my other option?" he asked.

"You turn the ship over to me and I'll provide you and one other crew member transport to within two kilometers of that hauler."

"How do I know I can trust you?"

"You don't, but I'd bet at least one of your crew's heard of me. I've made the same deal twice in the last two months with you guys. Ask 'em."

Marny looked at me in bewilderment. "Are you crazy? We can't let them go."

"Do the math, Marny. If they put their guns down right now, we've got a chance at getting Qiu. Not only that, I also reduce the chance of one of us getting hit. I'm not the frakking Navy. I don't like these guys, but I don't need to see 'em dead either."

"We've got 'em dead to rights, Cap." Her face was flush with anger.

"Trust me, just this one last time. Please."

She sighed audibly, "I sure hope you know what you're doing. It burns me bad to see these guys escape."

"Me and two others and you've got a deal," Captain Vilstrup finally returned.

HE WHO RUNS AWAY

I still had a knot in my stomach. We'd taken out the frigate and captured eight pirates. I'd also released three of their top brass to the big hauler crew. Tali, Jordy and Marny swept the ship and found two more pirates hiding, for a total of ten. As a group, they were fairly pathetic. I was a little surprised at how drastically my perception of them changed now that they weren't pointing weapons at me.

Ada pulled alongside the frigate and Nick joined us to help with the prisoners.

"Nick, Jordy, would you hold down the ship until the Navy gets here?"

Jordy looked at me like I'd grown a second head. "You suck, but yes, we'll hold 'em. Can't guarantee they'll all be here when you get back." He said the last loud enough for the prisoners to hear.

"Navy is less than eight hours out. We'll be back well before.

Nick nodded. I appreciated that he trusted me enough to let me do this.

"Ada, Tali, Marny I need you guys. I'll explain on the way."

"What's all the mystery?" Marny asked. I was leading them to the airlock where the *Adela Chen* was docked.

"We need to head back to the station. I've got a hunch," I said.

"Ada. Can you see if you can raise your buddy, Eldevurp?"

"Elvard."

I jumped into the pilot's chair next to Ada. "I've got the helm, see if you can get him."

She finally got him to answer his comm. "I've got him, what do you want to ask him."

"Put him on comm, please."

Marny and Talı had grabbed water pouches and meal bars and joined us in the cockpit. There wasn't really room for either on the bridge, but they improvised by dangling their legs down the hole where the ladder descended to the living quarters.

"Hey, E.V., here. We're in the middle of an emergency, what do you need?"

"E.V., any of you boys got ships?"

"Just little stuff, why?"

"Surely you've got some ore haulers around," I said.

"Well, duh, sure we do."

"So the Red Houzi's making off with all your ore and your asteroid. We've taken out their escort and their darts. About the only thing they'll have left will be stationary heavy blasters. Tell me your boys can't outfly that?"

"What do you mean?"

"I mean, what if you were to load up some containers, maybe take full ones even, and fly 'em at that hauler. If you let them go at the right time, I'd bet you could put it out of commission or at the very least get 'em to change their mind about things."

"Frak me. You say that frigate's down?" E.V. was starting to understand my plan.

"That's what I'm saying. And ... the hauler is out of darts."

"Let me round up my boys."

"Go get 'em, E.V.," Ada said.

End comm.

"They're gonna beat the ever-living shite out of that hauler," I said.

"How long you been planning that?" Marny asked.

"Forgiven?" I asked.

"Tell me you didn't just think of that," Marny said.

"I won't tell you anything of the sort."

"Ada, I want you to stay in the freighter. We need someone to stay mobile. I don't like Nick and Jordy being tied to a ship that isn't movable without some sort of backup. Okay?"

"Yes, can do. You know you've got a lot of blood on your face?"

I hadn't thought about it for a while, but my face and ear had taken a beating from Red and his buddy.

"It'll have to wait," I said.

"What are you thinking, Cap?" Marny asked.

"I'm taking a chance, but I think it's a good one. Flark still has crew on the station, I think that's where he'd go. He wants distance between him and that hauler."

"Wouldn't they just take him to where he was going?"

"If his destination is a base, I doubt whoever picked him up had the range. Flark's a rat jumping off the sinking ship. I bet anything he's holding onto Qiu as a bargaining chip."

Arriving back on station, we saw that the damage was significant. Between our missiles tearing apart the control station and the frigate's broadside, Jeratorn had seen better days. I hoped there wouldn't be any legal fallout for us.

"There's a short-term pier over on Tower B," Ada said.

"Want to take us in?" I asked.

Ada took the controls and expertly guided us in to what was nothing more than a ledge on the side of the tower. For our purposes, however, it would work just fine.

I hadn't brought my blaster rifle along, but still had my flechette pistol. Marny had her rifle and Tali was wearing a pair of pistols in holsters at her waist. I knew they both had more weapons. I was pretty sure I was down to the steel knife and my pistol. I'd removed my belt of grenades because I felt I was a lot more likely to do harm to myself than to someone else.

Inside the tower, the few people we saw in the open were running to their destinations. A soft red light pulsed at the top of the hallway but the warning klaxons had, fortunately, been turned off. I wanted to tell these people that most of the danger had passed and they should get back to business. But, I couldn't really guarantee that yet.

"Tali, how about we turn that nanite sniffer back on?" I said.

"I hope this works," Marny said.

"Agreed," I said.

I was disappointed to find that all of the nanite traces we found in this area looked to be secondarily planted - brought along on other people's clothing or shoes.

"I think we should work our way over to Tower A," Tali said.

We followed her to the airlock connecting the two towers. Surprisingly, the lock was once again functioning. During the attack, the first thing that should have happened was shutting down all of the connecting passages.

We were on the back side of Tower A and finally starting to pick up older nanites that were actual first-hand traces of Qiu. I was still disappointed that we couldn't see any current trace of her.

"Up or down?" Tali asked.

"Think they'd take her back to the brig?" I asked.

"No chance," Marny said. "Not with the Navy on the way. They'd need to hide her good."

"I've got an idea," I said. "Let's go check out The Welded Tongue."

"You want a drink?" Marny asked.

"Yeah, I'm feeling real thirsty right now." I punched the button to call the elevator car. We only had to go a few levels down to find the Welded Tongue. Once again, there was no new trace of Qiu anywhere.

"I'm hoping someone in the bar will have had contact with her," I said, giving away my big plan.

"It's more than I've got," Marny said.

The Welded Tongue was an amazing place. Two hours after being attacked by pirates, the restaurant/bar was at least thirty percent full.

"Maybe we should talk to Beth Anne, see if she knows anything," I said.

"I wouldn't trust her any further than I could throw her," Tali said.

I caught the arm of a server. He was a young kid, probably no older than twelve. "Could you ask Beth Anne if she has a moment? Tell her Liam Hoffen's asking."

"Okay." His voice was shaky.

I'd expected some attitude, but ... then I looked at my companions, decked out in armored vac-suits. I also considered my face, which was probably a bloody mess. We had to look like hell.

Beth Anne, dressed in another of her tight fitting dresses that displayed her feminine attributes to their best advantage, sauntered out from the doorway where the kid had disappeared.

"Captain Hoffen, you do look a fright. Oh, and we don't allow weapons in the bar. I'll have to ask you to take those outside."

"Just a quick question and we'll be on our way," I said.

"Nothing's free, Captain. What do you need to know, and how badly do you need to know it?" Her voice was sweet, but I wasn't at all fooled by it this time.

"Harry Flark has come back to the station and I need to know where he is," I said.

"Hmm, wish I knew that one. I'd be able to sell that info all day long. Afraid I can't help you. Maybe I could interest you in a cold drink?"

"No, we just need to find Flark. Anyone you can ask? Poke around for us?" I asked.

"Sure, I'll poke around." She stretched out the word 'poke' suggestively.

I sighed, "It'd be worth a lot to me."

"Well then, I'll pay it special attention. Anything else?"

"No. Thank you."

Beth Anne walked away. Hope drained out of me.

"You see that?" Tali asked.

"What?"

"Look at the carpet."

I looked at the carpet. There were bright-green, perfect-looking little shoe prints that led up to our table and back again to the bar. It'd been the path Beth Anne had walked.

"Why didn't she have any on her?"

"She's been wearing a vac-suit. Wherever she changed, she walked through a bunch of 'em," Tali said.

"Let's go," I said.

We started walking toward the bar, catching the attention of three large men who'd, up to this point, been hanging out, and ignoring us. They all had their hands on the butts of blaster pistols. They clearly didn't want to draw them, but were letting us know they had lethal power.

"You need to leave," the biggest one said to me.

Marny didn't even hesitate. She pulled her Bo Staff off her belt and snapped it to full length. The fastest of the three almost got his gun drawn before she thwacked his wrist, causing him to drop it. The other two were nursing the sides of their heads where Marny's staff had struck them.

"Two ways this can go boys," Marny said. "You can leave now, or I can finish it."

"She's getting away," I said.

One of the men started to bend down to pick up his weapon. I suspected he simply wanted to retrieve it to take with him, but Marny read the situation differently. She smashed the back of his head violently with her staff. He dropped on the ground hard, completely limp. The other two decided they didn't want to stick around to see what was going to happen next and made a run for the door.

Tali, pistols drawn, peeked into the back room. "Let's go," she said.

Marny stowed her staff and pulled the heavy blaster over her shoulder. "Take number two spot, Liam. I've got the rear. Just be careful of civilians."

The green tell-tales of Beth Anne's shoe prints led straight out of the back of the bar's storage area. Her strides had lengthened significantly. The woman was running in high heels.

We followed her trail right up to an airlock plastered with green nanites, way more than if they'd just come from the bottom of Beth Anne's shoes.

"Frak, we're right on her," I said.

We cycled through the airlock. It was a tight squeeze for the three of us in armor but time was not on our side if they escaped to a ship ...

Establish comm with Ada.

"Hiyas, Liam. Need me so soon?"

"Yes, we're chasing Flark down and I think they're going for a ship. Lower side of Tower A. Can you intercept?"

"On it," Ada said.

We made it through the airlock onto a private docking bay with a pressure barrier. There was enough room for three small runabout-class vehicles. An eight-meter boat was dropping through the pressure field.

"It's coming out now," I said.

"I see 'em."

I heard Ada talking to the AI. *Hail runabout.*

"Small craft, pull back into the dock or I'll be forced to fire."

The small ship ducked back up through the pressure field and into the docking bay. Marny aimed at the craft's forward view screen. She sidestepped around the bay, keeping aim on the pilot. Flark's enraged face shone through the glass.

Hail runabout, I instructed.

"Flark, give it up. You're not getting out of here."

"I've got Lieutenant Loo."

"Let's make a deal," I said.

"You can't do that," Marny said, a vein popping out on her forehead.

"My command, my rules, Bertrand. If you don't like it, then get another job."

"What the frak?"

"You let me pass, I'll give you Loo," Flark offered.

"I frakking quit," Marny said.

"I accept both offers," I said.

Tali looked from me to Marny and back. For the first time since I'd met her, she had a stumped look on her face.

"Cover me," I said to Tali. She nodded, holding her pistols on the door of the runabout.

Flark pushed the door open and green nanite trackers spilled out of the doorway and on to the docking bay floor. He didn't even have her in a vac-suit.

"Come out with your hands up. There're some itchy triggers out here," I said.

"I'm coming out. She's on the bench."

Flark's chubby frame exited the craft. He had green trackers all over him. Tali switched off the view, apparently it was bugging her as well. He stepped around me and looked over to Marny and Tali.

"I can't believe we're gonna let this happen," Marny said, pissed.

"Not sure what you're whining about," I said. "You don't work for me so you don't have to abide by my commitments." I looked over my shoulder at Marny, her anger turning to a smile.

"Why you little turd ..." She turned to Flark who was gingerly walking past her and jammed the butt of her gun into his face shield. Ordinarily, the helmet of a vac-suit can take a pretty good pop and to its credit this one didn't split open, but apparently the contents were jostled somewhat and Flark crumpled to the ground.

I rushed into the open vehicle. Qiu was slumped into the seat, breathing roughly. Perversely, the first thing that went through my mind was just how many nanite trackers were being sprayed all over my body.

"We got her Ada. Tell Nick and Jordy we found her," I was elated. Whatever came next, I would be okay with it.

CLEANUP

It was misery helping Qiu into her vac-suit. Flark had brought it along, but just hadn't taken the time to get her in it. She was burning up with fever and groaning painfully, so we worked as gently as possible.

"We'll take the runabout over to the frigate," I said. "They'll surely have medical kits on board." We loaded onto the small ship.

"Ada, we're coming out in the runabout, Qiu needs attention."

"Okay, right behind you," Ada said.

Establish comm with the frigate.

"What do you have, Liam?" Nick asked.

"We have Qiu on a small runabout. We're headed your way now," I said.

"There's an infirmary on deck three," Jordy said.

"Just don't shoot us,"

The little vehicle had good acceleration and we got to the frigate quickly. The large hauler was still not completely out of enhanced visual range and a flotilla of small ships was buzzing the behemoth. I suspected they would eventually be successful at destroying the hauler. What I wasn't sure of is if they would be able to bring the co-op's asteroid back. Personally, I'd try negotiating with the hauler at that point.

"Check Qiu's seal, I'm going to evacuate the atmo." We weren't going to land in a pressurized environment and it would take sixty seconds if I wanted to evacuate it without causing all of our ears to pop.

"We're all green," Marny said. I was glad she was talking to me.

"Qiu first? Then we can take Flark over?" I said.

245

"I've got Qiu. I'll take her right down to the infirmary," Marny said.

"I imagine Tali and I can handle Mr. Flark." It was a little bit of a joke since he was still unconscious. I hoped Marny hadn't killed him, but for all the death and destruction he'd caused, I wasn't sure I cared that much.

I also wondered what had happened to Beth Anne Hollise. We really didn't have anything on her directly. She'd stepped into some of the nanites, but then so had a lot of people. We'd chased her tracks straight to the docking bay, but when we'd gotten there, she was nowhere to be found. I'd thought she might be on the runabout, but that also wasn't the case. It was a mystery I wasn't interested in at this point.

I sidled up next to the larger ship and Tali pulled open the runabout's door and jetted across to the airlock to start it cycling. I was suspicious of Flark's prolonged unconsciousness, so I surreptitiously watched for him to make a move. Sure enough, with Tali out of the vehicle, he made a grab for Marny, just as she started to lift Qiu.

I pulled my flechette pistol and fired several times, point blank into his shoulder. I didn't want to kill him, but I'd be satisfied with a good maiming at this point. I was surprised at the impact the flechette darts had. I'd been shot several times with flechettes and aside from feeling like I'd been stuck by a needle – which, coincidentally, was the entire point - I hadn't taken too much damage.

To be fair, Marny had mentioned that this particular flechette pistol was not in the same class as those smaller weapons I was used to. She made sure this one carried a significant punch. I felt terrible as I watched Flark's body spin, out of control, into Marny's legs as she was trying to get out of the door, carrying Qiu.

"What in … You got him, Cap?" she asked.

"Yeah, sorry, more punch on this flechette than I'm used to."

"I told you. You've really got to start listening to me on these things."

Flark was drifting away from the vehicle and flailing, obviously in pain. His vac-suit had no doubt sealed back over the now well-embedded darts. I jetted out toward him and grabbed his arm to stop his spin. I'd removed his AGBs, so he had no capacity to steer himself. If I gave him a little toss in one direction or another, he'd just keep going that way until someone saw him or ... heck, it could be a long time.

I came even with his mask, "Try anything else and I won't come for you next time."

He nodded his understanding.

Tali and I cycled through the airlock with Flark. It was unnecessary with Tali along, but I kept the flechette pointed at Flark just the same.

"Should we segregate him?" I asked.

"I wouldn't think so. All the big boys went over to the hauler. Be good for him to spend some time with the rank and file," Tali said.

I put cuffs on his hands and sat him down next to one of the other prisoners. Once on the ground, I cuffed his ankles. We were getting low on restraints at this point, but I thought we were probably just about finished.

I hugged Nick when I saw him.

"Good to see you on the other side," I said.

"You too."

"Marny might be a little pissed at me. Maybe you could put in a good word with her?" I asked.

"Really?" He looked at me, surprised.

"Yeah. Any idea who the Navy sent?"

"*Kuznetsov.*"

"Seriously? Oh shite. She's gonna be pissed." Commander L. L. Sterra was in command of the Navy's Corvette *Kuznetsov*. She was the namesake of our now foundered ship.

"Probably not, since we recovered Qiu and Flark."

"Are you okay with all that?" I asked.

"My objection to the plan was never the ship. Does it suck that we ruined a ship we'd restored from the brink of the boneyard?

Yes. I estimate our loss to be just south of a million m-creds, none of which is insured, by the way. My objection was that it was too risky. We can't keep taking risks like this, Liam. The odds are going to catch up with us."

"I don't know how to step back. I couldn't leave Qiu. You saw her - she wouldn't have made it."

"I know. I get it. We shouldn't have been out here in the first place. I'm the one who wanted this job and it nearly cost us everything. I'm just saying we have to be more careful."

"Okay, we'll work it out. Let's get this thing mopped up."

"Agreed."

"Any thoughts on how to lash a frigate and cutter to a string of ore barges? I was thinking that if we got the Navy to give us this frigate as a prize, we might be able to raise enough capital to get another ship."

"Sure, we could totally do that," Nick said. I loved this little man. It was like he'd never been introduced to the word 'no'.

"How long before the Navy gets here?"

"Four hours," he said.

"Ada and I are going to hunt down *Sterra's Gift*. It can't have gotten far."

An hour later, Ada and I pulled up even with the tumbling *Sterra's Gift*. She looked so forlorn out here all by herself, tumbling with no power. My eyes burned as I thought about how far we'd come with this valiant little ship. It'd been worthwhile though and the circle was complete. Flark had no doubt been the mastermind of the attack on Colony 40. It was that attack that had given us *Sterra's Gift* and in return for that, we'd been able to use her to bring him down.

I didn't consider myself a sentimental person, but if I'd been asked to speak at that moment, I wouldn't have been able to. Ada seemed to sense that I was having a difficult time seeing the ship in this condition. It probably caused her pain, also, so soon after having seen her own freighter torn apart.

She reached over the console and just held my hand as we sat in the quiet.

After several minutes I broke our silence, "Think you can capture her and break her spin?"

"Do ducks fly?" Ada asked. She had me there. I remembered that ducks were like chickens, only wilder. And ... chickens didn't fly, or did they? I looked back at her blankly.

"Oh good Lord, Liam. You spacers are all the same. Let's just see what I can do."

The last time I'd had to stop a spinning object, I'd done it by allowing it to make contact with the flat side of my ship. Of course, that time was when I'd captured Ada's lifepod. Ada took a completely different approach. First she matched *Sterra's Gift's* tumble - I couldn't even begin to imagine what possessed her to do that. I felt like I might get sick and had to look down. Once my head cleared, I noticed she wasn't looking out of the armored glass but looking at a screen in the console.

Ada nudged the *Adela Chen* in close to *Sterra's Gift* and caught the longer ship on its frame. She slowly twisted and turned the joy sticks until both ships were no longer tumbling.

"That is the wackiest thing I've ever experienced," I said.

"You have a better idea?"

"Not at all, it was incredible. I've never heard of someone doing that."

"It's how the Navy ships recover debris."

"Those aren't manned ships though."

"Doesn't mean it doesn't work." Her logic was flawless, but I still thought she was crazy. I wondered how many pilots in the solar system could execute that maneuver.

"Where to, Captain?"

"Let's drop it inside one of our barges. For later."

"Can do." Ada slowly accelerated, gingerly keeping *Sterra's Gift's* hull in contact. She neatly decelerated on the other side of the first barge in the string, backing the carcass over the top. The string was currently generating a small amount of gravity to keep the ore from wandering, which it wouldn't do without an external stimulus. *Sterra's Gift* settled down on top of the ore.

"Think that'll be too much mass?"

"Nope. Each barge is holding about two-point-five kilo tonnes right now. What's her mass, another hundred fifty tonnes?"

"About a hundred."

"Won't even know she's there. Are you planning to do the same with that frigate?"

"If the Navy gives her to us."

"Won't matter. We can carry them both easily. This old girl has lots to give if you treat her right."

We flew back to the frigate just ahead of the *Kuznetsov*.

"Glad you're back, Cap. Navy's asking to board the frigate. Any issues?" Nick asked.

"None at all. Especially if they grab the prisoners. They know about Qiu?"

"Yes. They're in now. I gotta go." Marny cut the comm.

The *Kuznetsov* was a gorgeous ship by Navy standards. It was long and thin, shaped like an arrow. The body bristled with weapons. It was amazing to think that every bit of it could be retracted to reduce the sensor signature of the corvette to virtually nothing. It was made to sneak up on its enemies or simply outrun them. By the time you knew one was nearby, they were already well past you. If they decided to attack, then it would be a guerrilla, hit and run style fight.

Nick hailed me this time, "We've been invited to a meeting on the *Kuznetsov* with Commander Sterra."

"No rest for the weary," I said.

"They've dropped a gangway on the port side. Just come in the starboard airlock and I'll go over with you."

I was already familiar with the *Kuznetsov*, so I wasn't surprised when the corporal who was accompanying us led the way into a meeting room we'd seen before. It was a nice touch that a plate of sandwiches and pouches of juice had been left on the table. We'd made friends with the ship's steward, Polly Gellar, on previous visits and it seemed to be benefitting us now. The corporal bade us to dig in while we waited.

I found it impossible to stay seated when Commander Lavonne Sterra entered the room. She had what is referred to as 'command presence.' She held her hand out and shook both Nick's and my own. I felt grubby next to her. I couldn't estimate the number of hours we'd been in these suits and I believed the side of my face was still bloodied. I was embarrassed by my lack of decorum.

"It looks like you boys have been deep in it." It was a statement, not a question.

"Yes ma'am." It was all I could come up with, but it caused her to smile.

"Let's get business out of the way first and please don't stop eating on my account. You have no doubt earned a rest, not an appointment with a paper pusher. There is a matter of your firing missiles at a civilian structure. Do you have anything to say on this matter?" she asked.

"Should we retain counsel?" Nick asked.

"Let's start with a statement. If I think you're stepping into something, I'll stop the interview and we'll call Mr. Telish in."

I trusted the Commander and I knew Nick did as well.

"It wasn't something we had a lot of choice about. We'd have happily sat in the docking bay and let things play out, but the frigate was broadsiding the entire concourse. We couldn't survive. When we tried to run, the station's defensive guns started ripping us up."

"That's what we were able to gather from the recorded evidence, as well. I'm finding that your actions were justified."

"That's it?" Nick asked.

"All of the video evidence has already been filed. Mr. Telish had three officers analyze your actions and go on record as to their opinions of the necessity of firing your missiles at the station. All of the officers found that you acted well within your rights to defend your ship."

"We'd like to claim the frigate as a prize," Nick said.

"So awarded," Sterra responded. "Will you be filing a suit against the station for firing on your ship?"

"No. It was not station personnel that were operating the weapons," Nick said.

"Recorded. I'm very sorry to be so brief, gentlemen. It is a pleasure to see you again, but the news Qiu Loo brought back is not good."

"Anything you can share?" I asked.

"She brought back intelligence on a forward operations base for the Red Houzi in the Neutral Territory. Neither the PDC nor the Navy are willing to take a swipe at them. I'm hoping Qiu's testimony will change that."

"Qiu said that Flark had been expecting her. Have you made any progress on finding the leak?"

"No. And I'd ask you to keep that to yourself. There's a rat on our side, and if I'm going to find 'em I need to keep that information quiet."

"It will remain between us, Commander."

I'm sure you understand that if not for you boys, we'd have lost Qiu and we wouldn't know about this new threat. But listen to me - you need to lay low for a time. You've become a real threat to a powerful organization."

"Understood. One last thing? How'd those miners fare against the hauler that was stealing the co-op asteroid?" I asked.

Commander Sterra chuckled. "Their attack style was reminiscent of someone else's I've seen recently," she said, raising her eyebrows at us. "By the time we got there they'd tossed more than a dozen fully loaded containers of ore into the barge. The pirates were begging us to take them into custody. Did you have anything to do with that?"

"No, we were pretty busy with our own problems," Nick answered.

"Liam, Nick, thank you. The Navy owes you a debt they will most likely never repay nor acknowledge. Know this, however. You've made a difference today."

Sterra left the room as quickly as she'd entered it. The corporal allowed us to take the sandwiches and put them in a bag that was sitting, thoughtfully, next to the plate. She escorted us from the *Kuznetsov* and back onto the frigate.

By the time we returned, it was empty of prisoners and everyone else was sitting on the bridge eating ration bars and drinking pouches of water.

"We brought sandwiches," I said. I didn't have to say it twice. Marny unloaded the sandwiches and handed them out. I gave her back the one she handed me, I'd already had two while on the Kuznetsov.

"Any word on Qiu?" Marny asked.

"None yet," Nick said. "They have a full combat med-tank though."

"So what now?" Ada asked.

"Think you can push this tub over to the ore sleds?" I asked.

"Of course," she said.

"We should lash the frigate to the sled just like we did *Sterra's Gift*. Nick, do you think the gravity generator on the frigate will fight the ore-sled if we lay her down on her side?"

"Should be fine," Nick said.

"Marny, can we use the frigate's guns for defense if we do that?"

"Aye Cap, you'll only be able to use one side, but there isn't much out there that'd want to get in a scrape with even half a frigate."

"Sounds like a solid plan to me. Nick, any thoughts on how we're going to come out on this deal?"

"Not sure what you mean," he said.

"Well, we trashed *Sterra's Gift* but we have a scratch 'n' dent frigate and a load of ore."

"Ah. I haven't had a lot of time to do the math, but it's not as bad as it looks. Even a roached out frigate is worth more than *Sterra's Gift* to the right buyer and the auctioneers have moved most of our loot, I think you'll be surprised at how well that turned out."

I stood and mussed Nick's hair even though I knew he hated it when I did that. "Well little buddy, I think we're going to have to go ship shopping when we get back to Mars."

ABOUT THE AUTHOR

Jamie McFarlane has been writing short stories and telling tall tales for several decades. With a focus that only a bill collector could inspire, Jamie has finally relented to recording some of his most of requested stories.

During the day Jamie can be found at his home, writing in front of a neglected fire, with his two cats both conveniently named Dragon. When not writing, Jamie can be found at the local pub sharing his stories with any who will listen.

Thank you for reading, I'm so glad you enjoyed it. Please consider using one or more of the following links to learn about additional books in the Privateer Tales series or just to stay in contact with Jamie.

Blog and Website: fickledragon.com

Email: jamie@fickledragon.com

Facebook: facebook.com/jamiemcfarlaneauthor

Twitter: twitter.com/mcfarlaneauthor